The Siren of the Loch Gillelli

ALSO BY CHARLES KNOTTS

The Secret Storm
The Tenth Night

The Siren of the Loch Gillelli

Charles Knotts

The Siren of the Loch Gillelli © 2021 by Charles Knotts

Published in the United States by Amazon.com

ISBN 978-1-7323293-4-8 paperback
ISBN 978-1-7323293-5-5 eBook

The Siren of the Loch Gillelli is a novel. Any similarity of the storyline characters in the novel to persons living or dead is purely coincidental and not intended by the author

Cover & Interior Design by: Dru Knotts
DHK Kirkwood, Missouri

This book is dedicated to Brigadier General Gary Ambrose, USAF (ret), his wife Marcia, his daughter Alicia, and to the memory of his son, Bradley Ambrose. Few military families have sacrificed more in the service of their country.

Prologue

April 1912

The dull dark metal and wooden grip of the Webley revolver barely reflected the soft light from the small ornate lamp mounted above the dresser. As he had done a dozen times before during the past three days, Joshua Robinson had pulled open the top drawer and examined the gun. Its presence provided the reassurance to him that all was ready for the evening's event. Once again soothed, he slowly closed the drawer, nodding his head in satisfaction. Yes. They were ready.

Robinson squeezed past a small wooden chair and stood before the wash basin, the polished white carrara marble barely gleaming in the same soft light. He proceeded to wash his hands as if preparing to begin his usual work. After drying his hands, he wiped his face with the towel as he stared into the wash basin mirror. Robinson studied his face. He hated the moustache and beard. They broadened his facial features, making him look much heavier than his actual girth. It's just as well, he thought.

Robinson turned and retrieved his coat and fur felt bowler hat from the bed. As he donned the garments, he mused at the ambiance of his "luxurious" cabin. Although it had an elaborate old-Dutch décor adorned all in oak, it was embellished and ornamented to the point of being quite ostentatious. It was fancy, to be sure, but the cabin, for its hefty price, was also quite small.

It was a three-step accommodation, he thought. One could be anywhere in the cabin in just three steps.

Once again, Joshua Robinson pulled the watch from his vest pocket and checked the time. It was almost eleven o'clock in the evening. Somewhat both nervous and impatient, he decided to leave the cabin early and make his way to the First Class Smoke Room. Entering the main passageway of Bridge Deck B, Robinson walked to the Grand Staircase and up to Promenade Deck A. As he climbed the staircase, he noted the time on the grandiose clock. Just a few hours remaining.

Robinson noticed the main hallways and the grand reception areas were almost empty of crew members and passengers. Good, he concluded. Just as he had anticipated, late Sunday night would be the quietest moment of the voyage.

Deciding to remain indoors, Robinson strolled down the corridor leading to the First Class Lounge. He entered the lounge at the main entrance and wandered through a long room of sheer opulence. It was all but impossible to describe. The rich wood veneer, the white ceiling trimmed in patterns of gold, a grand chandelier in the center of the room, lush upholstered chairs surrounding intricately-cut cherry wood tables - all of the furnishings and accessories exuded magnificent luxury. The lounge is breath-taking, Robinson thought, absolutely breath-taking. It is also empty. The room was empty.

Quietly, Robinson exited the First Class Lounge and walked outside on the Promenade Deck to the First Class Smoke Room. This room, too, was richly adorned with dark mahogany paneling, mother of pearl inlays, and magnificent stained glass windows. Unlike the First Class Lounge, though, the room was reeking of pipe and cigar smoke. As Robinson walked to the rear of the room he noticed two tables where men in tuxedos and suits were playing cards. He greeted them with a polite smile and silent nod as he moved past them and sat on a couch facing a fireplace. Retrieving a cigar from his coat pocket, Robinson noticed the painting above the fireplace mantel. It appeared to portray a scene of New York Harbor. Below the painting on the mantel was a clock. As he lit the cigar, Joshua Robinson noted the time. He had almost a half-hour before the final meeting. Robinson smiled. That was more than enough time to enjoy a final smoke.

It seemed as if he was surrounded by stars. Robinson removed his hat briefly and looked skyward to the entire Milky Way Galaxy. Above him was a canopy of shining stars, the glittering points of light falling to an invisible horizon. He replaced his hat and again stepped back into the shadows.

Joshua Robinson had left the First Class Smoke Room by way of the rear entrance at eleven-thirty. He departed down a staircase and past the Restaurant Reception Area to the Restaurant Promenade Deck. He strolled to the starboard side of the ship and to a corner in the shadows that stopped at the drop-off to the Third Class Promenade Deck. He stood in darkness and in silence.

The bitter chill of the night air had settled over the ship. The ocean appeared to be a sea of glass, the cloud of stars reflecting from the mirror. It was as if the ship was sailing through the brightly illuminated universe. Suddenly, briefly, quietly, another man silhouetted in starlight entered the shadows.

"Good evening, Doctor . . ."

"*Mister*," Robinson interrupted in the darkness with a harsh whisper. "*Mister* Robinson. Remember that."

"Yes, of course. Forgive me. I again stand corrected." There was a brief pause. "Good evening, *Mister* Robinson."

"Good evening, Mr. Mayhew. Are you enjoying the night, sir?"

"Not particularly," the voice in the shadow replied. "Rather brisk, I'd say."

Robinson nodded his head. "Yes, I agree with you. Fortunately, though, the night air is keeping everyone indoors and in their cabins."

"That is beyond a doubt," came a voice from yet another dark silhouette entering the shadows. "Except for a Quartermaster Rowe strolling on the aft deck."

"Good evening, Mr. Porter," Robinson greeted the third man. "Thank you for joining us. Everything quiet down below?"

"Like a church yard cemetery at midnight," said the voice with a decidedly cockney accent. "The ship is asleep."

"Almost all of the ship is asleep," Robinson corrected Porter.

"They'll all be awake soon enough," Mayhew reminded them.

"Yes," Robinson agreed in a whisper. "Very soon, now." There was a silence among them as Robinson glanced about the deck. It was quiet. Empty.

"Are the men ready?" Robinson continued to whisper.

"Yes," Mayhew and Porter replied in unison. "Armed and ready to go,"

Mayhew added confidently.

"Very well," Robinson sighed.

"Have you received any messages today from the Captain or from Halifax?" Porter asked cautiously as if afraid of the answer.

"No," answered Robinson, "there have been no messages as of eleven o'clock this evening."

"That means the game is on," Mayhew concluded in a quiet voice.

"Yes," Porter agreed with an unseen nod, "and that also means *Elgie* is out there and waiting for us."

"Of that, Mr. Porter, I have absolutely no doubt," Joshua Robinson concurred. "*Elgie* is there, rest assured."

Robinson paused a moment, listening to the silence. All that could be heard was the deep, muffled noise of the ship's engines and the distant roiling of the sea in the ship's wake.

"Gentlemen," Robinson continued, "we have been planning and rehearsing this moment for months. I see no reason not to go forward. Mr. Mayhew, I will accompany you and your men to the Marconi Room on the boat deck and then to the ship's bridge. Remember – the ship's telegraph must be silenced. As anticipated, First Officer Murdock relieved Second Officer Lightoller a few hours ago. He has the watch. Captain Smith has retired to his quarters. You know what to do."

"We're ready, Mr. Robinson," Mayhew assured him. "We know what to do."

Robinson turned his attention to Porter. "Mr. Porter, after our initial efforts are completed on the bridge, I will join you at the Purser's Office on the starboard side of C Deck. We will have to act quickly. Time will be of the essence."

"We'll do it fine, Mr. Robinson," Porter assured him. "You'll see."

"All right, gentlemen," Robinson announced, "it will begin at twelve-thirty. Be here with your parties . . ."

At that precise moment, Robinson stopped talking as he and the two other men heard a distant yet distinctive sound of three bells emanating from the bow of the ship.

"Are those bells clanging?" Porter asked.

"Yes," Robinson replied quietly. Suddenly, they felt the ship begin a maneuver sharply to the left, the promenade deck listing to starboard in the turn.

"What's going on?" Mayhew wondered aloud.

"I'm not sure," Robinson uttered in surprise.

In a moment the three men felt rather than heard a strange grinding vibration coming from deep within the ship. It was as if the entire vessel was emitting a subdued groan from its soul.

"My God!" Porter exclaimed in fear and bewilderment. "What *is* that?"

Robinson turned and watched a huge, ghostly-white mountain passing before him. It towered above the superstructure of the ship. Small avalanches of ice poured down its side, some falling onto the edge of the Third Class Promenade Deck. To Robinson, staring through a cloud of frozen breath, it was as if he was in the Alps, the mountainside close enough to touch.

The mountain continued to move slowly past them and disappear into the darkness. In a moment, the constant subtle rhythmic rumbling of the ship's steam engines ceased. Again, all was quiet.

"It appears the ship has stopped," Mayhew remarked apprehensively.

"Yes," Robinson agreed. "I believe that was an iceberg, and I fear that we have struck it."

"What now?" Mayhew moaned. "What can we do?"

"Both of you go back to your rooms," Robinson instructed them. "Change into your suits and return here. With your revolvers. For now, have your men stay in their cabins." Mayhew and Porter seemed to have turned to stone. Neither moved. "Go!" Robinson chided them.

"What if the ship is damaged?" Porter wondered aloud. "What if she sinks?"

"Don't be silly, man!" Robinson angrily responded. "This ship is not going to sink. This is the *Titanic*!" He paused a moment in emphasis. "Now go! Quickly!"

There was no time to waste.

Joshua Robinson retraced his steps in returning to his cabin on Bridge Deck B. As he passed through the First Class Smoke Room, he noticed the card games were continuing. The gentlemen seemed unconcerned. Entering the First Class Lounge, he began to hear the ringing of the steward's bells.

"Why have we stopped?" Robinson asked a steward entering the lounge from the Grand Staircase corridor.

"There is some talk of an iceberg, sir," the steward replied as he rushed by. "I don't believe there are any problems."

Robinson quickly strode to the Grand Staircase and down to the passage-way that led to his cabin. Passengers from other staterooms slowly emerged into the hallway in curiosity.

"Sir, do you know what has happened?" an elderly lady in an evening gown and coat asked him as he was about to enter his cabin.

"No, ma'am," Robinson replied smiling. "I'm sure it is nothing of significance."

Entering his cabin, Robinson immediately went to the dresser and retrieved the revolver. He unbuttoned his vest and tucked the firearm in his waist. After he re-buttoned his vest, he reached into the drawer and collected a handful of cartridges for the gun and stuffed them in his coat pocket. Looking about the cabin, Robinson reassured himself that he was leaving nothing behind – at least for the moment.

Returning to the passageway, Robinson observed more passengers casually wandering about, searching for the source of the excitement. He entered the Grand Staircase Reception area, observing more passengers congregating about in small groups. They displayed an odd mixture of apparel for a late Sunday night. Men were in tuxedos, casual clothes, sweaters, smoking jackets, pajamas. Women wore everything from flannel nightgowns to fur coats. He decided to return to the meeting place by way of the B Deck passageways to the restaurant area.

Once back outside, Robinson noted a few more passengers were aimlessly strolling around the promenades or standing at the ship's railings. However, it appeared the bitter cold was keeping people inside to stay warm. Suddenly, as he was descending a ladder to the Second Class Promenade Deck, blasts of steam, released from the forward three funnels, shattered the silence. Startled, Robinson winced at the roar of the steam jets. Upon reaching the corner of the Second Class Promenade, he saw his two cohorts. They were in formal attire indicative of first class passengers. Both carried dark leather grips.

"What's the story, guv-nah?" Porter asked in his thick accent.

"It appears the *Titanic* has struck an iceberg," Robinson replied as he glanced about them. "I don't know the seriousness of the situation."

Perplexed, Mayhew stammered, "Wh-what is our plan now?"

"Well, we don't have to stop the ship. That has already been accomplished. I believe we can forego our actions at the wireless shack. It probably is quite busy at this moment." Robinson lifted the watch from his vest pocket and opened it. He squinted and shifted the watch in his hand. "It is hard to see in this poor light. It looks to be close to midnight." Robinson returned the watch to his vest pocket. "Let us proceed to the Purser's Office, shall we? We already are on C Deck. We can pretend that our business is with the Enquiry Office next door. I'm glad you brought your holdalls."

The three men, led by Robinson, walked past the entrance to the Second Class Library. They entered a long passageway on the starboard side of the ship that directly led to the Purser's Office. Slowly they moved past first class cabins and the Maids and Valets Saloon. As the men moved forward, more and more passengers were exiting their cabins, many of them in a confused state. As they approached the entrance to the Grand Staircase foyer, Robinson observed the area in front of the Purser's Office to be mobbed by first class passengers, mostly women, clamoring for their valuables.

Robinson turned to Mayhew and Porter. "We will push past them to the Enquiry Office entrance," he instructed with raised eyebrows. And that is exactly what they did.

Leading the way, Robinson politely, but firmly, pushed and prodded his way through the impatient and, at times, unruly gaggle, finally arriving at the large, open entrance to the Enquiry Office. Somewhat disheveled, Robinson reorganized himself as his two comrades emerged from the noisy mob. He glanced at the long counter in the Enquiry Office. It was lined by men, also impatient and unruly.

"I think we will wait here for a few minutes," Robinson concluded while observing the crowds.

Suddenly a voice cried out, "Ladies and gentlemen, I am Herbert McElroy, the Chief Purser. I regret to inform you the Purser's Office is now closed." The collective voice of the mob rose. McElroy continued. "Please! Please! I can assure that your valuables and personal items will remain quite secure in our safe. Now, *please* return to your cabins and await the instructions of the stewards."

Amidst the loud grumbling, the group in front of the Purser's Office began to disperse slowly. Robinson and the two other men briefly wandered away from the Enquiry Office and to the edge of the Grand Staircase foyer. They continued to watch the entrance of the Purser's Office. Robinson again checked his watch. It was almost a quarter after twelve. After a few minutes, Chief Purser McElroy left the office, closing the door behind him, and walked past the three men to the Grand Staircase. Robinson watched him disappear up the stairs.

"Finally," Robinson sighed. "Now, we go to the Purser's Office."

They moved quickly to the office door. After listening for a moment, Robinson knocked on the door once and opened it. The three men quickly entered and closed the door behind them. A young man stood behind a counter. "I'm sorry, gentlemen," he announced. "The Purser's Office is now closed."

"Do you work here in the office?" Robinson inquired quite sincerely.

"Yes, I am Mr. King, the Chief Purser's assistant. May I help you?"

"Yes, please," Robinson replied. "I have some valuables I would like to deposit in your safe. Is it still open?"

"Yes, sir," King smiled. "I can take care of that for you."

"Actually," Robinson quietly said smiling, "I would prefer to take care of it myself." Robinson produced the Webley revolver and pointed it at King. The smiles on both faces disappeared. "Now, if you would be so kind, please open the safe."

The young assistant turned and moved to the safe as Mayhew walked around the counter and joined him. Porter moved to the door, his gun drawn. As soon as the safe door was opened, Mayhew began loading its contents into the first leather bag. It took only a handful of seconds to fill the grip.

"Here you go," Mayhew grunted as he lifted the first bag onto the counter. "Let's have the second holdall."

Robinson handed him the second leather bag and lowered the first one to the floor. It was just a few more seconds before the second bag was filled.

"That's it," Mayew proudly announced. "All done. The safe is empty."

Robinson nodded. "Very well. Mr. King, if you will please squeeze yourself into the safe. There should be plenty of room for you - at least now that it has been emptied."

An expression of fear washed over King's face.

"I wouldn't worry," Mayhew reassured him. "I am sure you will be released from your temporary imprisonment quite soon."

With that, King squeezed into the safe and the heavy steel doors were slammed shut. "That should hold 'im for a while," Porter concluded.

"Yes," Robinson nodded in agreement. "Now, we will go to my cabin, at least for a few minutes. Mr. Porter, if you please . . ." Robinson handed him the first leather grip. "I will lead the way to my luxurious accommodations."

Robinson carefully opened the office door, waited a few seconds, then motioned the two men to follow him. Their work, for the moment, was done.

* * *

In the silent distance, the lights were no longer moving.

"There's no doubt about it, Captain. The *Titanic* is dead in the water."

Captain Artemus Pritchard moved past the quartermaster and stood beside him on the bridge deck. He raised his glasses and observed the brightly lit ship, its illumination reflecting off the still waters. "I'm afraid you're correct, Mr. Danker," Captain Pritchard agreed. "She has stopped moving."

"The *Titanic* stopped too early, didn't she?" Danker asked in rising trepidation. "I mean, she stopped a half-hour ago."

"Yes," the captain concurred. "It's only twelve-fifteen, much earlier than what was planned."

"Something must have gone wrong," asserted Danker. "Maybe the doctor had to stop the ship sooner than expected."

"Possibly," the captain sighed. "But why? It doesn't make sense."

"Should we try to contact her with the Morse lamp, sir?"

"No, no," the captain replied as he lowered his glasses and studied the invisible horizon. "Not at this time. We will remain lights out for the moment."

Captain Pritchard and Quartermaster Danker silently stood on the bridge and stared at the *Titanic's* lights for a few minutes, ignoring the bitter cold while pondering their next move. Suddenly, the ship's wireless operator appeared behind the captain.

"Beggin' your pardon, sir," the young man breathlessly announced. "I just received a message from the *Titanic*, a CQD message. It's to all ships in the area." He paused and looked down at his notes, trying to capture what little light emanated from the pilothouse. "It says '*Come at once. We have struck a berg.*' They gave their position, sir."

"What is it, lad? What is their position?"

"The message reads '*Position 41.46 North, 50.14 West'*," the wireless operator announced, still breathless.

"Thank you," the captain said. "Return to the wireless. Report to me immediately of any further messages."

As the wireless operator saluted and ran off, Captain Pritchard turned to his quartermaster. "Mr. Danker, plot our position and compare it to that of the *Titanic*. Then prepare the ship to get underway. Quickly, please."

Danker simply nodded and disappeared off the bridge. Pritchard returned his gaze to the far-off lights. Well, that explains why the *Titanic* stopped.

"So – now what?" Pritchard questioned aloud to himself. "What should I do?"

The cold, silent darkness of the ocean gave him no answer.

* * *

Joshua Robinson paced the floor in his cabin while Mayhew sat in the high-backed chair and Porter reclined on the horsehair sofa.

"The ship is beginning to go down by the bow," Mayhew noted as all three could sense the slant in the cabin floor. "This iceberg thing may be more serious than originally thought."

"Yes," Robinson agreed. "Possibly so."

Before Porter could add his opinion, a polite knock came at the door. Mayhew immediately reached for his revolver.

"Put that away!" Robinson admonished Mayhew before turning and opening the door.

"Excuse me, sir," a steward announced. "I've been instructed to tell all first class passengers to please put on their lifebelts and report to the Boat Deck. And, please, dress warmly." With that, the steward disappeared down the passageway.

"Wonderful!" Porter proclaimed, nodding at the two cases on the bed. "What do we do with all that?"

"Gentlemen," Robinson concluded, "I am afraid all we can do with our ill-gotten gains is to stuff as much of it into our pockets as possible."

With that, the three men opened the two grips and placed their contents on their persons, tucking as much as possible into each of their suit and coat pockets.

"What should I do with this?" Mayhew asked, holding up a box sealed in brown wax paper with no discernable label.

"Here. Give it to me," Robinson replied. "I'll carry it."

With that, the three men, pockets bulging with money and jewels and waistbands holding their firearms, exited the cabin and proceeded, as instructed, to the boat deck.

As they began plodding along the passageway to the Grand Staircase entrance, stewards were encouraging the passengers to stop milling about. As the three men approached the staircase, the stewards were no longer gently prodding the passengers. Their instructions took on a note of urgency.

Robinson led his two partners up the Grand Staircase in concert with other passengers wearing various stages of dress and speaking in hushed tones. When they reached the Boat Deck, they walked past the Gymnasium entrance and onto the starboard side of the First Class Promenade Deck. They stood adjacent to the raised roof of the First Class Smoking Room, watching the activities occurring around them.

The Boat Deck was teeming with passengers and ship's crew. Crewmen were uncovering the sixteen lifeboats and preparing them for launch.

"Are we going to try to enter one of the lifeboats?" Porter asked in a tone of pending panic.

"No," Robinson casually replied. "The lifeboats are reserved for women and children only."

"Then what are we going to do?"

"Porter, calm down," Robinson responded curtly. "For the moment, we are going to do nothing except stand here and observe the crewmen."

"There have been no boat drills on this voyage," Mayhew reminded Robinson, "and I believe the passengers were given no boat assignments."

"Yes," Robinson agreed. "That is true. The principle question now is whether or not the *Titanic* is going to sink."

"And if she sinks . . ." Mayhew wondered aloud.

Robinson turned his gaze to Mayhew and Porter. "Then, gentlemen, we all may very well sink with her."

At that moment, as the roar of the funnel steam jets ceased, a crewman carrying a crumpled-up canvas boat cover set the bundle on the deck beside them. Robinson returned his gaze to the lifeboats. The ship's crew was slowly cranking the lifeboat davits. The wooden boats began to rise from their cradles and swing outward, free from the ship. He then heard the ship's officers call for women and children to enter the boats. It appeared the passengers were either hesitant or unwilling to be loaded onto the small craft.

Robinson suddenly heard distant music being played by the ship's band. Then he noted the bow of the *Titanic* was dropping at a steeper slant into the water. He studied the bow slowly submerging beneath them when he was startled by a bright flash and whoosh coming from the ship's bridge. There was an explosion, and bright light filled the darkness above the ship.

"Blimey!" exclaimed a shaken Porter. "They're firing rockets now. We must be sinking!"

Once again Robinson retrieved his pocket watch and observed its dial in the rocket's glare. It was twelve-forty-five. Robinson uneasily concluded the *Titanic* indeed was sinking.

"Keep calm, gentlemen," Robinson again admonished Porter and Mayhew.

"Yes, I know. Be British." Mayhew chided Robinson. "That's fine for you and Porter. But I'm Canadian, and I would rather not go swimming tonight with a stiff upper lip."

Robinson laughed aloud. "You are correct, Mr. Mayhew. But before the end of the night - in *that* water - it may very well be more than our lips that will be stiff."

"What do you think *Elgie* is doing right now?" Porter wondered above the creak of the davits.

"Knowing Pritchard, probably just standing by and watching our fireworks display." Robinson turned to Porter. "Don't worry, Ernie," he quietly reassured Porter. "We will come out of this all right. You'll see." Porter showed Robinson a faint half-hearted smile and visibly shivered with trepidation in the cold.

The crewmen began to slowly lower the first lifeboat. Soon a second lifeboat disappeared beneath the edge of the boat deck. The three men observed the women and child passengers were more quickly entering the boats without any display of hesitation. Other passengers on the boat deck showed varying signs of uneasiness, if not outright fear.

One by one, more rockets were fired into the night, the bright light illuminating white canvas lifebelts covering dark, ghostly figures. Passengers on deck were calling out to their loved ones in the boats, some in encouragement, some in sadness, some in regret, some in farewell. The rockets' brilliance showed those lifeboats in the water slowly moving away from *Titanic's* sides.

Gradually, Joshua Robinson moved his two comrades towards the front of the Boat Deck. More of the lifeboats had disappeared from their davits. More of the passengers on deck were growing loud and unruly. The whoosh of the rockets had ceased. Robinson glanced at the bow of the ship. The sea began to wash over the Forward Well Deck and around the forward cargo hold hatches. Then the Forecastle Deck at the tip of the bow was awash, the anchor chains covered by the sea. The forward slant of the *Titanic* was rapidly steepening. Finally the last of the wooden lifeboats on the ship's starboard side was gone.

Robinson observed the crewmen wrestling with the first of the collapsible lifeboats. They finally maneuvered the boat to the first davit and connected it to the winch for lowering. There was a great deal of passenger unrest around the collapsible, with shouts and, finally, gunfire.

"All right, gentlemen," Robinson spoke in a whisper. "One of the remaining collapsible lifeboats will be our ticket off the *Titanic*. Be ready to move. Quickly."

Another collapsible was launched on the opposite side of the ship. There were two collapsible lifeboats remaining. Time was running out.

* * *

To Captain Pritchard, the lights of the *Titanic* appeared strange. In his glasses the ship appeared to be listing drastically. He had observed the firing of rockets from the *Titanic*, five of them before one o'clock. Quietly the quartermaster once again joined Pritchard on the bridge.

"Anything more from the wireless, Mr. Danker?"

"Just as before, Captain," Danker replied. "The *Titanic* is sinking by the bow. She's asking for all ships in the immediate vicinity to come to her aid as quickly as possible."

The Captain remained dispassionate.

"Captain, shouldn't we move in to help? We're just ten miles from *Titanic*. We may be able to help them."

"Quiet, Danker," the Captain said testily as he lowered his glasses. "I know where we are. I don't need you to tell me."

"What about the doctor and our men?" Danker reminded him.

"It's too late now to help them," Pritchard replied as he again raised his glasses and stared at the foundering ship. "This was an insane scheme to begin with. Those men knew the risks. The play has been completed, and their stage is sinking from beneath them. I'm done with the lot of them. My concern is with *this* ship. I will not become involved in their troubles."

"But, sir," implored the quartermaster, "all those passengers? And the crew . . ."

The Captain lowered his glasses and turned to Danker. "Damn it!" Pritchard snapped. "I will *not* have my orders, or my intentions, questioned on this ship. By anyone! Do you understand me?"

"Yes, Captain," Danker quietly replied.

"Besides," Pritchard continued, "the *Titanic* has plenty of lifeboats. Let them use their lifeboats. *Elgie* need not interfere."

"Yes, Captain," the quartermaster quietly concurred with a tinge of resignation and regret in his voice.

In the darkness before them the rocket display continued.

* * *

Robinson led his two men into the congregation of passengers at the front of the starboard Boat Deck. Crewmen were attempting to maneuver the last collapsible lifeboat from its cradle amidst the tangled moorings, the port list of the ship making it an almost impossible task. One crewmember propped wooden boards against the outside wall of the Officers Quarters. The attempt to carefully slide the collapsible down the planks and onto the Boat Deck faltered as the sea was washing over the Bridge Deck and into the Wheelhouse. A wave suddenly engulfed the men around the collapsible.

Robinson pushed past the passengers retreating from the oncoming rush of seawater and grabbed the stern of the collapsible. The boat began to float off the deck, its canvas sides still folded. Robinson threw the box into the boat and leapt in with Mayhew and Porter following behind him. But before they could jump into the craft, the two men were struck by another wave.

Mayhew managed to grab the stern lines just before they were cut. Porter, though, was overtaken by the water's surge and swept off the Boat Deck. For a moment, it appeared Porter was going to be washed out to sea, but then the suction of a newly-submerged ventilator shaft pulled him back toward the ship and the collapsible lifeboat. Grasping an oarlock, Robinson reached out and grabbed Porter as he was sucked towards the ventilator grating.

"Mayhew!" Robinson cried out. "Help me hold on to Porter!"

As Porter struggled in the water, Mayhew reached past Robinson and took ahold of the drowning man's overcoat collar. Together, Robinson and Mayhew pulled him into the collapsible just as other passengers were thrashing about the lifeboat, attempting to lift themselves out of the water.

"God!" Porter chattered. "It's so terribly cold. I'm freezing!"

"Lie down against me," Mayhew insisted. "I'll try to keep you warm."

The three men rested against the stern of the half-swamped collapsible. As other passengers in the water swam towards it, the boat slowly drifted away from *Titanic*. Occasionally, a swimmer would have the strength to lift himself into the boat. Gradually, the collapsible, its sides down, barely rode above the water. No one attempted to bail out the craft. The passengers simply sat on the tiny boat's planking, legs half-submerged in freezing water.

Robinson stared at *Titanic*. The promenade decks and portholes were ablaze with lights. The masts and ship's funnels seemed to tower above them. The bow was completely submerged, the lights below the water casting an eerie blue and green glow. The stern lifted higher and higher with each passing moment. Passengers still on board lined the railings, many of them migrating to the rising stern. There was a cacophony of sounds emanating from the ship. He could still hear the band's music drifting into the darkness. But now it was joined by countless human voices.

The *Titanic*, too, was given voice. In the distance, Robinson could detect deep groans echoing within its hull, accentuated by cracking and clattering and crashing. People, joined by planking, potted plants and deck furniture, slid down and splashed into the sea. The voices and the sounds rose as the ship's lights flickered out for the final time.

The people aboard the collapsible lifeboat said nothing. The silence in the boat was interrupted only by moans from Porter and some of the others. But across the water, it sounded as if thunder had been unleashed from the great ship, a virtual roar of destruction. In the din, Robinson heard a distinct, brief snapping noise. Suddenly the ship's forward funnel toppled into the ocean. It created a wave that nearly swamped the tiny lifeboat.

Now, the *Titanic* only could be seen by its dark silhouette against the stars. For a moment, in the thunder of the night, the ship's stern seemed briefly to settle. Then it arose again, almost straight into the night sky, the three huge bronze propellers gleaming in the starlight. For a few minutes, it remained there as if refusing to surrender to the sea. Then the stern slowly descended until it disappeared into the darkness.

"My God," Mayhew whispered. "She's gone."

"Yes," Robinson returned the whisper. "Yes. She is gone. God have mercy on us."

"What have we done?"

"Mr. Mayhew," Robinson sighed, "I believe what we have done is no less than releasing God's wrath upon us for all eternity. Our tiny piece of this world will pay for our sins. Forever."

The tiny boat floated on into the universe of stars around it. At the first light of morning, the occupants of the collapsible would be rescued by a ship named the *Carpathia*. For three of those saved, they would begin to pay a terrible price for their voyage.

* * *

The Captain lowered his glasses for the last time. The lights on the *Titanic* had finally disappeared on the distant dark horizon. The ship was gone, he concluded. Somewhere.

But that was not Captain Pritchard's problem. His work was done. He had carried out his orders as instructed. He still had his ship and damn all the others to hell. Pritchard strolled from the bridge to the wheelhouse. A welcome blast of warmth struck him as he entered the dimly lit room. Behind the helmsman stood the quartermaster.

"Mr. Danker, let's get underway. Set a course for return to St. Margarets Bay."

"Yes, Captain," came the reply. Danker was not about to mention the name of the *Titanic* again. Not ever.

"And, Mr. Danker, let's proceed very slowly with first light. There's a lot of field ice about. We need to be very cautious. Everyone is to keep awake and alert. Especially the lookouts. After all, we must take care of *Elgie*."

"Yes, Captain," Danker nodded. "As you wish."

"I'm going to retire now," Pritchard announced. "Wake me at sunrise."

"Yes, Captain."

With that, Pritchard went to his quarters. Soon the single screw of the nearly empty ship began to turn, the tips of the blades breaking the surface of the water. Slowly, she turned and made her trek north. This ship, too, as had *Titanic's* lifeboats, sailed on into the universe of stars around it.

And, thus, was born the Siren of the *Loch Gillelli*.

Chapter 1

The tapping on the glass was what awakened him. The eyelids briefly fluttered and then opened slightly, his eyes trying to focus on the bedroom window. The leaves on the tree limbs outside danced in the wind and the raindrops. The early morning sky was dark and threatening.

Rob Randall closed his eyes and let out a soft moan as he turned onto his back. He glanced at the pillow beside him. It was covered by a shapeless splay of dark hair.

"Well, Maggie," Randall whispered, "it looks like we're inside for another day. More rain, just like yesterday. No boat today." The dark mass of hair slowly rose from its perch. Then the furry shape stretched, its back arching high above Randall's face.

"Yeah, I know," Randall grunted. "You'd rather be on the boat than stuck in here with me." He watched the shadowy form saunter to the edge of the bed. "Tough luck, cat. Live with it." The cat's disappearance over the edge was followed by a thump and a disgruntled meow. "She left me," Randall sighed. "Story of my life."

He swung his legs out from under the sheet and sat upright on the bed. It was raining harder, the water flowing down the lower portion of the window pane. He shivered slightly, his arms folded about his chest. The cat padded around to his side of the bed and sat down. She glared at him with wide-open eyes. "What? What do you want?" Maggie let out a bellicose cry and trotted from the bedroom. "All right, all right," he assured her. "I'm coming. I'll feed you."

Randall donned a robe and stumbled from the bedroom to the kitchen. The cat sat next to her food bowl. Her bellowing continued unabated. He opened a glass container from the kitchen counter and filled her bowl, all the while the black head with pointed ears squawking and pushing his hand aside.

"Pig," Randall muttered. The bellowing had ended, replaced by slurping and snorting. The regular early morning ritual had ended. He shook his head as he opened the refrigerator door and poured himself a glass of orange juice. Taking a sip, he walked into the living room. He glanced at the living room bay window. Still darkened sky, still heavy rain. Setting down the juice glass, Randall opened the front door to the second story apartment and retrieved the newspaper from the hallway. He unfolded the paper and glanced at the headlines, noticing the paper was somewhat damp. I'll let it dry out a bit, he thought.

Randall returned to the juice glass and sat down on the sofa. The only light in the living room came from the front window and from the one opposite in the dining room. He yawned and fought to keep his eyes open. He had just drifted off when the phone rang.

Snapping awake, Randall glanced at the clock. It was almost nine. He leaned over and picked up the receiver, noticing the number on the call screen as being from overseas.

"Randall here," he announced, curious to know the caller on the other end of the line.

"Hello, Rob. This is Alex Sheffland. I hope I am not calling too early."

"Uh-h, no. No," he stammered. "Not at all."

Randall was stunned. Four months ago, he was partially responsible for the actions that led to the deaths of Alex Sheffland's sister and her husband and for incarcerating his brother Nigel on a myriad of criminal charges. After giving his depositions in the court cases, Randall expected never again to have contact with the Sheffland family.

"I have not talked to you since our flight to Reno," Sheffland continued. "Have you sufficiently recovered from our nasty altercation with the military drone aircraft?"

Randall instantly remembered the mid-air collision between one of British Sovereign's Boeing Triple Sevens and a remotely-piloted vehicle over Nevada. He and Alex Sheffland had suffered the misfortune of being on board the aircraft during the mid-air accident.

"Yes, Alex," Randall replied stiffly. "It could have been worse."

"Worse for you, maybe," Sheffland said coldly. "But not all that much for us."

Ouch, Randall thought. "Yes," he agreed, "I suppose that is true." He paused a moment. "How are you doing, Alex?"

"Oh, well enough to be expected," he replied somewhat curtly.

"And your father?"

"I suppose the same," Sheffland responded. "Well enough to be expected."

Randall suddenly felt trapped by a single phone call on a rainy morning. He tried to quell the sickening sense of panic. "Quite honestly, Alex, I feel terrible about what happened to you and your family." Randall quickly recovered his voice. "In many ways, it truly is a terrible tragedy. But a lot of lives were saved. And a lot more are and will be free from danger when they fly. As we said in the Navy, regardless of flying conditions, someone has to haul the mail. This time, I hauled the mail. No excuses. No apologies."

There was a long pause on the phone. "Yes, you're right, Rob," came Sheffland's response in weak resignation. "I know that. So does my father. I think I would have been disappointed had you responded in any other way. The Shefflands brought all of this on themselves. Deep down, I believe they have been doing it for decades. That is why I have called you."

"How so?" Randall cautiously asked.

"Rob, our family is in trouble. The airline is in trouble. My father and I want your help. We are asking for your help."

"Alex, I cannot help you with the pending court cases against Nigel or British Sovereign. The facts and circumstances speak for themselves. My contribution stands as is."

"Yes, Rob, I acknowledge that. It is not the court cases. Our difficulties go far beyond our legal problems. Far, far beyond them."

"I don't understand," Randall said somewhat confused, "but I will try to help you if I can."

"Thank you." Sheffland sounded relieved. "I do not wish to impose upon you, but would you be willing to fly to London to visit with my father and me? For a brief visit, anyway. If after we explain our current situation to you . . . if you wish to bow out, we will understand."

"Well," Randall explained, "before I agree to such a trip, I need to review some legal issues. You know, not step on anyone's toes, so to speak."

"Yes, I understand. Please let me know of your decision as soon as possible."

"I will, Alex. I'll talk with you soon." Randall returned the phone receiver to its cradle. He was filled both with curiosity and trepidation. He concluded whatever it was, it wasn't good.

He rose from the couch and walked back to the bedroom and to the bath. He stared into the mirror over the sink. His once thin face was now full with age, the paint faded and cracked from the years. I'm glad Laurel never saw me like this, Randall mused. Instantly he regretted the thought. No, no, that's wrong. I wish she were here. How long has it been? How long has she been gone? Thirty-three years? No? No. Thirty-four years. Yes. Thirty- four . . .

He looked down and gazed at his hands. At least they were not shaking.

* * *

Another football game – another disappointment. Will the Ravens ever get back to winning, Randall wondered. To quote the Raven, "Nevermore." He laughed out loud at his own joke.

"What's so funny?" Jack Kilby asked as he set his drink down on the coffee table.

"Ah, nothin'," Randall replied. "It's just if I'm not trying to figure out Baltimore's problems when they're in the red zone, I'm busy renaming the Washington Redskins. With all the bureaucracy there, my newest suggestion is the Washington Wildcrats. Their mascot can be a neutered tom cat with a front paw stuck in a cookie jar."

"I like it," Kilby nodded. "That name has a certain panache to it."

"Yeah," Randall agreed, "and they can rename the stadium the Big Litterbox."

"Yeah," Kilby concurred, "that works for me."

Both turned their attention back to the game. The Ravens were losing.

Again. Suddenly, Helen Kilby entered the family room carrying a large plate with both hands and set it down on the coffee table. "I made up some appetizers for you."

"What are they?" her husband asked casually, yet cautiously.

"They're homemade egg rolls," Helen smiled. "Chicken."

Randall crinkled his forehead. "Egg rolls? With pot roast?"

"Oh, I forgot to tell you," Kilby said half-heartedly. "Helen is making chicken chow mein for our Sunday dinner today."

"Yes," Helen confirmed with a breezy gesture and a smile, "and you'll love it. Can I get you fellows anything else?"

"No, dear," Kilby replied. "We're fine."

As she left the room, she asked over her shoulder, "Who's winning the game?"

"Cincinnati is crushing Baltimore," Randall chimed in.

"That's nice," Helen Kilby responded as she disappeared from view.

Randall stared at Kilby, one eyebrow raised. "Chicken chow mein?"

"Helen has a new recipe," Kilby sighed. "You know, angel hair pasta and teriyaki sauce. Some new concoction."

"But I *like* her pot roast," Randall protested mildly. "Okay," he acquiesced. "I'm game." He paused for a moment, glancing at the television screen. Then he turned to Kilby. "Jack, are you all ready for retirement?" Randall inquired sheepishly.

"No," Kilby replied. "I wasn't ready a month ago when you asked. And I'm still not ready."

"I was just wondering . . ." Randall innocently responded. "You've got only a few months left."

"Yeah, I know. It's just that I don't believe the Bureau recognizes the concept of retirement."

Randall laughed. "Well, why don't you do what I did. Just have the men in white drag you off to the big rubber room, you know, wearing a suit that buttons up the back."

Kilby stared at Randall for a moment. "You know, Rob," he said quietly, "I'm glad you can make light of that – now. It's been a long time."

They let the matter drop, each lost in his own private thoughts. Randall changed the subject. "Jack, you'll never guess who called me a few days ago."

"Olivia Brightmann," Kilby replied with a grin.

"No. And not Esther Craig, either."

"Boring," Kilby shrugged. "So, who?"

"Alex Sheffland."

The smile on Kilby's face faded quickly. "Is that right. No kidding." They weren't questions. Randall simply nodded. "What did he want?"

Randall shrugged his shoulders. "I really don't know what he wanted. I mean, not exactly. He told me his family is in trouble. Not the problems with Nigel or the counterfeit aircraft parts scheme. Something worse."

"Worse than murders and suicide and fraud on an international scale?" Kilby asked mystified.

"Apparently," Randall replied. "It was very strange. Alex sounded, well, he sounded almost desperate. He wants me to fly to London and meet with him and perhaps his father."

Kilby raised his drink glass from the table and stared down into it. "I wonder how Sir Geoffrey is doing?"

"From what I could gather, not so good." Randall shook his head. "I suppose that is to be expected."

"Rob, you know you can't do anything to help in the court trials. We've given our depositions on the murder case. And with the parts fraud, the airline company is hanging out to dry on that one. You couldn't do anything - even if you wanted to."

"Yeah, I know," Randall sighed. "I made that quite clear to Alex. I told him I could not and *would* not help them in either court case. He said that didn't matter – that the Shefflands needed my help on something else much more serious."

"But he wouldn't say what it was?" responded an incredulous Kilby. "That *is* strange."

"What do you think?" Randall asked. "Do you think I should go to London?"

"Well, I'm not sure," Kilby replied. "I can't imagine why they would need your assistance, that is, unless it *is* a matter of life or death."

"Or both," Randall said, "especially if it involves their airline."

"You're on your own on this one, pardner," Kilby responded in resignation. "I can't advise you on this one, pro or con."

Kilby set his drink down on the table. "At least, not until after we've had our chow mein dinner. Who knows? Maybe I'll be given the wisdom to figure out an answer for you after I've opened my fortune cookie."

Randall smiled. "Hopefully the message will be written in the proper King's English."

"Yes," Kilby agreed. "We can always hope."

At that moment Helen Kilby sauntered into the family room. "Here. I almost forgot the chopsticks."

Randall and Kilby stared at one another. It was going to be a Sunday meal of some duration.

Chapter 2

The night seemed to envelop the airfield. Randall glanced at his watch. It was almost ten-thirty. He looked outside the small waiting room at Manassas Regional Airport. He noticed the twinkling blue lights of the taxiways and, as always, thought of Laurel. Her stardust.

Randall had decided to make the trip to London. Whether out of guilt or just plain curiosity, he couldn't decide. Perhaps it was both. Now he was waiting to be picked up by a Cessna Citation business jet owned by the Sheffland's company, British Sovereign Airlines. He wondered if it was the same aircraft he stopped with a pickup truck on a New Hampshire airport taxiway four months ago. Randall did not have to wait long to get an answer.

He heard rather than saw the small jet taxi and park in front of two automatic doors that led to the terminal ramp. Randall stood and walked to a window. No sooner had the two engines been shut down than the jet's passenger door was opened and a man carrying small wheel chocks stepped down onto the concrete and placed the chocks at the nose wheels. It was the same aircraft, he concluded. Randall winced as he remembered the front radome of the aircraft coming to rest about three inches from the side of his head. Oh, well, he mused, better to *ride* in it than be *run* over by it.

He returned to his seat and slid his carry-on and briefcase in front of him. Randall contemplated his pending flight to London. It would take at least eight or nine hours, he surmised. A long trip. I hope the trip is worth it, he thought.

A dark haired man in a white shirt and dark blue slacks walked through the automatic doors and into the terminal. On his shoulders were black chevrons with gold stripes. A four-striper, he noted, his captain for the flight. He went to the counter and quietly chatted with the airport supervisor on duty. After a few minutes he turned and approached Randall. "Are you Mr. Randall?" Randall nodded. "My name is Alan Embry. I believe you will be accompanying us to England this evening. May I take your bag, sir?"

"Yes, thank you," Randall responded.

"Please follow me. We shan't be long. No dawdling tonight."

Together the two men walked past the doors and onto the tarmac. Embry allowed Randall to enter the aircraft first. He followed, stowing Randall's bag in a small closet. Randall's height forced him to lower his head and bend down at the waist as he entered the cabin of the corporate jet. He did not notice the single passenger already on board until he heard a familiar voice.

"Good Lord! Look what the cat dragged in!"

Randall raised his head just enough to find the source of the remark. Reclining in a seat was Don Wiltsey.

"Don? Geez! They gave you your own private jet?"

Wiltsey raised his seat back and stared at Randall with a wide grin. "Hell, yes. Only the best for an old SAC weenie."

Randall sat down in a plush leather seat facing Wiltsey. "I didn't expect to find you in here," Randall remarked as he fastened his seat belt. "What'd you do? Rob a bank?"

"No, nothing like that," Wiltsey replied as he reached into his shirt pocket and retrieved a toothpick in a cellophane wrapper. "They made me the new Manager of Maintenance for the British Sovereign – North American Operations." He opened the cellophane packet and placed the wooden toothpick in his mouth. "Like I said, not bad for an old Air Force retread."

"Not bad at all," Randall agreed.

The smile on Wiltsey's face faded. "I replaced Terry Chapman after his death. You remember Mac?"

"Mac McKuen?" Randall replied. "Yes, I remember him."

"Well, Mac's got my old job. He's the Maintenance Chief. And Byron Beauchamp began running the entire BSA operation here in North America after Alex Sheffland returned to London to take over Nigel's job."

"How are the Shefflands doing?" Randall cautiously asked, afraid of the answer.

"I guess they're doing all right," Wiltsey responded, shrugging his shoulders. "Don't see them much anymore." Randall simply nodded and said nothing. "But the company is doing well," Wiltsey continued, his voice trailing off.

"Good. That's good to hear." An uncomfortable silence followed.

"That parts deal?" Wiltsey resumed the conversation. "We've got that under control now. All the electrical parts from DyNational are being re-placed. They're being purged from the inventory. That's one of the reasons Mac was promoted. He's heading up the effort. The guy is a bull in a china shop. He'll clean up the house for sure."

Randall decided to change the subject. "What's taking you to London tonight?"

"Oh," Wiltsey casually shifted the toothpick in his mouth, "the big-wigs are calling a tribal pow-wow for a few days. They do that every once in a while. You know, flight operations and maintenance. New policies, new rules, more coordination, better communications, that sort of thing." Randall just nodded. "Why are you riding on this fancy taxi?" Wiltsey's eyes bored into Randall.

"Honestly, Don, I really don't know. Alex Sheffland asked me to visit them in London. It appears the Shefflands need my help on a matter of some importance." Randall paused for a moment. "You wouldn't happen to know anything about it, would you?"

"Nope," came a terse reply.

"I don't believe it has anything to do with the legal matters facing the Shefflands," Randall continued as he glanced out the cabin window and into the darkness. "At least, I hope not."

"A lot of bad business," Wiltsey sighed. "Bad business."

The cabin door banged closed and they heard the two jet engines start and spool up.

"Well, at least we've got each other's company on this flight," Wilt-sey brightened. "Won't be so boring." "Randall nodded and smiled. "I think we're going to return to Pease and refuel before going on to England," Wilt-sey concluded. "I suppose I'll have to watch you while we're there. You know, make sure you don't go speeding around the airport taxiways in an old pickup truck."

Randall smiled. "Not unless the plane tries to leave without me."

The Citation began to taxi to the runway. "Rob, before we take off," Wiltsey leaned forward, "I've got to ask you something. The triple-7, your flight to Reno. *How* did you know? How *did* you know that the plane was going to collide with a military drone in mid-air over Nevada?"

Randall gave Wiltsey a wry smile and a slight shrug of the shoulders.

"I've heard every supposition, every wild-ass guess under the sun," Wiltsey continued. "Soothsayers, psychics, tarot cards, dream catching, even reading tea leaves *and* coffee grounds! I've heard it *all*."

The jet turned onto the runway and briefly held its position.

"Don, I'm really not at liberty to say. But I will tell you this. The dried bones of a small chicken, thrown into a circle made of white string, work the best. Especially on Tuesdays."

With that, the plane roared off into the night.

* * *

Through the cabin window of the Cessna Citation jet, the English countryside below appeared lush and bright green, even for mid-September. Randall, recently awakened but not refreshed, wished he could crawl into a bed and sleep for another eight hours. He never was completely relaxed while flying, a carryover from his days as a pilot in Naval aviation.

"Looks like we're coming in on final," Wiltsey casually remarked. He and Randall had talked for a time after departing from Virginia, mostly about mutual military experiences and boat restorations. After leaving New Hampshire, however, the two slept on their flight to England. Both appeared slightly less than rested.

"Do you know where we're landing?" Randall asked as he looked off into the distance. "It seems like we are west of London."

"More like southwest," Wiltsey replied. "The Citation usually flies into and out of Farnborough Airport. That's where they keep the plane when it's here in England. Farnborough isn't far from the Sheffland's home and the British Sovereign headquarters in Littleton. Besides, Farnborough Airport caters to corporate jets like this one."

Randall nodded as he heard the landing gear drop into position. He watched out the window as the aircraft descended until he saw the runway asphalt over-run appear below them and then heard the thump of the tires hit the concrete.

Wiltsey smiled. "You know, I'm amazed at these little corporate jets. They are just about as hot as an Air Force fighter, the way they take off and land. All they need are afterburners and a drag chute."

"The key word is *little*," Randall responded. "I can't wait until I get out of this air machine and stand up straight. I think I've developed a permanent crook in my back."

"Yeah," Wiltsey agreed. "These things aren't built for guys our size. It's impossible to stretch out."

The Citation taxied from the runway and parked at the end of a line of other small business jets. Randall noticed two black limousines pull up to the plane as the engines spooled down to silence. Embry emerged from the cockpit and opened the cabin door. He passed the passengers' luggage to two men dressed in dark suits who emerged from the cars.

"Well, it looks like our rides are here," Wiltsey remarked as he crawled from his seat.

"Yeah," Randall agreed. "I hope they're not in a hurry. I need to stretch for a minute."

Wiltsey exited the aircraft followed by Randall. As he stepped from the plane, Randall thanked Embry for a nice flight. "Sorry about that last hour," Embry apologized. "We caught the edge of a nasty storm that is moving in tonight."

"No problem," Randall responded. "I've flown through weather a whole lot worse."

As Randall stepped onto the ramp, a young man greeted him with a broad smile. "Hello, Mr. Randall. I'm here to drive you to the Sheffland's home. Shall we?"

Randall nodded and turned to Wiltsey. "I guess this is where we part ways," Randall surmised.

"Yeah," Wiltsey said. "I've got my own ride. I'll be heading over to the BSA main office to meet with my counterpart here in Europe."

"Good seeing you again, Don," Randall smiled as they shook hands. "I hope your meetings go well."

"Yeah," Wiltsey replied with a tinge of wariness. "Maybe I'll see you around."

Randall watched as Wiltsey entered the limo. Barely visible through dark tinted windows, he saw Wiltsey give him a brief nod and a wave. Then the vehicle sped off. Randall suddenly felt a chill. Strange, he thought. During the entire trip, Don Wiltsey never once mentioned the events surrounding Nigel Sheffland four months ago. At once he regretted making this trip.

"Sir, shall we go?" The voice of his driver seemed to awaken him.

"Hum? What?"

"Mr. Randall," the young man repeated. "Shall we go?"

"Uh, yes. Yes, sure."

Randall slipped into the back seat of the limousine. The glass partition was up. He rode in silence as the vehicle left the aerodrome and proceeded east through Farnborough and into the countryside beyond. He felt weary. The ride through the English landscape, though beautiful, seemed somewhat monotonous. I'm just tired, he thought.

Moments before entering the village of Windlesham, the limo turned south from the main road and onto a narrow paved path framed at the entrance with two large granite posts. After crossing a small bridge, the ride continued through open country for almost a mile until the road entered the grounds of Banhaven, announced by nothing more than a modest stone marker. The limousine parked at the front entrance to the manor. The driver exited the vehicle and opened the rear door. "Welcome to Banhaven, Mr. Randall."

Randall emerged from the vehicle and looked at the estate. He was surprised that the manor was smaller than he had imagined although it was far larger than Fenwall, the Sheffland's home in New England. It was old and stately, and in a way, somewhat dreary. Perhaps it was the façade of sterile, grey stone.

"Please come with me," the limo driver instructed. Randall followed him to the front entrance. As they reached the massive wooden doors, the one on the right opened.

"Hello, Mr. Randall." A familiar face greeted him. "It is good to see you again." It was Simon, the caretaker of Fenwall Manor, whom Randall met during his visit to New Hampshire.

"Simon, what a wonderful surprise," Randall exclaimed. "You have returned to England. Is your wife Rose with you?"

"Oh, yes, sir," Simon replied. "I would not go anywhere without her."

"Is she here at Banhaven?"

"Indeed, sir. She is in the kitchen as we speak." Randall smiled and nodded.

Simon briefly addressed the limo driver, instructing him to deliver Randall's valise upstairs to the west wing guest room. Then he again returned his attention to Randall. "We have been expecting you. Was your flight satisfactory? Not too bumpy, I hope."

"The flight was fine," Randall replied. "Not too bumpy. Just the last hour or so."

"Good," Simon responded with a slight frown. "You know, I have never liked flying in that little jet. It's much too small, and it scares me, especially when flying across the ocean in it."

"I know what you mean," Randall agreed, "But it sure beats walking. Or swimming."

Simon laughed. "Yes, I suppose that is true, sir." He paused a moment. "Now, if you will come with me, I will lead you to our guest bedroom."

With that, Randall followed Simon to a staircase to the right of the main foyer. The floor was a light grey, almost white, marble that seemed to magnify the echoes of their footfalls. As they ascended the wide staircase, Randall noticed the ceiling braced by massive dark wood timbers. The manor appeared to be hundreds of years old.

When they reached the second floor, Simon turned right down a long corridor. They walked past several closed doors before coming to an open one. Randall entered the room first. It was splendidly furnished with a luxuriant canopy bed and rich, dark oak furniture. Unlike the manor's exterior, the guest room exuded warmth.

"Sir, it is almost two o'clock. Mr. Sheffland thought you would like to rest for a while before dinner. If you wish, I can call on you at seven."

"That would be fine, Simon." Simon bowed slightly and started for the door. "And Simon?" He stopped and turned to Randall. "It is good to see you again." Simon smiled and nodded as he closed the door behind him.

Randall walked to the window and stared out at the countryside. I hope that goes for the Shefflands, too, he mused.

Chapter 3

The darkness awakened him. He drew in his breath. The deathly silence magnified the night. At once, a sense of claustrophobia washed over him as if the canopy curtains were the drapes of a coffin.

Randall sprung from the bed, his chest heaving. He searched in the dark for a light. Finding a table lamp, the room was illuminated. He returned to the bed and sat on its edge, glancing at the bed's drapes. He shook his head and laughed to himself. Too many movies seen as a kid where the canopy of a bed came down and smothered the occupants, he thought.

Randall looked at his watch. It was nearly seven o'clock. He gazed out the bedroom window. The sun had long since set, the blanket of the night covering the grounds of the estate. He stood and walked to the bathroom. He felt awake after the long nap and refreshed after a splash of water on his face. He was drying his face and hands when a knock came at the door. He placed the towel on the bathroom sink and headed to the bedroom door.

"Alex!" Randall exclaimed as he opened the door. "I'm sorry. I was expecting Simon to be standing there!"

Alex Sheffland smiled and offered his hand. "Oh, I thought I would wake you from your slumber." The handshake from Alex was firm, the smile seemingly genuine and friendly. "Important guests always receive increased attention. Would you like to join me for dinner?" Randall nodded and returned the smile. "I hope our accommodations meet with your approval," Sheffland continued as they strolled down the hallway. "Some find the place somewhat bleak at times. It has been the family home for a number of years." Randall said nothing as he followed Sheffland down the staircase. "Was your flight satisfactory?"

"Yes," Randall replied, "very enjoyable."

"You will have to forgive Captain Embry," Sheffland chuckled. "He is a former Royal Air Force fighter pilot. Very sober and straight-laced when it comes to flying one of our Boeing Triple-7s, but when he flies the Citation, he reverts back to his days in the RAF. He truly believes he is flying one of their Tornados."

Randall laughed before responding. "No, nothing like that. No split-S maneuvers. No loops or rolls. Very sedate and proper flying."

"That is good to know." Suddenly they heard the distant rumble of thunder. "It appears you also made it in before the bad weather."

"Yes, I believe you're right," Randall agreed.

Sheffland ushered Randall into a plush dining room adorned with antique china cabinets. Above the long dining room table hung an ornate crystal and brass chandelier. Sheffland designated a chair at one end of the table for Randall as he strolled to the opposite end and sat. Randall felt as though he was staring down the length of a runway, the view of the end interrupted by a silver candelabrum.

"I believe I will need the use of a bullhorn to talk to you," Randall remarked loudly, "or perhaps a UHF radio."

"Yes," came a voice from behind the candelabrum. "You are correct. That is why I will be joining you at your end of the table momentarily. I simply do this to display a proper sense of British civility and decorum." At that moment, Simon entered the dining room carrying a tray holding another place setting.

"Just to let you know, Alex, I've slid down a saloon bar top that was longer than this table, so you really aren't impressing your American cousins."

Sheffland stood and walked towards Randall, laughing at the remark as he sat down next to his guest. "I suppose the bar room landing was accomplished during those days of your carefree and impetuous youth."

"Actually," Randall replied soberly, "it was just last week."

Sheffland's laughter became the true English guffaw. "You Americans .

. .” The frivolity slowly trailed off. “At least now we don't have to shout at each other,” Sheffland said smiling.

"I hope not," Randall responded. "Will Sir Geoffrey be joining us?"

The smile on Alex Sheffland's face instantly faded. "No. Father has been taking meals in his room. He will be joining us later."

Randall nodded before speaking again. "How is your father doing?" he asked quietly.

"Oh, as I said in our phone conversation, he has both good days and bad days. Work keeps him busy, his mind occupied. But there is such an impenetrable anguish. Losing Lydia and her husband . . . Nigel in prison, so much sadness . . ."

"Alex, that day in Reno, when we made the emergency landing, I didn't see you again. I never had the chance to express my condolences. My - my regrets."

"I know," Sheffland responded. "At first I was angry. Bitter. But then the enormity of the situation struck me. The attempt on our lives. The incredible extent of the counterfeit electrical parts scheme that could have destroyed British Sovereign. Lydia's death. Nigel's duplicity . . ." Sheffland shook his head.

Randall remained mute as Sheffland continued. "The mid-air collision with the military drone seems to pale in comparison with everything else. It would have been easy to blame you and Kilby for our trials and tribulations. But you saved our lives. Mine, you saved twice. You prevented the deaths of almost three hundred people. You saved British Sovereign. Simply said, our travails, our torments, were visited upon us by ourselves. We only have ourselves to blame. No one else."

Sheffland paused before continuing. "Now everything has changed. Nigel is in prison. I have returned to England to assume the reins of the company. Byron Beauchamp is managing our North American operations."

"He's a good man," Randall interrupted. "He and Don Wiltsey will help you and your father. You can be assured of that."

"Yes, you are right. They already have. We have been very fortunate in that regard. I wish that my father . . . I just wish I could help him more."

For a moment, there was a deafening silence between them. Randall decided to break it. "Alex, why did you ask me to come to London?"

"Because my father and I," Sheffland hesitated, "because we both need your help. Far more than you know. And you will know soon enough."

Simon and Rose chose that moment to serve dinner. The meal was consumed mostly in silence.

* * *

After a dinner of beef and potatoes, Sheffland and Randall retired to the study of Banhaven Manor. The high ceiling, the luxurious furnishings, and the wall-to-wall bookcases seemed to add to the grandeur of Banhaven. The huge stone fireplace was ablaze, the warmth permeating the recesses of the room and the glow brightening the dim light of a single lamp on the massive desk.

"This is a beautiful room," Randall commented as he sat on the couch in front of the fireplace.

"Yes," Sheffland agreed. "I love this old house. I was never truly comfortable at Fenwall. It seemed oddly cold, even forbidding. After . . ." he paused. "After Lydia and her husband died, we decided to sell Fenwall. We could not live there. Ever again."

Randall thought of Fenwall. Sheffland was right. The house did seem cold, almost menacing.

"But Banhaven," Sheffland continued as he prepared a drink, "Banhaven is home. We grew up here. My father was raised here. This is *our* home. I do not wish to leave it again."

"Perhaps you will have the opportunity to raise your own children here," Randall remarked as he glanced about the room. "I can think of worse places."

"Absolutely," Sheffland concurred, "as soon as I marry someone who will have me."

"Somehow, I don't think that will be a problem," Randall said with a faint smile.

"I hope not," Sheffland wished. "I am currently dating one of our flight attendants. She is, I believe you would say, a knock-out. Much better than I deserve."

"Hang in there," advised Randall. "Hopefully you will be as lucky as I was."

"Are you sure you do not want a drink?" Sheffland asked as he sat in a chair facing Randall.

"No," Randall replied. "I'm fine. But thank you."

Sheffland took a sip from his glass. He carefully set the glass down on the small table next to his chair. "Well, I suppose we should get down to business," Sheffland casually remarked. "That is, if you're up to it. After all, it is almost eight o'clock."

"No problem," Randall responded. "I slept on the plane. And the five hour nap helped. I'm fine."

"A number of years ago," Alex Sheffland began, "while working for the NTSB, you participated in the investigation of a commercial airliner crash in the Atlantic Ocean off the coast of Nova Scotia. Is that correct?"

"Yes," Randall replied. "You are correct. It was an accident involving a Swissair MD-11."

"Tell me about the crash," Sheffland said as he placed the fingertips of his hands together as if preparing for prayer. "All that you can remember."

"Well, like I said," Randall responded, "it was a Swissair flight. Uh, Flight 111, I believe. It was a scheduled commercial flight from JFK in New York to Cointain International Airport in Geneva, Switzerland. If my memory serves me right, I think it was a code-share flight with Delta Airlines." Randall paused momentarily, trying to recollect the past. "The accident occurred in early September of 1998," Randall continued. "Not long after departing JFK, the Swissair pilots reported they were experiencing some difficulties with the aircraft's electrical system. The electrical problems resulted in a fire that began in the ceiling of the plane near the cockpit bulkhead. The fire slowly spread into the cockpit, affecting controls and instrumentation and probably incapacitating the flight crew." Randall paused a moment.

"Please continue," prompted Sheffland. "What happened after the fire started?"

"The aircrew decided to divert the flight to Halifax, Nova Scotia. But the pilots had to remain off-shore to dump fuel, you know, reduce the plane's weight before landing. They never made it to Halifax. The aircraft went down in the Atlantic southwest of the airport. If I remember correctly, the plane crashed just five or six miles from shore."

Sheffland nodded. "A dreadful accident, to be sure."

"Yes," Randall agreed. "Second worse aviation disaster in Canadian history. Two hundred and twenty-nine lost their lives. Can't get much worse than that."

Sheffland sipped his drink. "What was found as the cause for the accident?" he asked, pursing his lips.

"Swissair modified the MD-11 after accepting the original aircraft from the manufacturer, McDonnell Douglas. The airline added entertainment centers to the airplane cabin, sort of after-market changes, I suppose. It appeared the electrical wiring for power to the entertainment equipment was not properly installed. Somehow, electrical modifications resulted in a fire that brought the plane down."

At that moment the fireplace emitted a loud pop and crackling sound. Randall turned and stared at the blaze, deep in thought.

"So how did you become involved in the accident investigation?"

"What?" Randall responded as if awakened from a dream.

"The accident," Sheffland repeated. "How did you become involved in the investigation?"

"Oh, yes," Randall said as he cleared the momentary cobwebs from his mind. "The investigation. At that time I was participating in the investigation of an airliner accident that occurred in 1996, two years before the Swissair crash. An American carrier had lost an airliner in a crash that was somewhat similar to the Swissair accident. A TWA Boeing 747 had departed JFK for Rome with a stop in Paris. The plane exploded soon after take-off and crashed in the Atlantic just a few miles off the southern coast of Long Island. That investigation began with the recovery of the airliner wreckage from the ocean floor and reassembly of the aircraft on shore. I was involved at the very beginning in those efforts. We recovered ninety-seven percent of the aircraft. The entire investigation lasted almost four years. Over a thousand people worked on it."

Randall's voice was interrupted by a rumble of thunder. He looked past Sheffland to the study windows. The glass panes were wet with rain. "Looks like a good night to be indoors," Randall casually remarked.

"No doubt," agreed Sheffland. "You were saying . . ."

"In the Swissair accident," Randall continued, "the MD-11 shattered on impact, scattering wreckage across the sea floor. Much like the crash off Long Island. The Canadian government asked the U.S. for assistance in the recovery and possible reassembly of the MD-11." Randall shifted in his chair before continuing. "You see, the NTSB had established procedures – protocols – for recovery of the crash victims' remains, analyzing the underwater crash site, identification and underwater recovery of wreckage, preparing it for reassembly, all of that work. Rather than reinventing the wheel, the Canadians asked the NTSB and the FAA to provide guidance on their initial investigative efforts. That is how I became involved in the Swissair accident investigation."

"I see," Sheffland nodded. "Helping out your neighbors to the north."

"That's about it," Randall said smiling. "I led an inspection team of six folks from the Board. We were the accredited NTSB representative along with the AAIB, Swissair, Boeing-McDonnell Douglas, and Pratt & Whitney. We were designated to assist the Canadian Transportation Safety Board in wreckage recovery, identification, sorting and reconstruction. And that is what we did."

Sheffland let out a loud sigh. "Tell me about *your* work there in Canada," Sheffland prodded Randall. "What do you remember about the recovery efforts?"

"Well, we were located in a hangar at CFB Shearwater, along with a number of the TSB folks. Shearwater is located right there on the east side of Halifax. The recovered wreckage was initially brought on shore and staged at a marine industrial park at, uh, Sheet Harbor, if I remember correctly. The wreckage was cleaned and then transported to the hangar at Shearwater. We weighed each piece, inspected and photographed them, identified them if we could, and then sorted the wreckage either for storage or for aircraft reassembly."

"What about the actual wreckage recovery from the water?" Sheffland asked. "Were you involved in those efforts also?"

At that moment the door to the study opened. A man in a dark, heavy robe shuffled in and closed the door behind him. Randall immediately recognized the figure. "Sir Geoffrey!" Randall exclaimed as he rose from the couch. "It's good to see you again."

Sir Geoffrey Sheffland walked to Randall, extending his hands in friendship. "Rob, thank you for traveling to our home on such short notice." The smile on Sir Geoffrey's face seemed warm and genuine. Other than some additional flecks of grey in his short, dark hair, he appeared surprisingly well – considering the events of the past few months.

Sir Geoffrey gestured to Randall. "Please, sit down," he told Randall as he moved to the opposite end of the sofa. "I did not mean to interrupt your conversation."

"Father," Alex said rising from the chair, "may I prepare a drink for you?"

"Yes, please. Thank you," came the reply. "The usual." He looked at Randall. "I trust the plane flight was satisfactory."

"Yes," Randall responded. "I had good company on the trip. I rode with Don Wiltsey."

Sir Geoffrey nodded. "To be sure." He turned to his son. "I suppose Don is here for the operations and maintenance conference?"

"That is correct," Alex replied, handing a glass of brandy to his father. "Beauchamp arrived yesterday. I have been meeting with him for most of the day."

"Everything up to snuff in North America?"

"They are doing very well," came the reply from Alex. "No problems to speak of."

"Good. Good." Sir Geoffrey again turned his attention to Randall. "And how have you been doing, Rob? Making progress on your boat?"

"Yes, actually," came the somewhat surprised response from Randall. "Still a fair amount of work to be done, but I am enjoying every bit of it."

"Father," Alex interjected, "Rob has been telling me about his work on the Swissair accident investigation. He was just telling me about the recovery of the airliner wreckage, weren't you, Rob?"

"Yes," Randall replied as he noticed a dark pallor sweep across Sir Geoffrey's face. "I explained to Alex the participation of the National Transportation Safety Board in providing assistance to the Canadian TSP in the initial recovery operations. We helped them in the aircraft wreckage recovery, identification, sorting and reconstruction."

"And you were just about to tell me of the ocean recovery operations," Alex reminded him.

"Yes, yes, that's correct." Strange, Randall thought, why such an interest in a seventeen-year-old airliner crash?

"To begin with," Randall continued, "the Royal Canadian Mounted Police, the RCMP, was in command of the recovery operation. The *HCMS Compass* was the on-scene command vessel. Guidance was provided to the

RCMP by the TSB and the Coast Guard of Canada. In addition, the recovery operational team was supplemented by the U.S. Navy. The *U.S.S. Surveyor* was sent in to assist in the recovery efforts. The *Surveyor* is the Navy's dedicated salvage ship. The American salvage vessel provided additional recovery heavy-lift equipment along with more than thirty salvage divers."

"The Canadian ship and the American vessel," Alex interrupted, "they worked together on the recovery operations?"

"Yes," Randall nodded. "You see, the *U.S.S. Surveyor* had provided the equipment and the divers for the recovery of the Boeing 747 wreckage in the waters off the Long Island coast two years earlier. They were experienced in every phase of aircraft underwater recovery and fully prepared to do it again."

The questioning shifted to Sir Geoffrey. "Rob," Sir Geoffrey quietly asked, "did you work with the crews on board either of the two ships?"

Randall noted the stark tone of the question. "Yes," he cautiously replied. "I worked with the crews of both ships."

The questioning quickly shifted back to Alex. "What did you do, this work, with the two ships?"

Randall paused, attempting to remember his efforts and organize his memories. "The initial aspect of any aircraft accident investigation," Randall continued, "after recovery of human remains, is to identify the exact location of the entire wreckage, the geographic positions of everything. The fuselage, the empennage, engines, wings, cockpit, landing gear – everything. The positions of each airplane piece needs to be placed on an arbitrary grid established over the crash site. I assisted the divers on each ship to develop one, unified grid pattern over the crash site in order for identifying positions of aircraft pieces and parts. In other words, I taught the recovery crews how to survey the crash site."

"How did they perform the survey work?" Sir Geoffrey asked.

"We developed a grid tied to global positioning. Then we surveyed the area. The surveying was accomplished by route survey techniques with divers, sonar, laser line scanners, even remotely operated vehicles. You know, ROVs."

"Did you perform any diving with the American or Canadian crews?" Alex asked.

Good grief, Randall thought, this questioning has become a tag-team match, except on this side, I've got no one to tag.

"Yes," Randall answered. "I dove on the wreckage twice with the Canadians and twice with the American divers. And, yes, I'm certified to dive."

"Who were the Canadian divers?" It was Sir Geoffrey's turn.

"Uh, if I remember correctly," Randall recalled, "they were from their Navy port inspection and clearance."

"And the American divers?" It was Alex's turn.

"Navy divers. They were assigned to the *Surveyor*. It was their billet."

"After the survey of the wreckage was completed, what happened next?" Back to Sir Geoffrey for the question.

"Well, the heavy lifting began in early October," Randall remembered. "The actual salvage work for recovery of the aircraft started at that time and continued for well over a month."

"How was the salvage work accomplished?" Sir Geoffrey continued the questioning. Randall wondered if that was an obvious breach of protocol.

"A number of techniques were used," Randall replied, displaying a slight impatience at the relentless questioning. "The wreckage was recovered by divers, dredging, and trawling. Some of the deeper recovery work was done by ROVs. There was wreckage as much as one hundred eighty feet below the surface."

"Were you still on board the recovery vessels during the recovery?" Sir Geoffrey – again.

"No," Randall shook his head. "By that time I was at the hangar at Shearwater. I was never again out at sea."

"Father," Alex interjected, "Rob already has explained his work on the accident investigation while at CFB Shearwater."

Sir Geoffrey smiled. "I see. That is what I deserve for arriving in the middle of a cricket match."

Cricket match? Used hay, Randall thought – more like the Spanish Inquisition. What gives?

Another rumble of thunder filled the study. The blaze in the fireplace remained bright amidst the popping of the burning logs. "Rob, thank you for your patience and for answering our myriad of questions," Sir Geoffrey said with a rueful smile that was more an expression of sadness and regret. "I have just one more question for you. When you were, as you phrased it, 'out at sea', did you learn of the discovery of an old shipwreck near the crash site of the Swissair plane? The ship wreck was discovered during the initial survey efforts before the recovery of the aircraft wreckage."

A long silence followed. Even the crackling of the fireplace abated as if waiting for an answer. "No," Randall replied softly. "No. I don't remember the discovery of an old shipwreck during the recovery efforts. I think I would have remembered that." Another long silence followed. Sir Geoffrey and his son quietly stared at one another, communicating only by their countenances. Finally, Alex simply shrugged his shoulders and sighed, an expression of resignation on his face.

"Being the only uninformed member of the audience," Randall said rather wryly yet impatiently, "would somebody please tell me what the hell this is all about?"

"Yes, that indeed is the question," Sir Geoffrey repeated. "What the hell is this all about?" He paused a moment before answering. "Honestly, Rob, I really am not sure." Sir Geoffrey shifted his gaze to the fireplace, the blaze fully illuminating a face in shadows. He continued. "When we first met, I briefly told you of my family. My grandfather, Cyril Sheffland, was a physician. He was born here at Banhaven in 1876. He grew up in this house. He received his education at King's College London School of Medicine."

Sir Geoffrey paused, smiling as he briefly glanced at Randall. "Growing up, I received the distinct impression that Grandfather Cyril was somewhat of a rogue – perhaps bordering on even being a scoundrel. He certainly was, as you would say, the black sheep of the family."

Sir Geoffrey returned to staring into the fire. "In late 1910, he emigrated from England to Canada. He took up residence in Halifax, Nova Scotia. Soon after arriving there, my grandfather purchased a ship, a steamship. The name of the ship was the *Loch Gillelli*. The ship was launched in 1907. The *Loch Gillelli* was a merchant ship of a slightly smaller size, about five or six thousand tons. Those types of merchant ships were known back then as tramp steamers or tramp freighters. When I was very young, I saw a picture of the *Loch Gillelli*. She was not of the standard mid-century merchant steamer design, a three-island ship design. I guess those ships came later during World War I."

Sir Geoffrey paused a moment, staring at the fireplace as if it were a theater screen. "No, the *Loch Gillelli* was of an earlier era. The engine room was aft in the stern of the vessel and not amid-ships. The wheel house, the bridge deck, the chart room – all of those were amid-ships. The coal bunkers, the holds – they were forward in the ship."

Randall remained transfixed at the face in the firelight. He stayed silent.

"I suppose the *Loch Gillelli* was a contract carrier. My grandfather was the ship's owner, the master, if you will. He employed a captain and crew to operate the vessel on charters to transport cargo between Canada and Great Britain or between England and the United States." Sir Geoffrey paused for a moment. He then sighed. "At least that was what I was led to believe."

The sound of thunder interrupted a momentary silence. Sir Geoffrey turned to Randall. "It was the understanding of the family that the *Loch Gillelli* sank in late 1912 during a terrible storm in the North Sea. She was sailing on a voyage charter, carrying a load of cargo to Wales, when she was lost at sea with all hands. After the loss of the ship, my grandfather Cyril remained in Halifax, practicing medicine until his death in 1944 at the age of sixty-eight. He never owned another ship."

A momentary pause quickly ended as Alex Sheffland resumed the story. "That should have been the ending for the saga of the *Loch Gillelli,*" Alex remarked ruefully. "But it wasn't. In March of 1999, the Canadian maritime authorities informed us that the wreck of the lost ship *Loch Gillelli* had been discovered. She was found eighty-six years after her sinking, not at the bottom of the North Sea but less than six miles off the shore of Nova Scotia."

Randall inhaled sharply. "Are you saying the shipwreck found during the recovery of the Swissair flight is that of your ship, the *Loch Gillelli*?"

"Precisely," Alex replied. "The shipwreck found during your airliner recovery in 1998 is the *Loch Gillelli.*"

Randall exhaled as if he had held his breath. "Are you sure?"

"Yes," came the reply from Alex Sheffland. "Quite sure."

"Before you begin asking a thousand questions," Sir Geoffrey interjected, "let me continue the story." Randall nodded and remained quiet. "When our family was notified of the discovery, we had no earthly idea of why the *Loch Gillelli* sank off the coast of Nova Scotia. Quite honestly, we still have no clear reason for it. But it is obvious that a false narrative concerning the sinking of the ship was concocted in order to hide the truth of her demise. Of that, there is no doubt."

Sir Geoffrey rose from the couch and walked to the fireplace. He retrieved a bronze poker from its pedestal standing to the side and repositioned the burning logs. The popping sound crackled throughout the study. Sheffland replaced the poker and returned to the couch. "My father, Howard Sheffland," Sir Geoffrey continued, "was born in Canada in 1916. He came to England in 1924 to complete his education. His home was here at Banhaven during those years until he joined the Royal Air Force in 1938. My father was not close to Cyril. Quite the contrary, once in England, he spent very little time in Canada with his father and mother. He had no siblings. I suppose he simply was happier here at Banhaven."

Sir Geoffrey paused, searching his robe pockets. "It seems I have forgotten my pipe. I must have left it upstairs. I will retrieve it later. Now, where was I?"

"You were talking about Grandfather," Alex reminded him.

"Oh, yes," Sir Geoffrey seemed tired and confused. "All that I knew of my grandfather Cyril and the *Loch Gillelli* came from my father and that was very little. My father rarely talked of his father. Sometimes, it was as if Cyril Sheffland had not existed. And once grown, I never dwelled upon our family history, that is, I never dwelled on the family *secrets.*"

"Until recently," Alex announced.

"Yes," repeated Sir Geoffrey. "Until recently." He paused as if collecting his thoughts. "In March of last year, a man contacted Nigel for the first time. I believe the man identifies himself as Devero. He claimed that he knew of a family secret, a very damning family secret. He claimed our family, the Sheffland family, was in possession of a vast treasure. The treasure of the *Titanic.*"

"The *Titanic?*" Randall interrupted. "*THE Titanic?*"

"Yes," Sir Geoffrey reiterated. "*THE Titanic. R.M.S. Titanic.*"

"You must be joking," Randall said. He was not smiling.

"I am quite serious," Sir Geoffrey reassured Randall. "I am not, as you would say, pulling your leg. And neither was Mr. Devero. He said he had specific, detailed knowledge of our family treasure trove, and Mr. Devero announced he wanted a portion of it. Fifty percent, to be exact."

"This Mr. Devero," Randall repeated, "he wants fifty percent of your treasure taken from the *Titanic*, I assume before she sank?"

"Correct," Alex confirmed Randall's assumption.

In the silence Randall shifted his gaze back and forth between Sir Geoffrey and his son, trying to decide if one, or both, was insane. "And this Mr.

Devero," Randall continued, "if he did not receive half of the so-called *Titanic* treasure, just what was he going to do?"

"At first," Sir Geoffrey answered, "if a portion of the *Titanic* treasure was not immediately forthcoming, Mr. Devero would reveal our family secret to the world. Of course, he received nothing."

"I see," Randall said nodding his head and not believing one word of the preposterous story.

"And after Mr. Devero did not receive his portion of the treasure post haste," Alex interjected, "he changed his tactic."

"Yes," Sir Geoffrey solemnly continued. "He informed Nigel that if he did not receive his cut of the fortune, he would bring down one of our airliners."

"You're serious," came from Randall more as a statement than a question.

"Quite serious," Sir Geoffrey assured Randall. "Nigel said nothing of this to me or to Alex - that is until one of our triple-7 cargo planes went down on approach to Brussels this past November."

"Yes," Randall nodded. "Sure, I remember that."

"The accident was the first for British Sovereign in which there was a loss of life. After the crash, Nigel told me the details of the extortion plot." Sir Geoffrey paused. "Alex, would you pour me another brandy? I can't seem to get warm."

Randall stared at the chilled Sir Geoffrey as he resumed the story. "After the crash in Belgium, we did not hear from Mr. Devero for a while. I convinced myself that the loss of our plane had nothing to do with Devero's attempt at extortion. Then, in late April, Devero again contacted Nigel. He told Nigel the crash was of his doing and that unless he received the money, another of our fleet would be brought down. Only this time it would be one of our passenger airliners."

Sir Geoffrey paused as Alex handed him another brandy snifter. He continued. "Imagine my surprise when, just a week later, Mr. Kilby of your Federal Bureau of Investigation informed me of a possible threat to one of our airliners." Sir Geoffrey smiled weakly. "And then you arrived, a former American transportation safety investigator. Truly, for the first time, I believed the extortion threat was real, that the FBI suspected there was a valid threat against British Sovereign from Mr. Devero."

"Do you still believe the threat exists against BSA?" Randall now was taking the story seriously.

"Well, after our airliner's collision with the military drone over Nevada," Sir Geoffrey replied, "I knew the particular threat you and Jack were investigating never was connected to the extortion plot. But the threat still exists. This past week, for the first time, Mr. Devero called me and again threatened the loss of another BSA airliner if, as you Americans say, the Shefflands did not 'play ball' - Devero's words, actually."

Randall did not hesitate to ask the obvious question. "Sir Geoffrey, have you reported this attempt at extortion to British or American law enforcement authorities?"

"No," Sir Geoffrey replied quietly.

"Why not?"

"Our family has its reasons."

Randall became flustered. "Well, they better be hellaciously good reasons. To me, having a Boeing Triple-7 turned into a ginormous bottle rocket seems to trump your possible personal motives."

After a moment of uncomfortable silence over Randall's obvious irritation, Sir Geoffrey sighed. "I wish it were as easy as that."

"Quite honestly, gentlemen," Randall concluded, "this entire story makes no sense. You talk of something that doesn't exist. A man threatens extortion over something that simply does not exist. Something that never existed. There was no treasure of the *Titanic*. There is no treasure. The ship sank in over twelve thousand feet of water. It's been gone a hundred years. Everyone knows the story of the *Titanic*."

A long silence was punctuated by the deep rumble of thunder and the crackling fireplace. The dying embers cast a ghostly hue over Sir Geoffrey and his son. They stared at each other, their faces glazed in sorrow.

"Rob, the Sheffland family has maintained a dark secret for over a century. A very dark and terrible secret." Sir Geoffrey's voice suddenly was weak, barely more than a whisper. "I became aware of it at my father's passing. My mother did not even know about it. My wife never knew, even at her passing five years ago. My sons learned of the secret only after Nigel told me of his contacts with Devero. It is a secret of something that is terrible beyond all measure."

Sir Geoffrey paused and closed his eyes as if a wave of pain had washed over him. After a moment, he continued. "Rob, have you ever heard of *The Rubaiyat of Omar Khayyam?*"

"Vaguely," Randall replied. "I believe it is a book of poems."

"Yes," Sir Geoffrey agreed. "In the mid-1800s, a man by the name of Edward Fitzgerald produced a translation of selected poems by the Persian poet and mathematician Omar Khayyam. Fitzgerald drew from over one thousand poems written at the end of the eleventh century. The title of his translation was *The Rubaiyat of Omar Khayyam.* The poems addressed the tenets of orthodox Islam, creationism, even mysticism." Randall nodded in understanding. "After Fitzgerald's translation was published, the Persian poems once again became famous and popular. So much so that in the early 1900s, the well-known book-binders Sangorski & Sudcliffe decided to create a single, magnificent copy of *The Rubaiyat.* Francis Sangorski, one of the publishing partners, took it upon himself to personally make the one-of-a-kind masterpiece. He transformed one of Elihu Vedders' illustrated editions of *The Rubaiyat* into a fabulously jeweled and gold-inlayed book. The cover of the book contained no less than fifteen hundred precious gems, each individually set in gold. Diamonds, rubies, emeralds and sapphires, all mounted in eighteen karat gold. The book was finished in 1911, and it became known in England as *The Great Omar.*"

"The book was considered priceless," Alex interjected.

Sir Geoffrey smiled and nodded in agreement. "Yes, the book is priceless," Sir Geoffrey reiterated. "It was sold at auction in early 1912 for a still-undisclosed sum, but the sale, to this day, has remained in dispute."

"This is a very interesting story, Sir Geoffrey," Randall remarked impatiently, questioning its meaning or relevance in his own mind, "but how does it apply to your 'family secret'? Or to the 'treasure of the *Titanic?*"

There was a long silence before Sir Geoffrey spoke "In April of 1912, *The Great Omar*, the jeweled copy of *The Rubaiyat*, was shipped to America on board the *R.M.S. Titanic.* The book was lost when the *Titanic* went down at twenty minutes after two o'clock in the morning on April 15, 1912."

Randall sat back, confused.

"Alex, would you please open the safe?" he asked in a fading voice.

Alex Sheffland stood and walked to the desk. On the wall behind it was a painting of a British RAF Lancaster bomber from World War II. He swung the large painting from the wall. Behind the painting was the door to a safe.

Alex worked the combination dial and then turned the handle and opened the safe. He retrieved an old wooden box from the safe and placed it on the desk. Removing the lid, he extracted what appeared to Randall to be a large book. Alex took the contents of the box and walked to Randall. He bent down and carefully placed it in Randall's hands.

Randall studied the object in his lap. It indeed was a book. The book's cover and spine were covered in precious gems, all glittering in the light of the fireplace. In the spaces between the jewels were reflections of gold, also shimmering in the firelight. To Randall, the book was instantly both mesmerizing and magical. It felt warm and alive.

"In your hands, Rob, you hold *The Great Omar*, the jeweled *Rubaiyat of Omar Khayyam*," Sir Geoffrey quietly announced, "the book that was carried on the *Titanic*. It was not lost at sea with the doomed luxury liner in 1912. Before you is the treasure of the *Titanic*. And, now, you also hold the terrible secret of the Sheffland family."

In the silence of the study, a distant rumble of thunder punctuated the night. At that moment the Siren of the *Loch Gillelli* was given voice.

Chapter 4

The storm had ended during the night. Frequent lightning and heavy rain was replaced with thick fog blanketing the English countryside. Randall stared out the bedroom window at the milky mist – soft, silent, barely swirling.

He had slept surprisingly well despite the revelations of the previous evening. Randall had held the book in his lap for the longest time, almost hypnotized by the sparkling stones and the glittering gold. He held it in silence of the secret until Alex Sheffland returned the book to the safe. No more was said after the safe door was closed, as if its metallic clunk erased the journey to the past, as if the journey had never been made. It was agreed by all to resume the discussion the next morning. And now it was morning.

A knock at the bedroom door snapped Randall from his reverie and reflection. Simon carefully opened the door and peeked into the room.

"Good morning, Simon," Randall greeted the gentleman's gentleman. "It appears somewhat foggy outside."

"Good morning, sir," came the response. "I beg your pardon. You were very quiet. I trust you slept well."

"Very much so," Randall smiled. "Refreshed, dressed, and rarin' to go."

Simon returned the smile. "We will be serving breakfast in ten minutes, sir. Sir Geoffrey and Master Alex wish for you to join them."

Randall nodded. "Very well. What is Rose whipping up in the kitchen this morning?"

"Kippers, sir."

"Salmon or herring?"

Simon seemed surprised. "Why, herring, sir."

Randall again smiled. "Sounds good. After you."

Simon escorted Randall from the bedroom and together they walked down the hallway to the staircase. As they descended the stairs, Sir Geoffrey and Alex Sheffland appeared, strolling companionably towards the dining room.

"Good morning, Rob," Alex called out. "Sleep well?"

"Yes, thank you," Randall replied. He quickly studied Sir Geoffrey. He seemed stronger and much more relaxed, more energetic, as if a weight had been lifted from his shoulders. They entered the dining room and Sir Geoffrey sat at the head of the table with Alex and Randall to either side. Randall decided to start the breakfast conversation honestly – if not bluntly.

"You're looking well this morning, Sir Geoffrey," Randall began, "at least much better than last night."

"Yes," Sir Geoffrey agreed, "and I am feeling much better, too."

"I believe our discussion of the previous evening proved to be therapeutic for both of us," added Alex. "The past few months have been very bleak, very dismal for the family. It was somewhat comforting to share our burden. Especially now."

"I understand," Randall responded, "but my visit to London, the revelations of last night, it begs the question. What do you want from *me*? Why am I here?"

Sir Geoffrey smiled. "You Americans. Forever impatient. Forever, as you say, cutting to the chase, as it were."

Randall sighed. "Forgive me, Sir Geoffrey. I didn't mean to doubt your sincerity. And I certainly appreciate any trust you place in me. I simply don't know why any of this should concern me. The *Titanic*. A treasure. A one-hundred-year-old shipwreck. I'm just an old stick jockey and tin-kicker from the colonies. None of this pertains to me."

"You are correct, Rob," Alex remarked. "None of this should be of concern to you."

At that moment, Simon and Rose entered the dining room bringing breakfast dishes of kippers and open range eggs with toast. A typical, traditional British breakfast, Randall concluded. No bacon, no sausage, no hash browns, no grits, no biscuits. And it would disappoint Don Wiltsey. No doughnuts. Bummer.

After Simon and Rose left the dining room, Sir Geoffrey continued. "Rob, you are here at our request for one reason. We need your help. It is as simple as that."

"Go on," Randall said warily. "I'm listening." Folding his arms, he sat back in the tall dining room chair.

"At this moment, the extortion threat against our family and against British Sovereign Airlines has been limited to a few phone calls and a single visit from this Devero character. In light of our current legal difficulties, I am sure you will understand that Alex and I are hesitant to approach the law enforcement authorities over a rather nebulous threat."

"Continue," nodded Randall.

"I believe all of this began with the discovery of the *Loch Gillelli* shipwreck in 1998," Sir Geoffrey said adamantly. "Somehow, in some way, I am sure our possession of *The Rubaiyat* and a belief we have some undefined treasure hoard from the *Titanic* are connected to the family ownership of the *Loch Gillelli* over one hundred years ago. Before we turn this over to the authorities, I want to know the true extent of the threat and our family's involvement with the *Titanic*."

"And that is why you are here, enjoying this scrumptious breakfast," Alex interjected. "Father and I firmly believe you are the man for the job."

Randall touched the fork that was lying on the plate of kippers and blotted his lips with a napkin. "And what makes you think I am the 'man for the job'?" Randall asked casually. "I have no real connection to your family, no real connection to the airline."

"That is exactly why we want you for the task at hand," Sir Geoffrey responded. "You have no connection to us. But you do have a connection to the people who discovered, and possibly explored, the wreck of the *Loch Gillelli*. You met divers and supervisory personnel from Canada, Great Britain, and the United States during your investigatory work in the Swissair crash. You can visit those people, ask them questions, perhaps find this Devero character."

"Not to mention having me do this work in order for you to preserve your family secret," Randall interrupted. "I would be inconspicuous, indistinct, even invisible, to those that wish to do you harm. Correct?"

Sir Geoffrey suddenly seemed uncomfortable.

"That is, until I meet up with Mr. Devero or one of his comrades," Randall declared. "Then, I'm the one in the firing line while the Sheffland family remains hidden from view. Such a deal."

"Yes," Sir Geoffrey responded in resignation. "I suppose that is true. I know we have absolutely no right to ask you to do this for me or for Alex or for anyone. As for the family secret, I'm not sure just exactly what *is* the secret, that is, beyond the possession of a priceless artifact taken from the *Titanic* before she sank. But I *do* know it's time the Shefflands meet the skeleton, or skeletons, in the family closet and finally say hello."

Randall smiled ruefully but remained silent.

"Rob, there is one other reason for requesting your assistance in this matter," Alex subtly pleaded. "Simply spoken, we trust you. You are one of the few people we truly trust. We know your conduct in this effort would be determined yet delicate and discreet."

"In other words," Randall smiled, "you want someone cunning and crafty, yet refined and reticent." He shook his head. "You British, you're all alike. You try to be so polite and subtle. Well, you're about as subtle as a brickbat."

Randall sighed and again shook his head. "I must be out of my mind, but I'll do it. As we colonials would say in the great American West of yesteryear, I will be a scout for you. I'll look around. But I will do it in my own way and on my own terms. To begin with, you will pay me for this work. In addition, I have the right to pull the plug on this little venture at any time of my choosing. And finally, if I find evidence of any criminal wrong-doing, I'm going straight to the authorities. Post haste."

Sir Geoffrey smiled like the cat that ate the canary. "I am agreeable to those terms. And I am sure we can successfully negotiate the financial terms of remuneration for your services."

"Oh, one other thing," Randall added. "As with the work I did a few months ago in New Hampshire, Inspector Kilby will be my back-up, my go-to guy. He will know my whereabouts and activities at all times. I will look to him for guidance and, hopefully, he will keep me out of trouble. Is that acceptable to you?"

"Yes," Sir Geoffrey nodded. "I have no problems with that arrangement."

"Good," Randall announced. "It appears we have a deal."

"Excellent," Sir Geoffrey proclaimed. "After breakfast, we will begin planning our efforts."

"I am afraid *you* will be planning your efforts," Alex remarked with regret. "I have the duty today to conduct a set of company-wide operations and maintenance meetings at Littleton." Alex looked at his watch. "And I better square things up or I will be tardy. Mustn't have that. If you'll excuse me . . ."

With that, Alex Sheffland stood and placed his napkin on the table. "Oh, yes, Father," Alex reminded Sir Geoffrey, "did you make the arrangements for Rob to meet with Nigel at Wandsworth?"

Sir Geoffrey grimaced as if in pain. Randall could not decide if his expression was the result of the question or the revelation. He remained uncomfortably silent.

"Oh, well, I must take your leave." With that, Alex was gone from the dining room.

Sir Geoffrey ruefully glanced at Randall. "Finish your breakfast, Rob. We will discuss *that* later."

This is wonderful, Randall thought, really swell. I get to visit the guy I put into prison. He already was beginning to regret his decision.

* * *

After breakfast was finished, Sir Geoffrey led Randall to the study. The embers in the fireplace had been reduced to a smoldering chalky white and grey ash. Sir Geoffrey gestured for Randall to sit on the sofa while he walked to the chair. After they were seated, Sheffland retrieved his pipe and tobacco pouch from his coat pocket and began the ritual of pipe preparation. He rapped the pipe bowl in the ashtray on the table next to him. He then placed the pipe stem in his mouth to make sure it was free of obstructions. "Rob, I am all too aware of what we have asked you to do. I am afraid our family has scant information on this matter." Sheffland carefully began filling his pipe with tobacco.

"Just what *do* you have, Sir Geoffrey?" Randall tried to remain cool and somewhat detached.

"Of course, we have *The Rubaiyat* that was shown to you last night. The only three items we believe came from the *Titanic* are the book, a single 1910 British sovereign, and an old handwritten piece of paper. Other than that, nothing else."

"What about papers, information from your grandfather or your father?"

"Nothing that we believe pertains to the *Titanic*," Sheffland responded, shaking his head.

"And what of the cargo ship, the *Loch Gillelli*? Any information on the steamer?"

"We do have information on the *Loch Gillelli*" Sheffland nodded. "Some of it has been kept in our family records, that is, information that has been passed down through the generations. A portion of it has been found through research done by Nigel, unbeknownst to me."

"Just what do you have?" prodded Randall.

"Our family possesses the original ship's papers, including the owner-ship and registry of the *Loch Gillelli*. We also have copies of a few cargo manifests."

"What about the ship's logs? Sailing records?" Randall casually asked.

"No," Sheffland replied. "We have no sailing or transport logs. I would assume those were maintained on board the ship and were lost when the *Loch Gillelli* sank."

"Not much to go on," Randall concluded.

"No," Sheffland agreed. "Not much."

"You mentioned a piece of paper kept with *The Rubaiyat*?" Randall re-membered. "May I look at it?"

"Certainly," Sheffland replied. He rose from the chair and moved to the desk. He opened the center drawer and retrieved a manila envelope. Shef-fland gave it to Randall as he returned to the chair. Randall opened the un-sealed envelope and peeked inside. He saw what appeared to be an old piece of yellowed paper and the unmistakable glitter of gold. He removed the pa-per and poured the golden object into his hand.

"I take it this is the single gold sovereign," Randall remarked as he ex-amined it. Sheffland simply nodded.

"The coin appears to be in pristine condition," Randall observed. "A portrait of King Edward VII on the face side. St. George slaying the dragon opposite. Dated 1910."

"From the mint mark," added Sheffland, "the coin was struck at the London Mint."

"I wonder if this particular coin was part of the *Titanic* treasure," Randall hypothesized. "Or perhaps it's simply a typical pound piece." He replaced the gold coin in the envelope and turned his attention to the slip of paper. It was old, almost brittle. On the paper, written in faded pencil, was a series of numbers, a few letters and nothing more. Randall read the numbers aloud:

"442930655507PC

M   W

443939633717C229

N   U"

"A lot of numbers. Know what they mean?"

Sheffland shook his head. "No earthly idea."

"The numbers are really difficult to read," Randall muttered as he examined the paper. "They're so faded. And the letters. They're all but impossible to make out." He shook his head. "Like I said," Randall repeated, "not much to go on."

Sheffland remained silent.

Randall puffed out his cheeks and exhaled. "I'll need copies of every scrap of paper in your possession that concerns the *Loch Gillelli*. Also, a copy of this one." Randall waved the paper in his hand. "That is, if it can even be copied. It's so faded."

"You will be given the originals of everything for your study and safekeeping," assured Sheffland.

"Very well," Randall responded. "Now, with regard to the subject your son Alex alluded to. You want *me* to visit Nigel. In prison. Do I understand that correctly?"

Sir Geoffrey affirmed Randall's understanding with a nod.

"With all due respect, Sir Geoffrey, have you and Alex taken leave of your senses? I'm the one who put Nigel in prison!"

"Rob, you are so polite for being American. Don't you really want to know if we have lost our collective minds – if we are crazy? Nuts? Bonkers, as it were?"

"Okay," Randall nodded. "Yeah. Have both of you had one too many hard landings? I cannot imagine accomplishing anything in a prison visit beyond getting my lights punched out. Maybe permanently."

Sheffland briefly laughed before becoming serious. "To begin with, Rob, *you* did not, as you phrased it, put Nigel in prison. *Nigel* put Nigel in prison. He is completely and totally responsible for his current plight. He has no one to blame but himself."

Sheffland momentarily paused to collect both his thoughts and his emotions. "You and I will be visiting Nigel this afternoon at Wandsworth Prison not far from here," Sheffland continued. "You will not recognize him. He is not the person you met just four short months ago. Nigel is – I suppose you could say – he is a broken man. He destroyed himself, he destroyed my daughter and her husband, and he nearly destroyed British Sovereign Airlines. I hope – I pray – that he will help in keeping this current matter from destroying what remains of our family."

Nigel Sheffland is not the only broken man, Randall thought. Sir Geoffrey was not just broken - he was shattered.

* * *

The ride from Banhaven to southwest London was quiet as the limousine sped through the pastoral English countryside. Sir Geoffrey sat beside Randall in the backseat of the car, staring out the window at the passing scenery. The morning fog had dissipated only to be replaced by dreary clouds and drizzle. Typical English flying weather, Randall mused.

It was a surprise to Randall that he felt no apprehension, no dread in visiting Nigel Sheffland. Sir Geoffrey's comments regarding Nigel during breakfast, and later in the study, had put Randall more at ease. But he still wondered how Nigel fit into the extortion picture and how he could be of help in finding this Devero character. I'll know soon enough, Randall thought.

The countryside scenes were gradually replaced with houses and buildings as the limousine entered the outskirts of London proper. Trees and grass changed to bricks and concrete. In the rain the landscape seemed to become dirty and depressing.

"Nigel has been incarcerated at Her Majesty's Prison Wandsworth since being extradited back to Great Britain," Sir Geoffrey said, returning Randall's attention back to the visit. "It is one of the largest prisons in southeast England. At least it is relatively close to Banhaven."

Randall nodded, but said nothing, preferring to remain quiet during the limo ride. The view out of the car's windows set the mood. Soon, the limousine turned right off the main highway and onto a street marked Heathfield Road. A few moments later, the prison came into view.

The building behind the main gate appeared huge and imposing. The façade was almost that of an ancient castle made of dark grey stone. The tall parapets in the center of the building stood like sentinels on each side of a stone arch above the main entrance to the medieval-like structure. Two additional parapets bracketed the ends of the façade. A high, dark stone wall behind the building extended for hundreds of feet in both directions. All that was missing was a moat, Randall thought, and maybe a dragon.

The limo turned into the main gate in front of the building and then immediately veered to the left, passing a sign directing cars and pedestrians to the prison visitor's center. After the driver parked the limousine, Sheffland and Randall exited the vehicle and entered the visitor's center. At a counter, Sir Geoffrey identified himself and his guest and confirmed their two o'clock appointment. After examining his American driver's license identification and passport, the attending guard displayed grudging acceptance of the documents and issued a visitor's badge to Randall. Upon signing in, Sheffland and Randall were escorted to the prison's main entrance by another guard. After passing through a metal detector, they walked outside on a sidewalk of cobblestones. They passed massive wooden doors and through the stone arch to Prison Wandsworth's Central Hall. In the middle of the circular hall was a visitor's kiosk. The guard led them to the kiosk and identified the visitors to a guard behind the counter. The guard briefly glanced at the two visitors, pointed past them to a door and simply said, "E Wing Conference." Sheffland thanked him and the escorting guard and, together with Randall, they walked to the door labeled E Wing Conference Room.

Randall glanced about the Central Hall. Four stories of brightly-lit walkways were connected to the huge circular room and trailed down various corridors like the spokes of a wheel. The central hall was capped with a round domed skylight. The walls were painted a cheery white and light blue and accented in bright yellow. The hall's décor belied the stark, forbidding, appearance of the prison's exterior façade. Sheffland and Randall entered the small conference room and sat on one side of a glass-partitioned table. A few minutes later, another door opened and Nigel Sheffland entered with yet another escort guard. He immediately claimed the chair on the other side of the desk partition and sat down. Sir Geoffrey gazed at Nigel and smiled. Randall stared at Nigel and drew in his breath.

Randall had not seen Nigel Sheffland since leaving Portsmouth, New Hampshire, four months previous. Now, Randall saw the visage of the dead. He was thin and pale, a shaven head accentuating a ghostly pallor. When Nigel glanced at Randall, he displayed no emotion. No anger. No bitterness. Not contempt. Only a blank stare and nothing more.

"How are you, son?" Sir Geoffrey began the conversation. "How are you feeling?"

"I am well, Father," Nigel answered in an emotionless voice. "At least, as well as can be expected." He smiled slightly.

"The barristers are pleased with their progress," Sir Geoffrey remarked uncomfortably as if searching for something to say.

"Yes, that is good news." Again, a response void of feeling, of life.

"As I said to you earlier, I have Rob Randall here with me. He has agreed to help us."

Nigel shifted his gaze to Randall. He again gave a slight smile. "Hello, Rob. How are you?"

Randall returned the half-smile. "I am fine, Nigel." He decided to try to break the visceral tension. "I wish we were meeting under different circumstances."

"Yes, I, too . . ." Nigel's voice trailed off as he shifted his gaze away from the two men on the other side of the glass.

"I have presented the story of the extortion attempt to Rob," Sir Geoffrey explained, "at least, what we know. I also showed him The *Rubaiyat*. He knows everything."

Nigel nodded slightly. "And now you know our dirty little family secret," he smirked. "The Shefflands robbed the *Titanic*, that is, before she sank. At this point, I would not be at all surprised to discover that we single-handedly plowed the ship into the iceberg."

There was an uncomfortable silence before Sir Geoffrey spoke. "Hopefully, Rob here will uncover the truth," he said ruefully. "It shouldn't be difficult. After all, it has only been one hundred years." Sir Geoffrey's attempt at subtle humor fell flat.

"Yes, Father," Nigel agreed stone-faced. "That fact alone should preclude Randall from suggesting *I* am the reason for *Titanic* ramming a berg during a gold heist."

Randall flushed, feeling the warmth rise under his collar. "Of that, Nigel, I have no doubt," Randall responded. "But it appears someone does believe you robbed the *Titanic* and now he is demanding his share of the loot."

Warily, Randall and Nigel Sheffland glared at each other through the glass partition. Sir Geoffrey interrupted. "Enough, gentlemen," he said, motioning with his hand to solicit calm. "Nigel, Rob has been gracious enough to listen to our plight and to try to help us. Please act accordingly."

Nigel seemed to visibly deflate. "Yes, of course," he sighed, looking down at his folded hands. "Please forgive me. I . . ." his voice once again trailed off.

"Son, let us start at the beginning," suggested Sir Geoffrey.

Nigel looked at Randall with an expression of resignation. He then returned his gaze to his hands, a blank stare on his face. "In March of last year, I received a phone call at my office. The caller identified himself as Reece Devero."

"Spell it," Randall ordered.

"Devero," Nigel responded, "*D-E-V-E-R-O*. Reece Devero. He wanted to make an appointment to visit me. When I inquired as to the nature of his business, he simply said it was personal and of the utmost urgency. He seemed so cold and detached over the phone. I suddenly became concerned that he knew of the airline purchasing counterfeit electrical parts and instrument replacements for our fleet. I immediately decided to see him. The next day, as a matter of fact."

"You saw him the next day?" Randall repeated. "Did he come alone?"

"No, actually," Nigel replied, "someone did come with him. But he remained in the outer office during our meeting."

"Did he have a name?" Randall asked, somewhat perplexed.

"Devero said his name only once. He referred to him as Pauly."

"Just Pauly?"

"Yes," Nigel recalled. "He didn't say a last name. Only Pauly."

"What did Devero look like?" Randall asked with mounting curiosity. "I mean, please describe him."

"He seemed to be in his late thirties, early forties," Nigel replied, his face scrunched in recollection. "He was thin, almost wiry. Blonde curly hair. Blue eyes. He had sharp features – nose, chin. He was quite well dressed."

"Was he British?"

"No. I don't think so. I believe he was Canadian. Accent, you know."

"Anything else?" Randall was now displaying more than passing interest.

"Yes. He walked with a very slight limp. Right leg, I believe." Nigel paused a moment. "One other thing." He suddenly remembered. "A strange thing happened during our meeting. He had a nose-bleed."

"A nose-bleed?" Randall sounded incredulous.

"Yes," Nigel responded. "A good old-fashioned nose-bleed, as if someone had bonked him on his nose. He seemed quite embarrassed by it."

"I'll bet," Randall smiled. "What about his compatriot – Pauly? Description?"

"I only managed a brief glimpse of him. He was much shorter. Heavier. He had a somewhat pudgy face. Very short hair – dark. He appeared quite disheveled. Almost sloppy. I didn't hear his voice." Nigel strained in recollection. "One thing stood out. His face was pink. Almost flushed. A splotchy pinkish complexion. That's all that I remember."

"Well," Randall concluded, "not a whole lot to go on. What did this guy Devero talk about during your meeting?"

"After introducing himself, Devero said that he had been doing research for years on a ship once owned by the Sheffland family. He said the ship was named the *Loch Gillelli* and that her hull was discovered off the coast of Nova Scotia in 1998. I knew that was true. He further informed me that his years of research had led him to the irrefutable conclusion that our steamer, the *Loch Gillelli* was involved in a plot to seize *R.M.S. Titanic* on her maiden voyage and to plunder the ship. Furthermore, he knew the *Titanic* was robbed prior to her sinking, and that our family still had the treasure, now worth millions, if not billions."

"And he wants a part of it," concluded Randall.

"Yes."

"And you and your father knew of the existence of the priceless *Rubaiyat*?"

"That is correct," Sir Geoffrey interjected. "Nigel knew of the book in our possession at Banhaven."

Randall smiled and shook his head. "So, simply put, you *do* have treasure from the *Titanic* and Mr. Devero wants at least part of it. Or else." Sir Geoffrey and Nigel both silently nodded in unison.

Randall pondered the story for a moment. "Nigel," Randall asked, "how did your initial meeting with this Devero character end? Did he threaten you with an '*or else*'?"

"No, not really," Nigel replied. "He made no direct threat, at least, not during his first contact with me. I pretended that I knew nothing of what he was talking about, which was mostly true. Devero concluded our conversation with just a suggestion that I think about it. You know, dragging our family name through this whole bloody affair with the *Titanic*. That sort of thing."

"Did you tell your father about this encounter with Devero?" Randall tried not to show skepticism.

"No," Nigel replied. "I decided against mentioning it to him."

"Why?"

"I just didn't want to bother him with it."

So many other secrets to keep, Randall thought. Why stack another one on the pile?

"When did Devero again contact you?"

"I did a fair amount of traveling during the spring, and so I didn't hear from him again until late May. By phone. I told Devero there was no connection between the Sheffland family and the *Titanic*, and, quite frankly, I told him to bugger off. He then informed me he had proof – definitive proof - that the Sheffland family was directly responsible for the loss of life aboard *Titanic*."

"And you said . . ." prodded Randall.

"I told him to *bugger off* anyway."

Randall turned to Sir Geoffrey. "And you knew nothing of this?"

Sir Geoffrey reluctantly shook his head. "Regrettably, no."

Randall returned his gaze to Nigel. "It appears Mr. Devero did not take your advice to – uh – 'bugger off'. When did you next hear from him?"

"It was mid-summer. Late July. He reiterated his demand that we turn over the *Titanic* treasure to him. All of it. But this time, his ultimatum had changed. He thought that perhaps the Sheffland family did not care if their name was sullied, but they certainly cared about British Sovereign Airlines. Devero informed me that if his demands were not met, he promised one of our aircraft would have an '*untimely demise*'. His words."

"And a few months later, British Sovereign has their first fatal crash of a Boeing 777 cargo plane in Belgium." Randall shook his head. "That must have gotten your attention?" He turned again to Sir Geoffrey. "And you still didn't know? You had no idea of the threat?"

"No," Sir Geoffrey quietly replied, shaking his head.

"Don't tell me," Randall said as he again looked at Nigel. "Let me guess. After the accident in Brussels, Devero calls and tells you he is responsible for the crash. Furthermore, if you don't cough up the goods, there will be another plane crash. Only this time, it will be worse. It will involve one of your passenger airliners. Am I right?"

Nigel didn't respond. He merely stared down at the table. His hands shook slightly.

"Great, just great," Randall remarked with disdain. "And then Jack Kilby and I arrived in Portsmouth, proclaiming there is a possible threat against one of your triple-7s. So, Nigel, *now* you're worried about your electrical equipment recycle racket, your family secret, your family name, the airlines, not to mention an extortion plot." Randall laughed. "And, *now*, here I am *again*. Man, I must be a real frog in the punch bowl."

Nigel remained silent.

"Okay, Sir Geoffrey, I think I've heard enough." Randall stared at Nigel through the glass partition. "I'll try to help you fellows as best I can. But I will tell you this. You have, as we Americans say, screwed the pooch on this one. Of all the . . ." Randall stopped, holding his hand up. "I won't say it. Sir Geoffrey, we will continue this conversation when we return to Banhaven." He stood, indicating the meeting was at an end. "Thank you, Nigel," Randall smiled through pursed lips. "We'll talk again."

As Randall and Sir Geoffrey returned to the prison parking lot and the car, the drizzle turned to heavy rain. It fits this place, Randall thought. It fits this day.

* * *

The return to Banhaven was as quiet as the ride to Wandsworth Prison. Randall stared at the soggy scenery as they left the congestion of London for the rural countryside. As they neared Banhaven, Randall turned his attention to Sheffland and began asking more questions. "Sir Geoffrey, you said Nigel told you of the extortion plot by this Devero character after the Belgian crash in November. When exactly did he inform you of this threat?"

Sheffland thought for a moment. "It was when you and Jack Kilby first contacted us about a possible threat against one of our passenger airliners."

"Was this before our arrival to Portsmouth?"

"No," Sheffland replied. "Actually, you had just visited me at our old operations building. Our first meeting. I told Nigel that evening after his arrival at Portsmouth."

"So Nigel told you of the extortion plot *after* you informed him of my visit?"

"That is correct," confirmed Sheffland.

"Strange," Randall said with furrowed brow. "Why do you think Nigel waited so long to tell you about Devero?"

"I don't know." Sheffland suddenly appeared confused. "Honestly, I don't know. Perhaps he didn't consider the extortion threat to be serious. Mind you, after I heard about it, I did take it seriously, especially in light of your warning."

"Or maybe Nigel simply did not want anyone to scrutinize British Sovereign Airlines," Randall remarked in conjecture. "When you suddenly shine a bright light in the darkness, rats caught out in the open try to scurry off before being noticed."

"Yes," Sheffland responded in resignation. "Perhaps that is so."

"Tell me," Randall continued, "has there been a report issued on the cargo plane crash in Belgium? Maybe an interim report from the Belgian or French investigators?"

Sheffland shook his head. "No. We have heard nothing from the Belgian or French authorities."

"In other words," Randall laughed, "no reviews. No previews. Typical. If there is no great loss of life, no big headlines, it's just business as usual. Regardless."

"I suppose that's the way of it." Sir Geoffrey's voice trailed off as the limousine entered the grounds of Banhaven.

The heavy rain kept falling, the many puddles like pieces of a living puzzle. Flowing. Ebbing. Forever changing. That is, until the sun returned.

* * *

Randall briefly paused as he examined the old documents spread before him in the study of Banhaven Manor. For about three hours, he had been slowly and methodically scrutinizing the ship's papers of the *Loch Gillelli*. He set aside the magnifying glass and leaned back in the plush leather chair, flexing his body before standing and stretching.

After returning from Wandsworth Prison to Banhaven the previous afternoon, Randall decided to dine alone in his room. The visit with Nigel Sheffland had been stressful and he felt tired beyond measure. Randall almost wished he had not made the journey to England. He simply wanted to be back at home working on his old boat.

After stretching, Randall again sat down at the desk and stared at the smattering of papers. At that moment, the door opened. Alex Sheffland entered the study. "Did I awaken you?" he asked, with a grin on his face.

"Yes," Randall replied, pretending to appear sleepy. "You interrupted me during a wonderful dream."

"I can only imagine," Alex said as he walked to one of the chairs facing the desk.

"I thought you were busy with a big company meeting," Randall casually noted. "I didn't expect to see you before I left."

"The planning meetings have been completed," Sheffland announced. "They went very well. Father informed me that you were returning home later this afternoon. I wanted to visit with you before you departed for the colonies."

"Yes," confirmed Randall. "Going home. I believe I have done enough damage here already."

Sheffland laughed briefly before becoming serious. "Father told me of the meeting yesterday with Nigel. He said it went well." He paused. "At least, better than expected."

"Yes," agreed Randall. "Better than *I* expected. Nigel was very cordial. Quite open."

"I'm glad," said a relieved Alex. "I was hoping it would go well. It has been quite difficult for him." Sheffland glanced at the papers strewn across the desk top. "I see you have been perusing our records on the *Loch Gillelli.* What have you learned?"

"Well, I learned a few things," Randall began. "There's not a whole lot of information in the ship's papers. The *Loch Gillelli* was rather small, not quite as large as a three-island vessel. Engine in the aft section. Raised structures at the stern. Open bridge on an exposed platform. Coal burner. Pretty typical for a turn-of-the-century tramp steamer, I suppose. Nothing remarkable."

Alex Sheffland frowned. "I guess it is not surprising there isn't much information on the ship, being a hundred years old and all."

"No," Randall agreed. "Not really surprising. I learned a little about the crew. The captain's name was Artemus Pritchard. He worked directly for your great-grandfather, Cyril Sheffland. Sheffland was designated as the ship's master." Randall paused briefly to look at his notes. "The ship's crew had a first mate. His name was Zachary Gable. But there's something strange. The crew roster also lists a fellow as the quartermaster. His name was Danker."

"What's so strange about that?" Sheffland wondered aloud.

Randall sighed. "Well, quartermasters normally are found only on large naval vessels, not on small cargo ships. You see, the crew roster listed only sixteen names in addition to the captain. A couple of deck officers, a few bo'sun mates, some ship's engineers and seamen – that's about it. A small ship and a smaller crew. There was no need for a quartermaster."

Randall paused a moment before continuing. "There is another thing that is strange, Alex. *The Loch Gillelli* was a coal-burner. So, where are the stokers? Why weren't firemen and stokers listed in the crew roster? The coal didn't walk into the boiler's firebox by itself. Somebody had to shovel it in."

"Hm-m," uttered Sheffland. "That *is* strange."

"Well, one thing's for sure," Randall casually remarked. "The *Loch Gillelli* made only a few voyages as a cargo ship. From the manifests, it appears the ship sailed under a few individual voyage charters carrying cotton and bales of cloth to England. One passing point of interest. There is no record of the ship making a voyage in 1912."

"And yet the family was formally notified by British maritime authorities that our ship, of Canadian registry, sank in the North Sea on a cargo voyage in 1912." Sheffland seemed perplexed. "How did that happen?"

Randall responded by simply shrugging his shoulders.

"Rob, anything else?"

"No," Randall replied. "Not really. I'm afraid that whatever I learn from now on will not come from the ship's papers of the *Loch Gillelli*. That is, unless I can find the ship's logs."

"I suppose this dearth of knowledge on the *Loch Gillelli* presents somewhat of a sticky wicket for you in completing your mission," Alex Sheffland remarked ruefully. "What now? Where do you go from here?"

Randall smiled. "I can go only one way. I can't start in 1912 and work my way forward. I can only start in the present and hopefully work my way to the past."

"How will you do that?" wondered Sheffland.

"I will begin with what I know, what I am familiar with, and that is the crash of the Swissair flight in 1998. This all seems to have started with the discovery of the *Loch Gillelli* shipwreck. I am convinced the ship is the key to your family's – uh-h – difficulties."

"And those family difficulties, as you say, began in North America."

Randall smiled. "That is correct. The answers to all of this will be found in Canada and possibly the United States. I will begin with those who participated in the recovery of the Swissair jet, Canadian and American. From there, we'll see where they lead me."

"How can I help you?" Alex Sheffland seemed genuinely sincere in his question.

"There's really not much you and your family can do right now," Randall replied, "at least, not until I've gotten a little further into this. I will keep you informed as progress in the investigation warrants. Just make sure I know when this Devero character contacts you again. Okay?"

Sheffland smiled and nodded in agreement. Randall glanced out the window at the morning sunshine. "Looks like the rain has passed," Randall concluded. "Good flying weather back to America, I hope."

"Yes," Sheffland agreed. "You should have smooth sailing."

Smooth sailing, Randall thought, better than that of the *Loch Gillelli*. Hopefully.

* * *

The sounds of Farnsborough Airport echoed through the open cabin
door of the Sheffland's Cessna Citation. Randall was staring out the passenger window half-asleep when he was suddenly startled by the clattering
arrival of another passenger.

"Well, look at what the cat dragged in," he proclaimed as Don Wiltsey
entered the aircraft cabin and sat opposite Randall.

"Yeah, yeah," Wiltsey responded, shifting the ever-present toothpick in
his mouth. "Right back at you."

"I guess the Shefflands aren't particularly choosey as to who they let on
board their business jet," Randall casually remarked.

Wiltsey glared at him. "That's for sure. Only the truly needy get a free
ride, especially the ones that can't afford a box of doughnuts."

"No, no," retorted Randall. "You're not sticking me with that. It was
your turn to buy."

Both men laughed as Wiltsey's luggage was stowed and the cabin door
was closed and secured.

"Well, I guess your big pow-wow in London finished up and you're heading home," Randall concluded.

"Yep," Wiltsey said rolling his eyes. "Time to get the hell outta Dodge."

"How were the meetings?" Randall asked as the jet engines started.

"They were okay," Wiltsey replied. "Some big changes coming."

"How so?"

"The company-wide system for the procurement and tracking of spare
parts is completely changing." Wiltsey responded, shaking his head. "Whole
new system. In a nutshell, everything is being done to prevent counterfeit
or re-used aircraft parts from ever again being purchased and distributed
by British Sovereign, especially the stuff for controls and instrumentation.
Never again. Thanks to you."

Randall quickly felt uncomfortable. Wiltsey sensed it. "Look, I meant
that in a good way," he continued. "If there was anything that ever needed
the light of day to be shined on it, if there was anything that needed to be
fixed, it was that counterfeit parts deal. You did what you had to do." Wiltsey

reached across and slapped his hand on Randall's knee. "Besides, it was the beginning of a beautiful friendship."

"I hope so," Randall smiled wistfully as the engine noise increased and the Citation began to taxi towards the runway.

"How was your meeting with the Shefflands?"

"It was interesting, Don. Very interesting."

"What do they have you working on now?" Wiltsey was obviously fishing.

"Don't worry," Randall laughed. "It's nothing to do with the airline." He paused a moment, searching for his words carefully. "It's a family issue. It has to do with – uh – well, I suppose you could say that the Shefflands have been considering their prior ventures with cargo ships."

The expression of disbelief on Wiltsey's face said it all. Whatever Randall was trying to sell, Don Wiltsey wasn't buying any of it. Not now. Not ever.

Chapter 5

"**R**ob, that is by far the damnedest story I've ever heard in my life, and I've heard some real winners!"

Rob Randall sat back in the recliner and gazed at Jack Kilby. The windows in the den were opened and a cool evening breeze fluttered the curtains, reminding him it was nearing October.

"I feel much better," Randall declared, smiling. "Now you know what I know."

"You sure this isn't all from jet lag?" Kilby asked in utter amazement. He wasn't about to ask if his friend of over forty years was inebriated. Or just plain out of his mind. Again.

"No, it isn't jet lag. And I'm not crazy and, no, I'm not drunker than a skunk." Randall had returned from England the previous day and now sat in the family room of Kilby's home. He had recounted every bit of his visit with the Shefflands. Everything.

Kilby sighed. "I really don't know what to say except maybe, 'Have fun – write if you get work!'."

Randall laughed. "See why I didn't want to visit you at your office. Sort of a long story, especially when I throw in all the details. And it remains *unofficial*."

Kilby shook his head. "I'm really at a loss for words. I can see why you wanted this unofficial and off the record."

"And I want it to stay that way, at least for the present," Randall reiterated.

"This is a strange one, all right," Kilby pondered. "*Titanic* treasure, lost ship, all of that. But the fact is you also have an extortion plot. A serious one. A threat to take down an airliner is not to be taken lightly."

"I'm not sure," Randall said. "Just one or two guys . . ."

"That's all it takes," interrupted Kilby. "You know that just about better than anyone, especially with your background."

"Yeah," Randall uttered in resignation. "You're right. I guess that's why I want to pursue this. Maybe I can stop something bad from happening."

At that moment, Randall and Kilby heard a sound of clattering coming from the kitchen. "Helen must be back. Helen, is that you?" Kilby called out.

"No," came a shrill voice from the darkened hallway. "It's just one of the ten most wanted."

Helen Kilby entered the den. "Rob, I didn't know you were here. Jack, why didn't you tell me Rob was going to be here? I wouldn't have gone to see Phyllis."

"How *is* Phyllis?" Kilby asked eager to change the subject.

"Oh, you know Phyllis," Helen replied. "She's happy. She just doesn't know it."

Kilby glanced at Randall and raised his eyebrows. Randall just smiled. "That's nice," Kilby responded somewhat impatiently. "Dear, if you don't mind, Rob and I are in the middle of a serious discussion."

"Oh, don't mind me," Helen cracked flippantly. "I'll just go back into the kitchen and throw dishes."

"Thank you, dear," Kilby said as Helen retreated from the den with a quick wave and a nod to Randall.

"Jack," Randall asked in a casual voice, "what *are* you going to do when you retire, you know, when you're home all the time?"

"I don't know," Kilby responded, shrugging his shoulders. "Drown myself in the bathtub. Live on your boat. Run off to Tahiti. Haven't decided yet." Randall joined Kilby in brief laughter. Then Kilby became serious. "I believe, at this moment, the real question is what are *you* going to do now?"

"Well," Randall replied, "as I told Alex Sheffland, I can't begin in 1912 and work my way forward. I can only begin in the present and go to the past."

"And how will you do that?" Kilby suddenly seemed hesitant, almost distant.

"I will begin with the crash of Swissair Flight 111 in 1998. I will try to contact the folks who participated in the aircraft recovery process, Canadian and American. I'll start with the Americans first. Hopefully, they will lead me to others."

"And what do you need from me?" Again, Kilby seemed distant.

Randall smiled. "From you, two things. First – a U.S. Navy ship participated in finding and recovering the Swissair airliner. The ship was the *U.S.S. Surveyor*. I need the name, address, and hopefully a phone number for the captain of the vessel during the recovery efforts. The FBI should be able to obtain that information without much trouble."

"I can do that," Kilby responded, nodding his head. "And the second thing?"

"I'll need a shoulder to cry on," Randall replied smiling. "A father confessor, reality checker, you know, someone to hold my hand."

"Yeah, right," Kilby seemed relieved. "Tell you what, I'll go one better. I'll obtain copies of the Swissair accident reports from the NTSB and the Canadian folks. I should be able to get those documents without stirring up too much interest."

"You mean *trouble*," Randall interjected. "Just so you know, I've already dreamed up a cover story for my work. I'm simply doing research for a book on the crash investigation of Swissair Flight 111."

"Sounds simple enough," agreed Kilby. "Better than telling everyone you're searching for the treasure of the *Titanic*. That might draw some attention."

"Yeah," Randall mused, "beyond a doubt."

"I'll get started on this tomorrow," Kilby said. "One other thing," he added. "In light of all that has happened this past year, you know, being shot, almost tossed *out of* a plane, almost run over *by* a plane, almost killed *in* a plane . . ."

"Twice!" Randall exclaimed. "Remember – *twice!*"

"Yeah," Kilby remembered, "*twice*. Not to mention other various and sundry attacks on your personhood. Try to keep from getting yourself dinged. In other words, be careful out there. Okay?"

"No sweat," was Randall's short, succinct reply.

Considering the past year, for Randall, that was easier said than done.

* * *

The area surrounding Norfolk, Virginia, had changed drastically during the past forty years. As he drove from Norfolk's airport to Virginia Beach, he realized it was now nothing but housing developments and strip malls. Traffic congestion abounded, especially around the naval air station at Oceana. Scratch this place for the retirement home, Randall mused.

It hadn't taken long for Jack Kilby to find the names and contact information of the ranking officers of the *U.S.S. Surveyor* during the Swissair jet recovery operations. The captain of the naval vessel resided in Massachusetts. The ship's operations officer was retired from the Navy and working overseas. However, one officer, the former ship's exec, lived in Virginia Beach. At least it was a place to begin.

Following the rental car's GPS and verbal instructions recorded on paper, Randall drove east into Virginia Beach and then briefly north along the ocean front searching for a condominium development. Eventually spotting it, he turned into the gated community of Sea Oats Shores. He drove past the unoccupied guard shack and open white wrought-iron gate and onto a brick-lined street. Winding through rows of condominiums, Randall finally arrived at his destination and turned into a driveway leading to a condo that appeared more like a house. He parked the car and proceeded to the front door. Before he could ring the doorbell, he heard, then saw through the screen door, a tiny - yet ferocious - Yorkshire terrier scrambling down the hallway, tiny toenails sounding a staccato of clicking taps on the tile floor. Once the dog spotted Randall, a high-pitch bellow came forth, announcing the territorial intruder. Randall then heard a gruff voice. "All right, Spike, knock it off." Randall immediately saw a man hurrying to the door. Through the screen door, he heard a greeting. "Mr. Randall?"

"Yes . . ."

"Come on in. You're right on time." The screen door opened to reveal a short, stocky man attempting to control the yappy dog. "Get back, Spike! He's not here to rob the place. You've done your job." The dog whimpered briefly then retreated down the hallway, tail wagging and head held high, silently proclaiming his superiority. "I remember you. Chet Blake." He held out his hand to Randall.

"Nice to see you again, Mr. Blake. Rob Randall." The handshake was firm, matching the man before him.

"Now that you've met Spike, c'mon back into the patio room. Can I offer you something to drink?"

"No," Randall replied, "thank you. I'm fine."

The patio room was a large, screened enclosure filled with indoor-outdoor furniture. As soon as he sat down in a chair with plush cushions, Randall was joined by Spike, the now not-so-ferocious watchdog. Blake immediately picked the dog up from Randall's lap and gently returned him to the floor. "Go on," Blake ordered. "Mr. Randall does not need you in his lap." Spike slowly padded to a dog bed in the corner and curled up, keeping a wary eye on Randall.

"That's one tough guard dog," Randall appraised as he studied Blake. The man appeared older but still solid as a rock. His large blue eyes, magnified by wire-rim glasses, dominated his square face and greying hair.

"You don't mess with Spike," Blake laughed. "Meaner than a junkyard dog." The dog's head momentarily popped up, looking at his master with curious eyes. "Yeah, you." Blake smiled as he turned his attention to Randall. "How was your flight? Did you have any problems finding this place?"

"No, not at all," Randall replied. "Norfolk sure is crowded, though. A lot different from forty years ago."

"Tell me about it," Blake responded. "I grew up in Hobson, just on the other side of Norfolk. It was bad forty years ago. Hampton, Newport News, Norfolk – it's now all grown together."

"Yeah, for sure," Randall agreed. "How long have you lived here?"

"Almost six years," Blake replied. "I retired from the Navy in 2009. My wife and I moved into this place a year later. We like it here, but you're right. It's pretty crowded. I take it you're retired from the NTSB?"

"Yes," Randall said. "Three years now."

"And you're writing a book?"

"Well, let's put it this way," Randall replied, "like I said in our phone conversation, I'm doing research for a book."

"On Flight 111?"

"Yes, on Swissair Flight 111."

Blake sighed. "I sure do remember that one. Awfully bad."

"Yes," Randall agreed. "About as bad as it can get."

"I met you right after our ship's arrival in Nova Scotia," Blake remembered. "I was the XO of the *Surveyor* at the time. I had been the operations officer on the ship and had just been promoted."

"Yes, I met you and Captain Sprague and your operations officer. I believe his name was Hewes."

"Yeah," Blake agreed, "Marty Hewes. Phil Sprague retired and he lives in Falmouth, Massachusetts. Hewes left the Navy before me. He started his own salvage consulting firm. I guess he spends a lot of time in Europe."

"What do you remember about the *Surveyor* work in Nova Scotia?"

Blake leaned back in his chair and stared outside the screen. "The *Surveyor* was in port in Philadelphia at the time when the call came in. Proceed ASAP to Nova Scotia. The Navy wanted us to assist the Canadians in the aircraft recovery effort."

"Did you participate in the Long Island crash recovery?"

Blake rubbed his face. "Sure did. Captain Sprague and I – well – we had the experience from that to help the Canadians. I guess you guys did, too. I mean, you were sent to Canada to help them like you helped us at Long Island."

"Yes, you're right," Randall responded. "The crash off Long Island was a real learning experience." He shifted the conversation back to the events in Canada. "Your ship arrived at St. Margarets Bay in something like a week after the accident. Correct?"

"Yes," Blake nodded. "September tenth. Eight days after the crash. We were sent there to search for the wreckage and recover it, along with the passengers. We had thirty-two divers from the Mobile Diving and Salvage Unit 22. I believe you helped prepare them for the survey and recovery work."

Randall nodded. "Yes, I trained them."

"The *Surveyor* had improved search-capabilities installed after the Long Island efforts two years earlier," Blake recalled. "We had what was called synthetic aperture sonar and a thing called laser electro-optics identification to scan the sea floor. We were able to define just about all of the aircraft wreckage. I remember you helped set up the underwater grid to map the debris."

"Yes," agreed Randall. "We established the grid and recorded the location of the wreckage prior to photographing and recovering it. Before that was completed, though, I went ashore to help in developing the procedures to identify and sort the pieces."

Blake shook his head. "I remember the guys recovering crash victims. God almighty! I don't know how you guys got used to it."

"Some of us didn't," Randall remarked dryly. He redirected the conversation. "Prior to recovering the wreckage, while you were completing the sonar survey, the *Surveyor* found the wreck of an old ship just west of the Swissair plane location. Do you remember that?"

"Yes," Blake replied, "vaguely. We were doing the sonar scan when we found the hulk. I guess that surprised some folks. The shipwreck wasn't recorded on any bathymetry documents. I really didn't pay much attention to it - you know, other fish to fry."

"Did you send any divers down to investigate the shipwreck?" Randall asked nonchalantly.

"I really couldn't tell you," Blake replied. "Hewes and Chief Norris would probably know that. They were responsible for the dive team activities. I'm sure you met Roland Norris when you were on board the *Surveyor* training the divers."

Randall leaned back in his chair and stared at the patio ceiling. "I'm sure I did. It's just hard for me to remember." Randall paused a moment. "Hewes. Norris. They would know?" He shook his head. "Dead end."

"Not really," Blake mused. "Hewes may be out of the country, but Norris surely isn't. Would you like to talk to him?"

"Absolutely," Randall responded enthusiastically. "That would be great."

"I'll be right back," Blake announced as he rose from his chair and walked into the house. Spike raised his head warily and stared at Randall, silently threatening to attack at the slightest provocation.

"Relax, Spike," Randall said in a soothing tone. "Go back to sleep."

Blake soon returned with a phone, punching numbers with beefy fingers as he resumed his seat. "Norris lives up the coast near Williamsburg. I hope he's home." Blake finished entering the numbers and listened for an answer.

"Chief, this is Chet Blake!" he greeted. "How's my favorite naval petty officer?" Blake paused and then laughed. "No, I'm not calling about any money you owe me." Blake winked at Randall. "But thanks for reminding me. We'll discuss that later." Another pause and more laughter. "No, that's not it. The reason I called you is I have a visitor here with me. His name is Rob Randall. He's a retired National Transportation Safety Board investigator. You may have met him. He visited the *Surveyor* during our work in Nova Scotia on the Swissair plane crash back in '98." Blake paused a moment. "Yeah, that's him. He did the training so you and your guys wouldn't screw it up too badly. Look – I'm going to place you on speakerphone." Blake placed the phone on the table next to him. "Hear us okay?"

"Yeah," came the electronic voice reply. "I got you."

"Say hello to Rob. Rob, this is Chief Petty Officer Roland Norris, retired. Rollie, for short."

"Hey, Chief," Randall began. "I believe we met a number of years ago. It's nice to visit with you again."

"Same here," Norris responded.

"Rollie, Rob is doing some research for a book on the Swissair Flight 111 accident. He has some questions that I can't answer. Perhaps you can help him."

"Well, I'll try," Norris responded. "Fire away."

"Chief," Randall began, "during the initial sonar scanning of the ocean floor for the survey of the crash site, an old shipwreck was discovered just west of the aircraft wreckage. Do you remember that?"

"Sure do," came the reply. "We found it right off the bat."

"Did you have divers go down on the wreck?"

"As a matter of fact, yes," Chief Norris replied. "Two divers were sent down on each of two separate dives to check on the proximity of airliner wreckage in relation to the shipwreck. You know, make sure that pieces of the jetliner weren't mingled in with the shipwreck debris."

"Were the two divers the same for both dives down to the shipwreck?"

There was a brief pause before Norris answered. "Yes, yes, they were as a matter of fact."

Now, the big question, Randall thought. "Chief, do you remember their names?"

Another pause, palpably longer this time. Randall held his breath. "Yes. Yes, I remember them. One of the two was Danny Latham."

"Aw, shit," Blake interrupted in exclamation.

"Yeah, I know," Norris said in almost a whisper.

"What's wrong?" Randall asked.

In a low voice, Blake said, "I'll tell you later." After a brief pause, "Who was the other diver?" Blake asked in a louder voice.

"Uh, McDowell. McDowell was the other diver."

"Do you remember his first name?" Randall asked, again holding his breath.

"Paul," Norris responded. "Paul McDowell."

Paul, Randall thought. Pauly? I wonder.

"Chief, did you review the two dives on the shipwreck with Latham and McDowell?"

"I'm sure I did," Norris replied, "but I don't remember anything remarkable about the dives. The shipwreck had no impact on our work surveying the aircraft wreckage."

"Rollie, I'll explain about Latham after we're done with our call," Blake instructed.

"Fine by me," Norris agreed.

Randall remained silent. Not much to go on, he thought. Two names and that's it.

"Any other questions, Mr. Randall?" Blake asked.

"No, I think that's it for right now."

"Fair enough," Blake announced to Randall and Norris. "Thanks, Rollie. Say hi to the missus for me. We'll talk soon."

"You bet," came the response from the phone. "See ya." A distinctive click and the call ended. Blake picked up the phone to check it and returned it to the table.

"Hope that helped," he said, satisfied that Randall found the information he was wishing to find.

"Interesting," Randall said aloud to himself as much as to Blake. He gazed at Blake, silently asking another question.

"You want to know about Latham," Blake responded, anticipating the query.

"You got it," Randall answered.

Blake sighed heavily. "Danny Latham is the only sailor who died while under my command. He was lost on my watch."

"What happened?"

Blake sighed again, not wanting to answer. But he did. "I had become the commanding officer of the *Surveyor* after Phil Sprague was promoted. About a year after I assumed command, the *Surveyor* was ordered to recover an F-14 Tomcat from Oceana that had plopped into the Atlantic only about twelve miles off of Virginia Beach. The two air crewmen ejected from the airplane and were rescued, so it was just a matter of recovering the plane. We found it with sonar pretty quickly. The jet was down about two hundred feet, not really a big deal for the divers. On the first reconnaissance dive, Latham had some type of problem. He lost consciousness. The dive team quickly got him back on the ship, but it was too late. He didn't make it."

Randall remained silent, transfixed by the story. Blake continued. "There was an inquiry, of course. When you first phoned me, you said you had been in the Navy for nine years, so you know what 'Board of Inquiry' means."

"Yeah," Randall smiled, "Board of Inquisition."

Blake nodded. "The inquiry never really figured out what happened, and they never assigned blame. But you know how it is. The captain of a ship is responsible for everything. Period."

"Yep," Randall said. "That's the way of the sea. Always has been. Always will be."

"I remember McDowell, now," Blake continued. "He was on that dive with Latham. He was interviewed during the inquiry. I remember McDowell was chosen to accompany the body home. He and Latham were best buddies. They returned Latham to his home in Maine."

"They?" Randall interrupted.

"Yeah. Marty Hewes was the officer that was in charge of the military funeral arrangements. He traveled to Maine with McDowell."

"Do you remember anything else about Paul McDowell?"

"Not really. I do remember he had an unusual nickname. The dive team guys called him 'Beach Ball'."

Randall laughed. "Beach Ball! You're kidding!"

"No, that was his nickname. I think it was because that when he wore a wet suit, he looked like he had a beach ball stuffed in it."

"Big guy?" Randall perceived.

"Yeah," Blake responded. "Sort of rotund for being a Navy diver."

"I've got one more question for you," Randall announced. "After the shipwreck was discovered, did you discuss it with the Canadian folks?"

"*I* sure didn't," Blake replied. "I think you would have to ask Phil Sprague about that. He was the captain of *Surveyor*. It would have been his job."

"Yes," Randall agreed, "I suppose you're right."

"You know," Blake said, "you seem more interested in that shipwreck than you do in the plane wreck."

"Oh," Randall lied, "I'm just trying to be as thorough as possible. It will make for an interesting side note in the book."

Randall remained there at Blake's home for another hour, the two of them reminiscing about their days in the Navy and their mutual military experiences. By the time Randall was ready to leave, Spike had become his lap dog and they were now fast friends.

* * *

"Well, it sounds like you had an interesting visit," Jack Kilby remarked.

Rob Randall sat on his living room sofa, phone in one hand and Maggie the cat in the other. He stroked her head between her ears, the purr loud enough to be heard on the phone by Kilby.

"I think so," Randall agreed. "At least I have a bit more to go on."

"Not much," Kilby concluded. "A couple of names and that's about it. Not a whole lot to go on."

"Yeah," Randall responded. "I guess you're right. I think the key to this whole extortion plot will be found in Canada. But I do find it curious that it was an American ship that discovered the *Loch Gillelli*. There has to be some American connection to this thing. There has to be."

"So what's your next move?" Kilby asked.

"My next move is that tomorrow I'm going to the boat to drop off the new bilge pump that was delivered to the apartment yesterday while I was gone. After that, I'll probably travel up to New England and maybe then on to Nova Scotia. Maybe."

"Okay," Kilby responded. "So, tomorrow, while you're frolicking on your yacht, I'll try to dig up the contact information for this seaman Paul McDowell. I should be able to find it without much trouble since you gave me his assignment to Mobile Diving and Salvage Unit 22. And I have already given you the contact info for Captain Sprague in Massachusetts. Pretty slim pickin's for an investigation, though."

"No kidding," Randall said curtly. "Tell me something I don't know."

"Yeah, you're right," Kilby responded in a tone of surrender. "Call me if you decide to travel up north."

"No sweat. See you later."

Randall ended the call and gazed at the cat. An American connection, he wondered. Slim pickings, for sure.

Chapter 6

"Maggie, what's wrong with you this morning?" Randall negotiated the backstairs leading to the first floor and detached garage, a rolled-up trouble-light in one hand and squirming cat in the other. He pushed the back landing door open and walked across the concrete drive to the garage building. The trunk to his car was open, the new bilge pump already placed in the compartment. He threw the trouble-light on top of the pump box and closed the trunk lid.

"Calm down, Maggie," Randall said, frustrated at the cat's strange, panic-stricken behavior. "You like going to the boat." He opened the car door just as Maggie jumped out of his arms, making a bee-line for the back door. "Maggie, get back here!" Randall yelled as he trotted behind the retreating cat. Maggie stopped at the apartment door, wary, acting frightened.

"What's wrong with you today, youngster?" Randall asked the cowering feline. "When did you become a scared-y-cat?" He picked up Maggie and returned to his apartment. He set the cat down on the kitchen floor and grabbed his phone.

"It's okay, Maggie," Randall said as he closed the apartment door. "You stay here and guard the place. I'll be back in a little while."

Randall headed back down the stairs and to the garage. He walked to the side of the car. Fumbling for the keys, he was starting to climb into the little blue Ford Mustang when he noticed something peculiar. The short two-by-four wooden board he used as a front wheel-stop had been partially kicked away. That's strange, he thought. Why is that moved?

The apartment garage was a short building containing six individual single garages, partitioned only by the separate roll-up doors. The apartment tenants could freely move through the garage building once a single garage door was opened.

Randall walked to the front of his car and, with his left foot, kicked the board back into position. He then looked at the car. He furrowed his brow as he noticed some smudge marks on the edge of the hood. Okay, why are those there, he wondered. Car guys don't leave grimy fingerprints on immaculate paint. He went to the car door, bent down and pulled the hood latch, hearing the familiar pop of a hood release. Randall returned to the front of the car, raised the hood and propped it up. Even with three open doors, the garage was dark.

He glanced into the engine compartment. Nothing seems amiss, he judged, moving his head from side to side in the poor lighting. He moved to the right side of the engine. He looked down towards the rear of the engine and the firewall. Between the car battery and the engine block, Randall could observe the light-grey concrete garage floor. It was then that he saw it. A single strand of wire was silhouetted in the faint light reflecting off the concrete. All right, he thought, that shouldn't be there. Randall moved to the back of the Mustang and retrieved a flashlight. The moment he illuminated the engine compartment Randall knew something was terribly wrong.

The wire was one of two taped to the side of the exhaust manifold, the ends of the wires almost touching as they rested on the steel pipe. The wires were routed under the car. He moved to the side of the vehicle and lay down on the concrete, shining the light under the car. He found a small package taped to the side of the vehicle frame. No doubt about it, he concluded. I'm pretty sure that's a bomb.

Randall stood and proceeded to carefully lower the hood of the car and gently close the driver's door and trunk lid. Then he gingerly walked out of the garage and to the back door of the apartment building. He retrieved the cellphone from his coat pocket and dialed 9-1-1.

"9-1-1," the nasally woman's voice announced, "what is your emergency?"

"My name is Robert Randall. I live at 3804 Woodmont. I found what I believe to be an explosive device attached to my car."

"What type of car?"

"Ford Mustang. Two-door Ford coupe."

"Do you own the vehicle?" The inflection of the voice never changed. It seemed as if the 9-1-1 operator routinely fielded phone calls on bombs every day.

"Yes, for the moment," Randall replied, mustering his fleeting patience.

"What type of explosive device is it?"

At that moment Randall lost his patience along with all sense of decorum. "It's a car bomb, lady," he responded, raising his voice an octave. "It goes boom. How the hell should I know what type of explosive device it is? I didn't yank it out and examine it, for God's sake. Send the police out here. Now. Got it?"

"Yes, sir." Her tone never wavered.

After he repeated the name and address to her, Randall decided to call Jack Kilby. "Hey, Rob. Good morning," Kilby greeted him, seeming to be all bright-eyed and bushy-tailed. "How you doin'? Are you on your boat?"

"Hey, Jack," Randall replied sarcastically. "I'm doing great. Happier than a pig in mud. I wanted to call and let you know that I just got done talking to 9-1-1. I found a bomb under my car just a little while ago. I'm waiting for the police and Lord knows who else to arrive. They should be here at any moment. I hope."

Randall's proclamation was met with complete silence. Finally, after what seemed like an eternity, Kilby squeaked out a response. "Is that right? Interesting. Hey, I'll talk to you later." Click.

* * *

A sudden cool morning breeze stirred the leaves above him, the sunlight obscured in the shade. Randall briefly cracked open an eye, squinting at the flashing lights a few hundred yards away. It looks like the apartment building is still standing, he thought. He closed his eye again, wishing to continue sleeping under the tree. He shifted his back against the tree trunk before dozing off.

"I swear to God, you could sleep in the middle of a battlefield at high noon." Randall opened his eyes and glanced up at Jack Kilby, his arms folded and his face glaring.

"I'm not sleeping, Jack," he responded. "I'm just meditating on the goodness of the day. You should try it."

Kilby plopped down on the grass next to Randall. "Great! You almost get blown into soup mix and then turn around and act like a Buddhist monk at a yoga class."

"Like I said, you should try it," Randall reiterated. "And the key word is *almost*."

"Well, it won't blow up now," announced Kilby. "The bomb squad disarmed it."

"That's nice," Randall said as he once again closed his eyes.

"You know, Rob, in the past year, you've been shot twice, almost murdered in a sabotaged plane, almost killed in a plane crash."

"Don't forget the kidnapping and walking the plank at ten thousand feet," Randall reminded him.

"Yeah, that, too. And now a car bomb. Really, have you ever thought of finding a new circle of friends?"

"Jack, are you my best friend?" Before Kilby could reply, Randall answered his own question. "Enough said."

At that moment, a large flat-bed truck carrying a single massive steel cylinder rumbled past Randall and Kilby. Randall opened his eyes and waved his right hand weakly. "Bye-bye, bomb," he said casually.

"Rob, we have to talk."

Randall snapped awake as a voice from a distant loudspeaker announced it was safe for the residents standing in the streets to return to their domiciles. "Yeah, I know," Randall said in resignation. He and Kilby stood and slowly strolled down the sidewalk toward the apartment.

"Got any idea as to who would want to turn you into bird feed?" Kilby asked.

"No, not really," Randall replied.

"Remember yesterday when I said I didn't think there was an American connection to this *Titanic* treasure thing?" Kilby reminded him. "It's possible that I may have spoken prematurely."

Randall stopped and gazed at Kilby. "No fooling. You don't say. After some guy tries to pop me into burger bits over an extortion threat against an international air carrier, now you're interested."

"Yeah, I guess I had that coming," Kilby sighed.

As they reached the apartment building, Randall and Kilby were met by the ranking police officer on scene and a sergeant on the bomb squad. "Well, Mr. Randall," the sergeant began, "that was a particularly nasty little device. A battery, a block of C4, and some wires. Simple yet sophisticated."

"How so?" Kilby interrupted.

"Well, the fuse was ingenious. The ends of two leads were mounted on top of the engine manifold like so." The sergeant held the index fingers of both hands together, the fingertips almost touching. "The wiring insulation was half stripped at the end of each wire, the bare wire surface facing up. At the end of one wire was a dab of solder. When the exhaust manifold heated up, the solder would flow, touching the other wire and completing the circuit. Like I said, simple, yet sophisticated. You'd be driving down the road and boom! It would have ruined your day as well as your car, and I guarantee you would have turned into well done hash."

"Professional job?" Kilby asked.

"Might as well be," the sergeant replied. "The guy who installed that device sure knew what he was doing. He was thorough, for sure. There was a second device, a blasting cap in the gas tank. When you opened the gas cap cover to fill up the tank – bang! Very messy."

"They would have got me, coming or going," Randall surmised.

"You bet," the sergeant agreed. "Somebody doesn't like you."

"Mr. Randall," the police officer interjected, "you will have to come down to the police precinct station and make out a report. I'm sure we'll have a lot of questions for you. We will also have to impound your car for further examination. You know, fingerprints and such. Okay?"

"Sure, sure," Randall replied. "Just let me know when I can get it back."

"It will be just a couple of days." The officer turned to Kilby. "Inspector, this will be a federal beef, too. Bureau of Alcohol, Tobacco, Firearms and Explosives. You might want to accompany Mr. Randall."

Kilby simply nodded as the two policemen walked away. He turned to Randall. "Rob, just how did you know to look under the hood of the Mustang?"

"It's strange, Jack," Randall answered. "I carried Maggie down to the car so she could go with me to the boat. But she was having none of it. She didn't want near that car. Somehow, I guess she knew. I put her back in the apartment. When I returned to the car, I noticed the stop-board in front of the wheel was kicked out of place. While I was putting it back into position, I noticed smudges of dirt on the edge of the hood. When I saw that, I knew something was wrong."

"So you're saying Maggie saved your life?"

Randall smiled. "No. What I'm saying is Maggie saved her own life, and in doing so, she saved my life, too."

"The cat gods must have been looking kindly upon you today," Kilby concluded.

"Well," Randall responded. "Some God was looking out for me."

Kilby laughed. "If I were you, I'd hang on to Maggie,"

"Don't worry," Randall smiled. "I will. We're best buddies for life."

Randall and Kilby watched as the little blue Mustang, Randall's pride and joy, was unceremoniously loaded onto the bed of a tow truck and hauled away. I'm glad the car is okay, Randall thought. I would hate it had it blown up.

He did not want to think about the other part of that.

* * *

Rob Randall stared at the breakfast menu trying to decide if it was going to be eggs or oatmeal. "Well, Rob, what are you having this morning?" Jack Kilby briefly gazed about his menu, catching a glimpse of Randall's face furrowed in concentration.

"Decisions, decisions," Randall replied. "What about you?"

"I'm not sure yet," Kilby responded. "Maybe an omelet."

Randall closed his menu. "I'm going for the gusto this morning. A man can eat only so much oatmeal in his life. Bacon and eggs, over easy. Hash-browns, too."

"Wow," Kilby exclaimed in surprise, "you're hungry this morning. A last meal before the police interrogation?"

"Actually, Jack, I'm famished," Randall remarked. "I think it's like what

Winston Churchill observed. There is nothing more exhilarating than being shot at and living through it."

"Uh, huh," Kilby agreed dryly. "Swell."

The waitress arrived at their table and took their breakfast orders. As she returned to the kitchen, Kilby started the interrogation early. "Okay, Rob," he began, clasping his hands together in front of him, "who do *you* think tried to pull your meal ticket?"

"Honestly, Jack, I don't know. Very few people know of my trip to England *and* have knowledge of the extortion plot. Sir Geoffrey and Alex Sheffland, of course. Nigel Sheffland, too, but he's locked up in prison. Don Wiltsey knows I traveled to London, but I'm sure he knows nothing of this *Titanic* treasure business. That's it. I don't believe the Shefflands would hire me to look into the extortion plot and then immediately turn around and yank the plug on me with a bomb. That doesn't make sense."

"Yeah," Kilby sighed quietly. "You're right. It doesn't make sense." He paused a moment before continuing. "What about the two Navy guys you talked to a few days ago?"

"No," Randall replied, shaking his head. "I didn't say a thing to them about my trip to England or the *Titanic* treasure. And neither of them struck me as being suspicious. As far as they were concerned, I was simply doing research on an event that happened a long time ago." Kilby shook his head briefly and remained silent. "And on top of that," Randall continued, "I saw them just two days ago. That's hardly enough time to contact a guy and arrange for a hit the next morning - especially with an explosive device. Mad bombers aren't exactly listed in the phone book or advertising on-line."

"Oh, you'd be surprised," Kilby laughed. "So that's it? Those are the only folks that know about the *Loch Gillelli?*"

"Just about," Randall replied.

"What do you mean?"

"There is one other person who knows about the extortion plot," Randall announced. "About all of it."

"Who?"

"You, Jack." Randall wasn't smiling.

Kilby's face was expressionless for a moment. He was mute. Randall silently stared at him.

"You, you think . . ." Kilby finally sputtered, pointing to himself, "you think I have something to do with this?"

Randall raised his eyebrows. "Well, I became suspicious of you last night. I remembered your behavior the last time I had dinner at your house. You got pretty bent out of shape because I said I liked Helen's pot roast better than the chicken chop suey . . ."

"It was chow mein!" Kilby interrupted in a loud voice.

"Whatever . . ." Randall responded equally loud. "Look what's happened to me in the past year. You've been in the middle of all the crazy life-threatening shenanigans."

Kilby began protesting but Randall kept up the accusation. "And don't think I haven't noticed you constantly hitting me up to change my will in order to bequeath my boat to you in case of my *untimely* demise. What do you say to that?"

Kilby sat there at the table, mouth agape and in shock.

"Well, believe me." Randall concluded, "when the police ask me who I think master-minded the plot to spread me around the countryside, take a guess at my answer." Randall then proceeded to flash a wide smile at his friend of more than forty years. "There," Randall ended his rant. "I feel much better now."

"So you feel better now . . ." repeated Kilby.

"Um-hum," Randall nodded.

Kilby exploded into laughter. "Okay. Okay, you got me going on that one," a loud guffaw coming from Kilby as their meals were delivered to their table.

Kilby and Randall finished breakfast before the morning meeting with the police was again discussed. Kilby started the questioning. "So, Rob, just what *are* you going to tell the police?"

"Exactly what I've been telling folks. My cover story. I'm doing research for a book on a seventeen-year-old plane crash in Nova Scotia. I am not going to say one word about the Shefflands, the sunken ship, the *Titanic*, or about the extortion plot. If the police, or the FBI, want to figure any of this out, they will have to begin at the bottom and work their way up. First – find the hitman with a strong penchant for using explosive devices. Period. I'll do the legwork on the folks at the top."

"Do you think that's wise?"

"*That* I don't know," Randall replied. "But *that* is what I'm planning to do. I don't believe anyone will attempt an organized hit on yours truly, now that the law enforcement folks have been alerted. Besides, from now on, I'll be traveling. It will be difficult to hit a moving target, at least for a hired hit-man."

"Are you going to inform the Shefflands of yesterday's events?"

"I'm tempted to," Randall said with a tinge of doubt. "I believe they should know about it if only for their own safety."

"Yeah, you're probably right," Kilby agreed. "Maybe just Sir Geoffrey or Alex, though."

Randall silently nodded. He fully understood the implications.

* * *

Two pointed ears protruded from the nest of clothes packed in the open suitcase. A casual flick of her tail indicated Maggie the cat was quite comfortable and content.

"Get out of there, youngster," Randall commanded. "You are not going with me to New England. Or Canada." He chased Maggie from the suitcase as he placed another shirt on top of her newly-commandeered bed. "You're staying here. You know the routine. Mrs. Phelps from across the hall will be looking in on you." The cat yawned, jumped from the bed and sauntered out of the bedroom. Randall shook his head.

The police interview from the previous day indeed was more of an interrogation. Kilby had warned Randall he would receive the "third degree" from the police investigator. The only things absent during the questioning were blinding lights and a rubber hose. However, as far as Randall was concerned, he was through with it. The entire matter now rested with the police. And the Federal Bureau of Investigation. It was their job to find the perpetrator, or perpetrators, of the attempt on his life. He would not be deterred. Next stop – New England.

Jack Kilby had provided the location and contact information for the commanding officer of the *U.S.S. Surveyor* during the Swissair plane recovery. Captain Daniel Sprague was retired and resided in Massachusetts. For the seaman Paul McDowell, the only information available was his last known address in Maine. Again, it was not much to go on, but Randall nevertheless was going. He had an early morning flight to Boston the next day.

Randall strolled into the living room and sat down on the sofa. Before him were individual stacks of notes and reports laying on the coffee table. He began to segregate the piles of information and select those that were to be carried with him on his trip. His briefcase gradually was filled with airliner accident investigation information, from both Canada and the United States, on Swissair Flight 111. The final stack of papers to be reviewed was his notes recorded during the visit to England.

Randall once again studied his scribbled handwritten records taken from his conversations with Sir Geoffrey and Alex Sheffland. He also found his notes of the meeting with Nigel Sheffland. He enclosed them in a file folder and placed them in the briefcase along with a folder of information from the ship's papers on the *Loch Gillelli*. As he finished the selection of information to accompany him, he found a single piece of paper with numbers and letters written on it. Randall had copied them from the faded slip of paper found with *The Rubaiyat of Omar Khayyam* in the possession of Sir Geoffrey Sheffland. He read them again with renewed curiosity.

"442930655507PC

M   W

443939633717C229

N   U"

The arrangement of the numbers seemed random, Randall concluded. And the letters made no sense. It did not appear to be some type of coded message.

He stared at the numbers for more than an hour, continually playing with them in his mind. Then Randall considered the actual piece of paper he first read by the dim light of the fireplace. The letters were so faded, he remembered, so difficult to decipher. What if they were different from those that he wrote? It wasn't until he changed the "M" to an "N" and the "U" to a "W" that the patterns of the numbers fell into place. He knew exactly what the numbers were and what they meant.

Another piece of the puzzle fell into place. Where would the numbers lead him?

Chapter 7

The trees along the road were beginning to display their fall colors, the hills of New England slowly being covered in autumn splendor. Another summer was past, Randall thought. Soon the hills would be blanketed in snow. Another summer gone. Another summer less.

The urban sprawl of Boston retreated in the rear view mirror of the rental car. Before Randall was the rural pastoral scenery of Massachusetts as he drove down the Atlantic coast toward Cape Cod. The first step of his sojourn was taking him to Falmouth, the home of retired Navy Captain Daniel Sprague, former commanding officer of the *U.S.S. Surveyor*. The journey carried him through small towns with quaint New England names like Middleborough and Plymouth and Wareham, all steeped with history and enriched with tradition. Finally, as he passed the entrance to the Otis Military Reservation, Randall knew he was entering the northern outskirts of Falmouth.

Entering the town, Randall turned east onto Main Street. The road was lined with picturesque buildings and houses displaying a unique, old-fashioned refinement. Strange, Randall mused. If you replaced all of the cars with carriages and the pavement with brick, one would be transported back to the year 1715. The more things change, the more they stay the same.

Randall finally found the small strip shopping area off of Main Street and turned into the parking lot, immediately seeing the sign Cape Lighthouse Books above still another quaint, refined shop. He parked the car and walked to the book store entrance. As he opened the door, a tiny bell tinkled above him, repeating the brief ringing as he closed the door behind him.

"Be with you in a second," came a voice from behind a curtain leading to a presumed back room. Randall glanced about as he unzipped his coat. To his left was a wall of white bookshelves lined with fictional literature. Smaller shelves were spread throughout the store. To his immediate right was a small circular oak wood table with three matching chairs. The curtain moved and a man appeared behind the store counter against the wall opposite Randall.

"Captain Sprague?" Randall asked as he instantly recognized the face.

"Mr. Randall," the man deduced. "I remember you." Daniel Sprague returned the expression of recognition. "I was wondering if I'd recognize you. You haven't changed a bit since '98." He walked around the end of the counter and towards Randall.

"You haven't changed either, Captain," Randall said, returning the compliment.

"Heck, I thought I was better looking now," Sprague responded with a broad smile. "Well, now that we've both identified ourselves as blind liars, come on in and sit a spell." The two shook hands, then sat down at the oak table.

"Welcome to Falmouth. Did you have any trouble finding the store?" Sprague asked.

"Nope, not at all," Randall replied.

"Being located on Main Street makes it easy to find us," Sprague remarked. "Have you ever been to Falmouth?"

"I flew into Otis a few times, but that was years ago."

"Yeah, I remember now. You told me you were once a Navy pilot. Sub hunters, I think." Sprague smiled at the recollection. "Back during the Cold War. They sure kept you guys busy, especially here on the east coast."

"That they did," Randall agreed. "Got a lot of flying time in back then."

"Yes. Different era, for sure," Sprague sighed. "The Navy of the past." He paused and gazed at Randall. "So, what brings you to Falmouth? You mentioned something about doing research for a book?"

Randall nodded. "That's correct. I'm doing research for a book on the

Swissair Flight 111 crash investigation. I'm here because I wanted to review the efforts to recover the plane with you. I've already had the opportunity to visit with Chet Blake."

"Oh, my gosh," Sprague exclaimed. "How's Chet doing?"

"He's doing very well," Randall replied. "Living the good life in Virginia Beach."

"Blake was our ops officer," Sprague recalled, "and later he was my exec when I was commander of the *Surveyor*. A truly fine officer."

Randall smiled and nodded. "I also talked with Chief Norris."

"Good grief. Rollie Norris," Sprague reminisced. "We could not have done what we did had it not been for Chief Petty Officer Roland Norris. He pulled my bacon out of the fire more than once."

Randall laughed. "It's funny how Navy chiefs used to do that all the time."

"They've always done it," Sprague agreed, "and they always will. Thank God." Sprague shifted in his chair. "You know if you've already spoken to Blake and Norris, you probably have heard the whole story. I doubt if I can add anything."

"I suppose that's possible," Randall responded. "I just have some questions about your particular efforts and perspective during the survey work and the aircraft recovery."

"Well, go ahead, but I'm sure you know what happened. The Swissair plane crashed and we received the request for assistance from Canada just a few days later. The *Surveyor* was asked to perform the underwater survey work of the crash site and help in the recovery of bodies and wreckage. You were there to give our guys some guidance, so you know all of that."

"Yes," Randall agreed, "I remember it well." Randall redirected the conversation. "Who were your Canadian contacts during your time there in Nova Scotia?"

Sprague paused for a moment before replying. "Just about all of our coordination on the survey and recovery work was with our counterparts on the Canadian ship, the *Compass*."

"Who were they?" pressed Randall. "Do you remember them?"

"Yeah, I guess," Sprague replied. "The captain of the *Compass* was a fellow by the name of Foster. I don't remember his first name. It might have been Kurt. His first officer was a guy – oh, what was his name? – Toven? I think it was Toven."

"You dealt with Foster most of the time?"

Sprague nodded yes.

"The dive team, Unit 22," Randall continued, "did they have much interaction with the Canadian divers?"

"I suppose so. I believe Chief Norris is in a better position to answer that one, he and Marty Hewes. Hewes was our operations officer during that time."

Randall nodded. "I've heard the name. I guess he's out of the country right now."

Sprague snorted. "Yeah, that I can believe."

"What do you mean?" Randall asked with a puzzled expression.

"Oh, nothing," Sprague replied. "It's just that Hewes was sort of a slimy eel. He was wiggly, cagey. I never really trusted him. He seemed more interested in working the angles than doing the job." He paused for a moment. "Of course, that's just my opinion."

Randall smiled. "What else do you know about him?"

"Not much," Sprague strained to recall. "Salvage diver. He came to us with an EOD background."

"Explosive ordinance disposal?" Randall's query was more like a statement of confirmation.

"Yeah, you know, like mines, torpedoes, that sort of thing."

"Hewes knew his stuff?" Randall pressed for more details.

Sprague nodded. "I think he did. At least he didn't blow himself up on my watch."

Randall had a brief flash-of-lightning moment. I wonder if Hewes tried to blow *me* up on *my* watch, he thought.

Randall decided to shift the conversation. "Captain, do you remember a fellow by the name of Paul McDowell? He was a diver on your ship during the Swissair recovery operations. He was assigned to Unit 22."

Sprague gave Randall a brief, lopsided smile. "Yeah, I remember McDowell. He came up before me once. Captain's mast. He had an altercation with another diver and a member of the ship's crew."

"Who was the other diver?"

"That's the funny thing about that whole episode," Sprague recalled.

"The other diver was his best friend, at least from what I was told. His name was Latham."

"Danny Latham," Randall sighed.

"You've heard of him then?"

"Yes," Randall responded. "Chet Blake told me about him."

"Poor Chet," Sprague said sadly. "He lost Latham in a dive accident a year after he took command of the *Surveyor*. A terrible tragedy."

"I guess the inquiry never did figure out what happened." Randall began fishing.

"Yes," Sprague agreed. "I managed to lay my hands on the final report. It was inconclusive as to the cause of his death." Before Randall could ask another question, Sprague continued. "That's another strange one. You'll never guess who was on that final dive with Latham." Sprague paused, perhaps adding to the dramatic effect. "None other than Paul McDowell. I always wondered about . . ." His voice trailed off to silence. After a moment lost in recollection, Sprague shrugged his shoulders. "Oh, well. That was a long time ago."

Randall nodded and smiled. Time to try a new fishing spot. "Back to the work the *Surveyor* did during the Swissair crash recovery. The initial survey efforts were completed by your ship. Correct?"

Sprague nodded. "With your help, we mapped the entire sea floor in and around the crash site. I believe it made the recovery efforts a lot easier. At least, it was way more efficient."

"While the survey work was being completed, a shipwreck was discovered just west of the crash site. Do you remember when that happened?" More trolling by Randall.

"Yes," Sprague replied. "Actually, I do. There's a reason the shipwreck has stuck in my mind all these years. The discovery seemed so unexpected. It quickly became obvious the Canadians had no idea there was the hull of an old ship in that particular location. We had some folks dive on the wreck and report their findings. Then the Canadian Coast Guard came out and tossed some divers into the water to see if we were telling them the truth. Needless to say, we were."

"Do you remember anything else about the discovery?"

Sprague shook his head. "Not really. After the survey work was completed, we immediately began the recovery. The *Surveyor* was a great platform to conduct the heavy lifting efforts. I was consumed by that work until the recovery operation was completed." Sprague smiled. "I remember you and the other folks from the NTSB really helped us a lot. All that mapping you did. And I know your assistance to the Canadians was greatly appreciated as the wreckage was hauled to the surface. You helped put the pieces of the puzzle together."

"Well," Randall responded, "after your ship's work was completed, it was the Canadians who did the heavy lifting. Their efforts were second to none. They did an outstanding job on the crash investigation. No doubt about it."

Sprague became solemn. "Years later, I read about the results of the crash investigation. I guess it was some type of electrical problem that caused a fire in the cockpit. The fire brought the plane down."

"That's correct," confirmed Randall. "Some wiring installations were completed after the aircraft was delivered to the Swissair by McDonnell Douglas. Something went terribly wrong."

"I remember when the guys were bringing the victims to the surface," Sprague said, almost choking. "It was horrible . . . horrible."

Randall realized the moment had arrived to end the inquiry. Just as with Chet Blake, the conversation with Dan Sprague turned to mutual memories of their time at Annapolis and their experiences as officers in the U.S. Navy. And they talked about retirement and the business of owning a bookstore in Falmouth, Massachusetts. Before the end of the afternoon, it was if they had known each other their entire lives.

Chapter 8

After spending the night in Falmouth, Rob Randall retraced the previous day's drive during the return trip to Boston. Passing quickly, the roads in the urban sprawl again became congested. He negotiated the route around the west side of the city and proceeded north towards New Hampshire and Maine.

Despite Jack Kilby's advice, Randall had decided to inform the Shefflands of the attempt on his life. By happenstance, Alex Sheffland was visiting the North American operations of British Sovereign Airlines in Portsmouth, New Hampshire, the site of Randall's previous adventures with the Shefflands four months earlier. It was just as well he was telling Sheffland in a personal meeting rather than by phone. Besides, it would be interesting to observe Alex Sheffland's reaction to the bomb plot.

Once north of Boston, Randall again enjoyed the rural scenery of New England. The colors of the fall foliage were even more pronounced as he drove north towards Portsmouth. If anything, Randall thought, at least it would be an enjoyable drive to Maine and perhaps beyond.

The drive ended too soon as Randall entered the southern edge of Portsmouth. Considering the memories of his past visit, the brief stop to see Sheffland made him uncomfortable. He exited the interstate highway and made his way to the old Pease Air Force Base, now a municipal airport and industrial park. According to Don Wiltsey, British Sovereign Airlines had just moved their North American operations center into a new building on the flight line adjacent to their hangar. He parked near the guard gate and walked to the main entrance of the operations office. He entered the building and was immediately escorted to Alex Sheffland's office. As Randall entered the room, he found that Sheffland was not alone. Sitting opposite him was Byron Beauchamp, now the director of the airline operations in North America. "Ah, the man that saved my life," Beauchamp exclaimed as Randall entered Sheffland's office. He stood, and before Randall could shake his hand, Beauchamp enfolded him in a bear hug.

"Forgive Byron for not displaying a traditional British greeting," Sheffland mused. "I believe he is happy to see you."

"After that Sunday morning," Beauchamp laughed, "I'm happy to see anyone." He released Randall from the bear hug.

"Well, you look fit," Beauchamp observed as he gazed at Randall, "considering we almost lost you in Nevada. Along with Alex."

"I can't complain," retorted Randall. "It's nice to see you again. How do you like your new position as Director of Operations here in America?"

"It suits me well," Beauchamp answered, "thanks to Alex and Sir Geoffrey."

"And he is doing a marvelous job," Sheffland chimed in. "We would not know what to do without him."

Before the idle chit-chat could continue, Alex Sheffland became serious. "Byron, would you excuse us? Rob and I have some issues to discuss, and I believe his time here is limited."

"Sure, Alex," Beauchamp said, somewhat surprised but still smiling. "Rob, if you have time, stop by my office before you depart. It is good to see you again." They shook hands warmly as Beauchamp left the office. Without being asked, he closed the door behind him.

"Good man, Byron," Sheffland said almost in a whisper. "Decidedly indispensable."

"I'm glad to hear that," Randall responded.

"You know, Rob, Byron is right. I'm not sure I really ever thanked you for saving my life. Twice."

Randall smiled as he immediately thought of Maggie, the cat. "Alex, you have to remember one thing. That's not quite correct. It just so happens that in the process of saving my own life, I also saved your life. Twice. It was strictly by coincidence."

"Well, whatever," Sheffland reiterated, "thank you."

"No sweat." Randall changed the subject. "How is Sir Geoffrey getting along? Is he doing better?"

"Yes, actually, I believe he is. Thank you for asking. Your agreeing to help us has made a difference. He seems . . ." Sheffland paused, searching for the appropriate word. "He seems encouraged now."

"I'm glad," Randall responded.

"Rob, when you called me yesterday, you said you wanted to review your initial efforts in resolving some of our family matters. What has happened so far?" Sheffland leaned back in his chair.

"To begin with, I've interviewed a few American naval officers and enlisted personnel who participated in the recovery operations for the Swissair accident. They were also the folks who originally discovered the shipwreck of the *Loch Gillelli*."

"Did they provide you with any important information?" Sheffland asked.

"They gave me the names of two American naval divers who actually made the original dives on the shipwreck after its discovery. Unfortunately one of them is dead. The other diver resides in Maine. That's where I'm heading after I leave Portsmouth. I want to talk with him." Randall paused briefly. "I should tell you his name is Paul McDowell. I have no idea if he is the 'Pauly' that accompanied Mr. Devero on his visit to your brother Nigel. I hope to find out."

Sheffland nodded his head. "Well, at least it's a start."

"It's a beginning," Randall agreed. "But I believe the key to all of this subterfuge will be found in Canada. Regardless of what Mr. McDowell tells me, my next stop will be Nova Scotia."

"Very well," Sheffland seemed satisfied.

At the moment, Randall decided not to tell Sheffland about deciphering the numbers and letters on the piece of paper found with *The Rubaiyat*. For now, he would keep that to himself.

"Alex, there is another reason for my visit with you while I'm here in New England. I debated the necessity for telling you this, but I believe you should know. A few days ago, there was an attempt made on my life. A serious one, beyond any doubt."

Sheffland instantly appeared stricken, a genuine expression of horror on his face. He seemed speechless, almost paralyzed with sudden fear. Randall continued. "Considering the element of time, there are only four people who knew of me visiting London and the specific reasons for doing so and also had the time to arrange for what we in America call a professional hit. Jack Kilby is one. He doesn't count. That leaves Sir Geoffrey and Nigel. And you." Randall's eyes bore through Sheffland. There was no questioning the implications.

"How did they . . ." Sheffland stammered. "What did they do?"

"They placed an explosive device in my car. Very neat. Very tidy."

It appeared Sheffland was on the edge of being physically ill. "I can't believe it. I don't know what to say."

"Well, you can begin by informing your father that a physical threat may exist towards members of your family. Also, it appears the extortion plot is quite real. If I were you, I would behave accordingly. Finally, placing an explosive device in a car is a federal offense in the States. There will be a criminal investigation. How far that goes is anyone's guess. But be aware those folks may eventually end up on your doorstep, whether you like it or not."

Sheffland grimaced and shook his head. "I can't believe this. It can't be." His voice cracked, choking as he tried to swallow Randall's words. "We never wanted to place you in danger. Never."

"I know that," Randall reassured him. "But I also believe this is going to get worse before it gets better."

"I don't know what I can do." Sheffland seemed lost, foundering on the shoals of reality.

"Well, to begin with, tell your father. He needs to know. Also, at this moment, there is one thing you *can* do for me."

"Anything. Just name it." Sheffland said.

"I'm sure Wandsworth Prison maintains records of people who visit the inmates. If you could, I would like to know the names of the individuals who visited your brother in the days immediately following the meeting your father and I had with Nigel."

"That might be important?" Sheffland seemed clueless.

"Yes," Randall replied. "It may be very important."

"Very well," Sheffland uttered in resignation. "I will find the information for you."

Randall had no desire to belabor the record of his activities. He simply wished to continue his journey to Maine. He decided to end the conversation. "Alex, you now know what I know. Before I leave, I would like to see Don Wiltsey if that's possible. Just a brief chat."

"I believe that can be arranged," Sheffland said with a faint smile. "He is around here somewhere. Perhaps Don is in his office."

Alex Sheffland led Randall down a hallway of the new operations building to a corner office. Above the door hung a sign marked Manager of Maintenance. Wiltsey was sitting at his desk. Sheffland knocked quietly on the door. "Don, I have someone here to visit you." Wiltsey glanced up and recognized Randall standing behind Sheffland.

"Whoop, there goes the neighborhood!" Wiltsey exclaimed. "C'mon in, Rob. I didn't know you were here in town. Have a seat."

"I'll leave you two at it." With that, Sheffland retreated down the corridor.

"Wow," Randall said smiling as he looked about the office, "you're in the high-rent district."

"Oh, yeah," Wiltsey responded, "I'm in tall cotton now. The world is my oyster."

"Yes," Randall mused, "but it will take a long time to get rid of the grease from under your fingernails."

Wiltsey shook his head and became serious. "That will never happen, Rob. Never. I may be sitting in a fancy office and having a fancy title, but I'll always be just a wrench monkey crewin' an airplane."

Randall smiled and nodded. "I suppose you're right."

"So," Wiltsey continued, "what brings you up to our neck of the woods?"

"Actually," Randall replied, carefully choosing his words, "I'm on my way to Maine and probably Canada. Since I was in the neighborhood, I thought I'd stop by and say hey to everyone."

"Well, I'm glad you did. You on vacation?"

"Sort of," Randall responded. "I'm doing research for a book I'm writing."

"What's the book about?" questioned Wiltsey.

"The book concerns the crash of a Swissair passenger airliner off the coast of Nova Scotia back in 1998." Randall hoped Wiltsey was buying it.

"I remember that," Wiltsey nodded. "The aircraft was brought down by an electrical fire. They were trying to make an emergency landing in Halifax. Didn't make it."

"Yes," Randall agreed. "The aircraft crashed just off the coast. I'm writing an account of the aircraft recovery operations and the subsequent crash investigation."

"Sounds like a lot of work for someone who is retired," perceived Wiltsey, "especially someone who has been trying to forget the past."

Rats, Randall thought. He ain't buyin' what I'm sellin'. Time to change the subject. "Well, the reason I wanted to visit with you doesn't have anything to do with my book. But the reason does involve a plane crash."

Wiltsey shrugged his shoulders. "Fair enough. Shoot."

"I didn't ask you about this during our flight to and from London," Randall began, "but I wanted to know about what you might have heard while you were visiting England with regards to the British Sovereign cargo aircraft crash in Belgium last November. The investigative authorities from France and Great Britain have not published a final report yet. In fact, they have not even issued an interim report. It seems like they've put a lid on the investigation."

Wiltsey gave Randall a somewhat quizzical look. "Yeah, you're right. There's been no final report, at least none that I've heard about. What's your interest in it?"

"Let's just say," Randall stammered, "let's just say I'd like to know - if only for old time's sake."

Wiltsey was sharp enough to realize something was afoot and it had to do with the Sheffland family. A trip to London. Now this visit. Research for a book, my ass, he thought. Randall's up to something and he's working for the Shefflands. "Well, Rob, I can give you the latrine talk I overheard while I was in London. I guess you Navy guys call it scuttlebutt. You've heard enough about the accident, you know, the triple-7 cargo plane crashing short of the runway on final approach into Brussels. At first I believe everyone thought it was strictly pilot error. The pilot reached the missed approach point at the minimum-allowed altitude and didn't perform a go-around when he still didn't see the runway. But it appears something was fouled up in the flight management computer or the control system. They were performing a precision approach to the runway but, somehow, the aircrew was being given an incorrect rate of descent or glideslope information. In fact, I heard the aircrew did not even receive any ground proximity warnings. When they broke through the fog, it was too late. The pilot fire-walled the throttles, but he almost instantly slammed into a dike. That was it."

"Bad ECI parts?" Randall wondered aloud.

"Electrics. Controls. Instrumentation. Bad parts somewhere. The investigators recovered all of the cockpit ECI stuff and the computer control center cabinets down below in the equipment bay. They were untouched by the fire. By this time, I'm sure the investigation team knows exactly what happened, and I believe the cause of the crash will be traced to reused or counterfeit ECI parts."

"Nigel Sheffland brought down his own plane," Randall sighed.

"Nigel. And others." Wiltsey shrugged his shoulders. "It was bound to happen. Sooner or later."

"I'm sure we will find out in the next few months," Randall said. "The final report should be published shortly."

"And I believe there will be hell to pay when it hits the streets," concluded Wiltsey. There was a long moment of silence, each lost in his thoughts. "Hey, Rob," Wiltsey continued, wishing to change the subject, "will you be staying in town tonight?"

"Yes," Randall replied. "I've got hotel reservations here in Portsmouth. I was planning on an early start in the morning."

"Why don't you come over to our house for dinner this evening? You haven't met my wife yet, but she's heard a whole lot about you. What do you say?"

"I'd like that, but I'll go one better. How about if you allow me to take you guys out to dinner? You can choose the restaurant. Your choice. How about it?"

"Even better," Wiltsey laughed. "Instead of doughnuts, I'll have an appetizer."

"Sounds good," Randall chimed in smiling.

After their discussion, Wiltsey drove Randall to the flight line to visit with folks he had met four months earlier. Randall noticed nothing had changed. Don Wiltsey may have been christened King of the Hangar, but to the guys, he was still just the master mechanic.

* * *

Except for the voice of the woman behind the reservations counter, the hotel lobby was eerily quiet. Randall glanced at his watch. It was just past nine o'clock in the evening. Late September, he thought, off-season for the tourists. He walked to the counter, suitcase in tow, and announced his arrival to the hotel clerk. The young lady began tapping on a keyboard while looking at a computer screen. After pauses and additional taps, the computer decided his reservation indeed was legitimate. "Yes, Mr. Randall," she announced, "we have you down for one night. One person, king-sized bed, no smoking. Credit card and ID, please."

"Okay," Randall wondered if they required fingerprints, his mother's maiden name, and a DNA sample, too.

The clerk waited for the computer print-out, then gave it to him while explaining the numerous locations for initials and signatures. After signing away his life, Randall returned the form to the clerk. "All right, you're all checked in." She handed him the key card. "Anything else we can do for you?"

"Nope," Randall said dryly.

"Enjoy your stay."

"Yep," Randall said dryly.

He walked a few steps towards the elevator when the hotel clerk called out, "Mr. Randall? I almost forgot. I have a package for you." He returned to the counter and waited as the clerk disappeared into a back room. She returned carrying a brown cardboard box. "Here you go, sir. Sorry about that." She smiled as she gave the box to Randall. "This was delivered during the afternoon."

"No problem" he responded. "I appreciate it."

Randall returned to his suitcase and walked to the elevators. He headed to his room on the third floor. Entering, he immediately placed his suitcase and the package onto the bed. Then he closed the door, wondering the entire time if there was an explosive device in the box. I hope it doesn't take down the building, he mused.

Randall sat on the bed and stared at the cardboard container. It was addressed to him in care of the hotel. The return address on the box was his home address. Randall opened his suitcase and retrieved his pocket knife, pondering if he should open the package. Open at your own discretion, he thought. But, just remember one thing. Discretion is the better part of valor.

"Here goes," he announced to himself. Randall slit open the clear packing tape and carefully folded back the flaps. Inside was another smaller box and, underneath it, a large sealed manila envelope. He removed the smaller box and tore open the envelope. He pulled out bound copies of what appeared to be two different reports. One report was completed by the NTSB on their participation in the recovery of Swissair Flight 111 in 1998. The other document was the complete report by the Canadian Transportation Safety Board on the Swissair accident, including a detailed description of the wreckage survey and recovery efforts. Outstanding, Randall thought. Jack Kilby came through.

Randall then turned his attention to the smaller box. He carefully lifted the lid and gasped in surprise. Inside was a leather holster containing his Smith & Wesson thirty-eight caliber snub nose revolver. Along with the gun was a federal license for the firearm and a folded note. He unfolded the paper and read it aloud:

Rob,
After the bomb scare, I decided you better have this. It's your revolver. I ransacked your apartment trying to find it. Don't worry. I cleaned up the mess.
Enclosed is a CCW permit that's good for all fifty states. Authorized by the FBI under Law Enforcement Safety. Just keep it stashed in your suitcase if you decide to visit Canada. Be careful. Don't shoot your eye out.

Jack

P.S. Maggie says hey.

Randall smiled briefly and then grew solemn. He gazed at the holstered handgun. He thought of Jack. He thought of Alex Sheffland and his father, Sir Geoffrey. He thought of Don Wiltsey and his wife during dinner a few hours ago. Friends and acquaintances, all.

Tomorrow, it would end. Tomorrow, he would be traveling into "bad-lands" territory. There would be no friends and acquaintances there. And someone wanted him dead. Randall pulled the revolver from its holster and opened the cylinder. All five chambers were loaded. He carefully closed the cylinder and returned the gun to its holster. He suddenly felt cold but only for a moment.

Good to go, Randall decided. I'm good to go.

Chapter 9

From the instant he entered Maine, Rob Randall was vaguely uncomfortable as if he had finally encroached in enemy airspace. The dreary day added to his uneasiness, the hills and forests cloaked in rain and fog. Perhaps Randall felt he had returned to England.

Jack Kilby had sent to Randall the last known address of Paul McDowell after his departure from the U.S. Navy in 2007. He lived in the small town of Calais, located on the Maine coastline just south and west of the Canadian border. As for McDowell's friend Danny Latham, his home had been in Presque Isle, north of Calais at the top of the state. Except for flying above it, Randall had never visited the Maine seacoast.

The drive north on Interstate 95 carried him past Portland and Augusta before finally reaching Bangor. There he left the interstate and drove on an old two-lane state road for seventy miles until he reached the quiet portside community of Calais. As with the rest of Maine, it, too, was shrouded in fog and mist. If Indian summer was to be found in Calais, it was certainly hidden from view.

Randall drove into the south side of the hamlet. Following his GPS, he turned onto a side avenue searching for Hamel Street. Finally reaching Hamel, he turned and slowly proceeded along the street, trying to find the address listed as 3105 A.

"Let's see," Randall said to himself, "here's 3113, 3111 . . . " He looked to his right outside the windshield, counting the house numbers as they passed. He stopped in front of 3107 Hamel. The next house was 3105 Hamel. But no 3105A.

"Hm-m, no 3105 A," Randall sighed aloud. "Okay. What's the deal?" Parking the car, he got out and cautiously walked towards the house. The fog and mist and silence seemed to swirl about him as he moved, the street devoid of any sounds. As he passed a gravel driveway, he noticed a large detached garage behind and to the right of the house. It was a two-story garage with steps on the left side leading up to the second floor. On a large post at the foot of the stairs, a street number was attached. It read 3105A.

There it is, Randall thought. I wonder if Mr. McDowell is home. He quickly got his answer.

"If you're looking for Paul, he's not there." Randall was startled as he slowly walked on the gravel drive towards the out building. He quickly turned and confronted a woman quietly following behind him.

"Beg pardon, ma'am?" Randall stared at an old woman. She wore a faded green sweater over a faded print dress. Faded white hair framed a faded face, her skin covered in a mass of wrinkles.

"I said if you're looking for Paul, he's not here anymore." She had a unique voice. It was if she possessed a New England accent accentuated by a southern drawl.

"Do you know where he can be found?" Randall smiled softly, trying to appear friendly and non-threatening.

"Yes, sir," she said with curious inflections in her voice. She paused a moment. "I guess I mean no, sir. Paul died about a month ago."

"What happened?" asked a stunned Randall.

"I don't know - for sure," the old woman replied. "I guess he was stabbed. They found him in an alley off of Main Street."

"Do they know . . . do the police know who killed him?" asked a stammering Randall.

"No, I don't think so," she replied, again with the curious inflections. "I'm sorry, sir," she continued. "Did you have business with him?"

"No, not really," Randall responded with a fleeting smile. "Just a mutual acquaintance, that's all."

The old woman stood there, one arm across her chest, the other arm propped on it with her hand extended up to her neck, the fingers wrapped about her throat, her head cocked to one side. "Well, his belongings are still in his room above the garage. The police won't allow anyone to remove them yet. But if you want to see his room, you can go up there. The key to the door is under the mat. I don't think the police would mind, at least not now."

"Thank you," Randall responded while shaking his head. "That's not necessary. By the way, are you his landlady?"

"Yes, sir. I mean, no sir, not anymore."

"Ma'am, I have one last question if you don't mind. Do you know where Paul worked?"

She paused a moment. "He had a job at a boatyard here in town. The name of the place is Calais Harbor, um-m, Calais Harbor Boat Repair. The boatyard is right along the St. Croix River. Just go back down to the end of Hamel, turn left, go east until you run out of road, turn left again and go north. The place is on the right side of the road. You'll see it just as you hit the edge of town."

"Thanks," Randall nodded. "I appreciate it. Maybe I'll see you again."

Randall returned to the car as the old woman watched. She wished the stranger could have arranged to have Paul McDowell's possessions removed from the garage loft. No sense in mourning him, she thought. The old woman needed a new tenant.

* * *

The road meandered along the western edge of the St. Croix River as it led Randall to the south side of Calais. He searched the right side of the road for the boatyard, noticing small, individual docks and boat ramps. Suddenly visible in the thick fog was a sign for Calais Harbor Boat Repair. Randall turned off the road and entered an unpaved parking lot.

The repair yard had dozens of boats of various types and sizes on cradles and trailers to the right of two buildings. A small brown-brick office was attached to a much larger prefabricated structure made of sheet metal and painted a dull blue color. Randall parked the car and walked across the hard-packed dirt lot to the office entrance. He entered and was immediately confronted by a long counter at the front of the room. A young woman sat at a desk behind the counter facing Randall. At the front of the desk was a nameplate that identified the woman as Paula. She stopped tapping on a keyboard and glanced over a computer screen. "May I help you?" she asked, her doe eyes appearing above the rims of funky red-rimmed glasses.

"Yes. My name is Robert Randall. Is it possible I could talk to the manager of the boatyard?"

The young woman tilted her head back in order to see Randall through the eyeglasses parked at the tip of her nose. "What's the nature of your business?" She studied Randall with expressionless eyes.

"It's with regards to one of your former employees," Randall answered. "His name was Paul McDowell."

Her doe eyes were no longer expressionless. The tip of a nervous tongue instantly appeared between pursed lips. He immediately noticed a sharp intake of breath. "Are you a cop?" she asked brusquely.

"No," Randall replied, displaying a faint forced smile. "I'm just an acquaintance of an acquaintance from his days in the Navy."

He watched the young woman mulling it over in her mind. Then she turned and picked up a microphone. "Ralph," she announced, "come to the office, please. You have a visitor." Randall could hear the loudspeaker announcement reverberating inside the big steel building and across the repair yard. "The manager's name is Ralph Englehart," she said warily. "He's around here somewhere."

"Thank you," Randall responded. He leaned against the counter, gazing at the young woman, studying her. "I didn't find out until earlier this morning that Paul had passed away a month ago. And under such tragic circumstances. Did you know him well?"

The young woman hesitated for a moment. "No," she finally answered, "he was just one of the guys who worked here."

As he was about to ask another question, a heavy-set man with a short, scraggly red goatee matching short, scraggly red hair entered the office. He quickly made eye contact with Randall.

"Ralph, this is Mr. Randall," she announced. "He would like to talk to you about Paul."

"Are you from the cops?" Englehart asked suspiciously. "Cuz if you're from the cops, I ain't answerin' no more questions about Paul. I'm done with the questions."

"No, no," Randall explained. "As I told Paula here, I'm just an acquaintance of a friend from his Navy days."

"Oh, okay," Englehart said warily. "C'mon back to my office." He lifted the hinged end of the counter and gestured to Randall. "Follow me."

Randall strolled past the young woman as she watched him with more than curious eyes. She displayed a countenance of suspicion. He trailed behind Englehart to his office. "Have a seat, Randall. How can I help you?"

"Well, honestly, I don't know if you can," Randall replied. "I did not know that Paul had passed away until earlier this morning. What happened to him?"

"Beats me," Englehart responded with a shrug of the shoulders. "Somebody killed him with a knife."

"That's terrible," Randall said grimacing. "Do the police have any inkling of who did it?"

"Not to my knowledge," Englehart replied, again with a shrug of the shoulders. Before any additional questions could be asked by Randall, Englehart interrupted him, displaying some degree of impatience. "Mr. Randall, why did you want to see Pauly?"

That's it, Randall thought. *Pauly.* Pauly plus murder equals Devero.

"In 1998 Paul McDowell was a diver in the U.S. Navy. During that time, he and his dive team were assigned to a salvage ship, the *U.S.S. Surveyor.* In October of that year, he participated in the recovery operation of a commercial airliner that crashed off the coast of Nova Scotia. I wanted to interview him for a book I'm writing on the crash investigation."

"Yeah," Englehart responded, "I remember Pauly talking about that. He told me he was in the water so much during that time that it took a month to get rid of the wrinkles in his fingers. He said they looked like prunes."

Randall smiled at the remark. "Did he ever say anything else about his work in Nova Scotia?"

"Nah, not really," Englehart responded, still seeming fidgety. "I remember he said the plane was in a million pieces and that it took a lot of work to recover the wreckage."

"And the victims?"

"No," Englehart replied adamantly. "He didn't say nothin' about that. I think it upset him."

"I can imagine," Randall grimaced. "Pretty bad stuff." Time for another tack, he thought. "Did Paul ever mention any shipwrecks he explored during the recovery efforts?"

"Nope," Englehart said evenly. "Not that I can remember."

"Did you know him well? I mean, did he have any close friends here?"

The fidgeting increased. "I guess I knew him about as well as anybody. He sorta kept to himself. Know what I mean?"

"Yeah," Randall replied, staring at Englehart, "I got it." Randall realized he wasn't getting anywhere with the boatyard folks. "Well, thanks for your time. I appreciate it." He stood, looking down at Englehart. "I'll see myself out."

As Randall turned to leave the office, he stopped and faced the fidgety boatyard manager. "You know, I hope the police find the guy who killed Pauly. I'm sure you all here feel the same way." With that, Randall headed for the main entrance. He passed Paula's desk. She was nowhere to be seen.

Randall returned to the fog and the mist. As he walked to his car, he was stopped by a voice emanating from behind him. "Mr. Randall?"

He turned and glanced at a man, wearing a blue uniform, walking behind him. "Yes," he replied, "I'm Randall."

"I'm Robert Cork," the man in the blue uniform announced, holding open a folder of identification and a badge. "I'm the police chief of Calais."

Randall nodded. "Chief, may I help you?"

"I was informed that you were looking for Paul McDowell."

"Yes," Randall responded, "that's correct."

"What business did you have with him?"

Randall paused and stared at the Calais Chief of Police, studying him. He appeared none too jovial or friendly. "I wanted to talk to him. That's all."

"About what?"

"About a private matter, "Randall replied evenly but firmly. "Now, if you will excuse me . . ."

"Just wait one moment, Mr. Randall. I'll ask again. Why did you want to visit Paul McDowell?"

"Chief, since I have been informed of Mr. McDowell's passing, your question is no longer germane. Again, if you will excuse me . . ."

Cork held up his hand. "Not so fast. I think you need to come to the police station so we can further discuss this."

Randall tried not to show his anger. "Am I being arrested?"

"Not if you don't want me to. Either way, you're coming with me."

Randall glared at the threatening face. "All right, Chief. We'll have it your way. Let's go to your station." With that, Randall followed Chief Cork to an unmarked police car. He was shown the back seat. The ride to the police station was brief, quiet and most certainly frosty.

Randall was seething inside as he followed Cork into the police station. He was immediately led into a room marked Interrogation 1. He marveled that a town the size of Calais would need more than one interrogation room in police headquarters.

"Chief," Randall began, "before you commence your interrogation, I want you to call this man. I am sure he will answer many of your questions." He removed Jack Kilby's business card from his wallet and gave it to Cork. "His name is Jack Kilby. He is an inspector with the Federal Bureau of Investigation at the headquarters in Washington, D.C. Let's call him now. Please."

Cork examined the card and then glanced at Randall. "Okay, c'mon." Cork led him to his office and closed the door. He gestured to Randall to be seated in front of the chief's desk. Cork sat on the edge of the desk and called Kilby. "Uh, Inspector John Kilby, please," requested Cork. After a pause, "Yes, I'll hold."

Randall glanced about the office as Cork waited. It was rather nondescript. A shooting trophy on top of a file cabinet. A large map of the town of Calais on the wall behind the chief's desk. A dry-ink easel on another wall. Randall smiled faintly when he noticed the ornate brass nameplate on the desk. It read Chief Robert "Bobber" Cork.

"Yes, Inspector, my name is Robert Cork. I am the Chief of Police for Calais, Maine. I have brought a man in for questioning. His name is Robert Randall. He insisted that I contact you prior to him answering any questions."

Cork paused for a moment. "Yes, sir. I brought him to the police station."

A pause. "No, sir. He is not under arrest."

Another pause. Cork started to look beleaguered. "No, sir. He has not been formally charged."

Still another pause. More beleaguering. "Yes, sir, I understand. You are aware of his visit to Maine. It's just that . . ."

Once again, a pause. "Well, Inspector, I wouldn't call it rousting a citizen . . ."

A final pause. "Yes, sir. I'll cooperate fully. Thank you."

Cork gave the phone receiver to Randall. "Inspector Kilby would like a word with you."

Randall took the phone. "Hey, Jack. How's it going?"

Laughter was the response on the phone. "Rob, it seems that every time you leave town, you end up in a police station. Or a hospital." More laughter. "I keep telling you. You've got to figure out a different way to win friends and influence people. The way you're doing it now – it just ain't workin' for you."

"Yes," Randall apologized, "sorry about this."

"What's the deal?" Kilby asked, becoming serious.

"The fellow I wanted to visit with, you know, Paul McDowell? He was murdered about a month ago here in Calais."

"Good Lord," Kilby sighed. "Do the police know who did it?"

"Not yet," Randall replied. "I guess that's why I got dragged in here."

"Look," Kilby exclaimed over the phone, "first the car bomb and now this. *Attempted* murder is not good. Murder is *really* not good. Maybe you should reconsider this whole thing, before you end up on ice."

"Yeah, I suppose you're right." Randall glanced at Chief Cork as he stood and sauntered to the other side of the desk. "Look, Jack, I'll call you later after I've completed my interview with Chief Cork. Thanks."

Randall returned the phone receiver to Cork. He took it and simply said, "Thank you, Inspector. Good talking to you." Cork replaced the receiver on its cradle and gave Kilby's card back to Randall. "Well, I guess I should begin with an apology," Cork admitted. "It seems you *did* have some business to discuss with Paul McDowell."

"Chief, I would have answered any of your questions back at the boatyard, but you sort of came on like Eliot Ness and the Untouchables." Randall smiled. "If you have questions, fire away."

"Look, before I ask you anything," Cork said, "let me explain. This case is as cold as a one-month-old dead flounder in a freezer. It just seemed strange that some guy should appear out of nowhere and start asking questions about McDowell."

"I understand," Randall assured him. "I came to Calais specifically to see Paul McDowell. In 1998, while he was an enlisted sailor in the U.S. Navy, he participated as a diver in the survey and recovery of a commercial airliner that crashed off the coast of Canada. I am a retired investigator with the National Transportation Safety Board. I, too, worked in Canada at that time assisting the Canadian folks during the investigation. I wanted to ask McDowell about the surveying dives he made at the beginning of the recovery."

"So you really were *not* aware of his death," Chief Cork ascertained.

"No, not until this morning," Randall responded. "I was given his name by a few of his shipmates in Virginia and Massachusetts. I simply stopped by here on my way to Nova Scotia. That's all."

"For a book you're writing, according to Inspector Kilby." For the first time, Cork smiled at Randall.

"That's correct," Randall said, returning the smile.

"Well," Cork announced, "when I put my foot in it, I am the first to admit I'm wrong. Sorry."

"No sweat, Chief. You're just doing your job."

"Yeah," Cork laughed, "and here I was planning on beating a confession out of you."

Randall smiled, now knowing he had the upper hand. Might as well go for the gusto, he thought. "Chief, what *did* happen to Paul McDowell?"

"We don't know," came the reply with a shrug of the shoulders. "We just don't know. He was found stabbed to death in a downtown alley about a month ago. No motive. No suspects."

"And no one has any ideas," Randall responded with a declaration as much as a question.

"Yep. Nobody knew of anyone that wanted him dead. He didn't seem to have any real close friends. But it also appeared he didn't have any real enemies either. No leads."

Randall decided to press the issue. "Did you find anything on a computer or maybe a pad or phone?"

"That's just it. When we went through his personal belongings, there was no computer. No pad. No phone," Chief Cork grumbled in frustration.

"Nothing that could give us a clue."

"What about the folks where he worked, you know, at the boat repair company?"

Cork rolled his eyes. "Those people were less than forthright," he declared in exasperation. "To talk to them, it seemed like they never knew him. I mean, like some of them never even heard of the guy."

"Yes," Randall agreed. "I noticed they were none too friendly during my visit. Those folks definitely did not want to talk to me."

"Uh-huh," Cork said in resignation. "I don't understand that. McDowell had no family around here, at least since his mother died years ago. It seems like he had no friends. It's really strange."

Randall had one more question for Chief Cork. "Do you know if McDowell did a lot of traveling? I mean like going to Canada or maybe even Great Britain?" Randall immediately prayed he had not put *his* foot in it.

Cork gave him a quizzical look. "No, I don't know anything about that. Should I?"

"I'm not sure, Chief," Randall replied, returning the quizzical expression. "A couple of his acquaintances in the Navy thought he was traveling quite a bit. That's all."

Cork nodded his head. "Thanks. I appreciate the heads-up. Maybe that's important."

"Maybe it is," Randall agreed. "Maybe it is."

After we're done here, Randall thought, I have one more task to perform while I'm in Calais. But first, I need to stop and buy a flashlight.

* * *

Except for a lone dog howling in the distance, the neighborhood was quiet. It was almost midnight as Randall left his car and casually strolled down the sidewalk, passing a few houses before coming to the gravel driveway. The house at 3105 Hamel was dark. He stopped and listened. There was only silence. Carefully, he crept along the edge of the gravel, trying to make as little noise as possible as he approached the detached garage apartment of Paul McDowell.

Randall had informed Chief Cork that he intended to peruse McDowell's personal papers before departing Calais, hoping to find records on the survey and recovery dive operations in 1998. He just didn't tell Cork that his perusal was to be conducted in the dead of night.

When he reached the apartment staircase, Randall illuminated the flashlight, shining it up the steps. He slowly climbed them, attempting to keep the wooden creaks and groans to a minimum. Upon reaching the top, he flicked the doormat away with his shoe. As he was told, the door key was under the mat. Randall picked up the key and unlocked the door. Then he returned the key to under the mat. Slowly he opened the door.

Immediately Randall was struck with the odor of mildew and stale cigarette smoke. He quietly closed the door behind him. He shone the light about the floor. The apartment was one large room. To his left was a bed against the back wall. Next to it, under the back window, was a desk and chair. He noticed the bed was stripped of blankets and sheets and pillows. In the far corner was an entrance to what appeared to be a bathroom. To his right in the corner was a bar in front of a small kitchenette. A large empty closet framed the far side of the front window. On the floor in front of the kitchenette and bar was a pile of packing boxes. Randall approached them, studying the markings on each box. The boxes appeared to contain all of Paul McDowell's earthly possessions.

Randall knelt down in front of the boxes. He pulled one aside and opened it. The box was filled with folded clothing. He slid a second box from the pile and removed the lid. More clothing. He proceeded to open each box. Clothing, kitchenware, toiletries, old issues of boat and dive magazines - all possessions and property of a man and a life. But other than some old bills and junk mail, there were no personal papers. Randall closed and returned each box to the pile. Nothing, he thought, absolutely nothing.

Randall stood and again shone the light around the room. He moved to the kitchenette and casually opened the drawers. All were empty. He then walked to the desk at the back of the room. Pulling out the chair, Randall sat down and opened each desk drawer, shining the light inside. Nothing. The desk was empty. Randall sighed and shook his head. Then he had a thought. "You know," he whispered to himself, "in all the television detective shows, they always find something hidden in the desk."

Randall carefully proceeded to remove each drawer from the desk and peek in the empty openings. He first checked the left drawers. Nothing. He then tried the right side. He removed the top drawer and shone the flashlight into the opening. "Well, I'll be a . . ." he whispered. Behind the drawer, Randall saw an envelope taped to the wood. He reached into the opening and pulled it out, the tape making it difficult to extract the paper envelope without damaging it. In the dim light, he examined it. The envelope was unmarked and sealed. Carefully tearing the flap, he opened it and removed the contents.

The envelope contained a United States passport. Randall opened the cover and placed the passport on the desk top, shining the light down upon it. He immediately saw the face of a heavy-set man with black curly hair. He then glanced at the name. The passport belonged to Paul McDowell.

Randall proceeded to page slowly through the passport, examining the locations of his travels. "Bingo," he said aloud. Paul McDowell had traveled to Great Britain in March and September of the previous year. He also had made numerous trips to Canada.

"Well, I got Pauly," Randall quietly proclaimed. Randall replaced the top drawer and checked the remainder of the desk. Nothing more was found.

As he looked about the room for a final time, he suddenly froze. He heard a car on the gravel driveway approaching the garage, the stones crunching under the tires. Glancing through the front window, it was obvious the car's headlights were off. He listened as the noise of the idling engine ceased.

Randall immediately doused his flashlight and listened. For a moment, there was only silence. Then he heard the creaking noise from the stairs. He quickly pressed himself against the corner of the room next to the bed. He heard the key being inserted into the door knob. Randall held his breath.

In the darkness the door slowly opened. A person entered and quietly closed the door. Randall saw the silhouette of a figure glide towards the front window and close the curtains. Then he heard the click of a light switch and the room was bathed in the dim light of a single ceiling fixture. Randall, as yet unseen, watched as the figure moved to the pile of boxes and knelt.

"Looking for this?" Randall quietly asked, waving the passport in front of him.

"Oh!" she cried out as she fell back onto the floor, cowering at the man behind her.

"Well, what do you know?" he said smiling. "None other than Paula. Paula from the boatyard. It's late. Shouldn't you be in bed?"

"What – what are you doing here?" she stammered.

Randall shrugged his shoulders as he emerged from the corner of the room and approached her. "I could ask you the same thing," he said with a smirk. "But then again, I don't think this is the first time you've been here. Am I right?"

"Yes," Paula grumbled. "I mean no. This isn't the first time I've been here."

Randall sat on the edge of the bed as the young woman gathered herself up and plopped down on one of the boxes. "It's not what you think," she continued. "We were just friends."

"Sure," Randall said. "Just friends."

Disgruntled, she rolled her eyes. "I mean it," she repeated. "We were. Just friends." She glanced at the passport in Randall's hand. "Where did you find it?" she asked in resignation.

"It was hidden in the desk," Randall replied as he gestured behind him. "Stuff is always hidden in desks."

Paula pursed her lips. "I don't suppose you'd give it to me?"

"You suppose right," he responded. "This goes to the police." Randall paused a moment before continuing. "Just why do you want it?"

"Cause." More grumbling.

"Cause why?" prodded Randall.

"Because I went with him to Canada. A couple of times."

"So you knew what Pauly was up to?" Randall surmised.

"Not really," she said as she picked at a fingernail. "Pauly just kept tellin' me he was goin' to be rich. He was searchin' for some big treasure. He said he was goin' to give me some of it."

"So I guess you were more interested in the treasure than in Pauly." Randall laughed. "Ah, young love." He became serious. "You didn't want to be tied into his death. This passport may have done that."

Paula said nothing. She stared at the floor.

"Who killed him, Paula?"

"I don't know," she replied with a sneer.

"Don't give me that," Randall shot back.

"I told you! I don't know." Paula sighed. "He didn't tell me much."

"Who was he working with on this so-called treasure hunt?"

"Oh, there was some guy. His name was Reece. I don't know his last name. I only saw him once or twice. He lives somewhere in Canada."

"Nova Scotia?"

"Yeah, I guess." Paula glared at Randall. "Seems like you know more than I do."

"Not really." Randall returned the expression of contempt. "Do you remember any other names?"

"Yeah, one," she replied reluctantly. "Pauly called him Huey the Duck."

"Huey the Duck? You're joking?"

"Nah, that's what Pauly called him. I never met the man."

Randall stared at the young woman. "Was he the one running the show?"

"Yeah, I guess so."

Great, Randall thought. Pauly, Reece and Huey the Duck. Sounds like a kid's show on Saturday morning. For a moment, he studied the young woman. "Paul and Paula," he mused. "Together again."

"What?" Paula asked, confused.

"Oh, just a song from long ago," he explained. "Long, long ago. I guess love was different back then."

Randall tossed the passport to the young woman. It landed on the floor in front of her. She glanced at it and then gazed at Randall, a look of disbelief on her face. "Go on," he said softly. "Get out of here before both of us get caught. Try to stay out of trouble."

She lifted the passport from the floor and quickly stuffed it in her coat pocket. "Thanks, Mr. Randall," she said, an expression of sudden relief on her face.

"You know, Paula, you need to let the police know about McDowell's trips and about Reece. You owe him that much. After all, he loved you."

Her expression of relief changed to one of disbelief. Paula, the boatyard girl, quickly left the apartment. Randall watched as the door closed behind her. He listened as her footfalls faded down the creaking steps.

Randall glanced about the room one final time. Nothing more to be found here, he thought. Nothing more to be learned. He went to the door, flashlight in hand, and turned off the ceiling light. Descending the steps, he stopped at the foot of the stairs and listened. All was quiet. He heard no sounds.

Rob Randall had not yet heard the voice. He had not yet heard the Siren of the *Loch Gillelli*.

Chapter 10

Just as he had anticipated, the drive from Maine to Halifax, Nova Scotia, took most of the day. After departing Calais early that morning, Randall entered New Brunswick, driving along the northern shoreline of the Bay of Fundy. The landscape was, for the most part, flat and forested. At least, though, the rain and fog of the previous day had given way to bright sunshine and a cloudless sky.

Passing through Saint John, Randall felt tired and discouraged. Not enough sleep last night, he concluded. Out late and an early call did not make for a decent night's rest. And he decided not to contact Jack Kilby. Whatever had happened on his journey so far Randall had decided the call could wait for a few days. Then he thought about Paul McDowell. Pauly. Who murdered him? And why? And what about Paula? Hell, he didn't even know her last name. In considering the girl, two things were certain. Paula did not want to be tied in with McDowell, and Paula did not want to end up dead in the same Main Street back alley with a shiv in her ribs. What a mess, he thought.

The monotonous scenery of Saint John gradually gave way to the rolling mountains and valleys of the Caledonia Hills. The leaves were almost in full color, portending an early winter for eastern Canada. Randall continued his journey through New Brunswick, finally turning south towards Nova Scotia as he neared the town of Dorchester. Driving to the south and southeast, Randall passed the eastern tip of Cobequid Bay and then headed south for his destination, the city of Halifax. The landscape had again returned to that of relatively flat, empty topography. The land was unvarying, boring and added to the tedium of the trip. As Randall entered the outskirts of Halifax, he felt exhausted. All he wanted to do was check into his hotel, make a few phone calls, grab something to eat, and hit the rack.

And that is exactly what he did.

* * *

Randall awakened relaxed and refreshed the next morning. A good night's sleep had done the job. Even though he was staying at a hotel near the center of town, the noise of the city traffic went unnoticed. His exhaustion turned that which was apparent to oblivion. Since arriving in Massachusetts a few days earlier, Randall had felt vaguely uneasy. Now, after reaching Halifax, the feeling was more pronounced. This was the port of the *Loch Gillelli* he thought, and this is her grave.

As he dressed for the day, he opened the window curtains and gazed out at downtown Halifax from his sixth floor perch. The city looked much the same as he remembered it seventeen years ago. The skyline was more crowded with new buildings. The area around the Citadel, however, appeared as before. He looked to the north, observing the area along the southern end of the Narrows. It appeared that Her Majesty's Canadian Dockyard-Halifax had a full quota of naval ships tied up at the dock facilities. In the far distance, he could see an airliner on approach to Halifax Stanfield Airport, the emergency destination of the ill-fated Swissair flight. Randall then turned his eyes to the east.

On the other side of Halifax Harbour, Randall saw Canadian Forces Base Shearwater, the Canadian base that was his home during the recovery operations for the Swissair plane wreckage. He could pick out the hangar where the debris was stored and where a portion of the airliner was reassembled. Sadly, he contemplated the ultimate fate of the aircraft wreckage. Randall closed his eyes and shook his head, trying to rid himself of the memories.

He had an appointment in the afternoon to meet with a Canadian naval officer whom he had worked with during the Shearwater recovery operation. Her name was Commander, now Captain, Robin Holland. She was currently in command of the CFB Shearwater Annex, home to the Shearwater Jetty and to the Fleet Diving Unit Atlantic. Perhaps she would have some knowledge on the Canadian dive team in 1998.

But before Randall was to visit with her, he had to perform his very first task in Halifax. He knew where he was going. But he didn't know where it would take him.

* * *

The road toward the Nova Scotia coastline west of Halifax was at times winding and narrow. Randall caught intermittent glimpses of the Atlantic Ocean and inlets along the route. Otherwise, the scenery was one of trees and fields that more resembled wetlands. Occasionally he glanced at his GPS, anticipating numbers already known to him.

The faded piece of paper, shown to Randall that stormy night at the Sheffland's estate, did not contain a code. Once the letters were changed, the challenge of deciphering the patterns of the numbers was easy. The two sets of numbers were geographic coordinates. He was traveling to the first one:

> 44 degrees, 29 minutes, 30 seconds North
> 65 degrees, 55 minutes, 07 seconds West

It was the location of Peggys Cove.

Randall finally arrived at the small seaside resort community. But he quickly concluded Peggys Cove was as much a tourist trap as it was a resort area for summer vacationers. The quaint seaside village seemed to be surrounded by swaths of gift shops and parking lots. It was obvious, though, Randall had arrived at Peggys Cove in the off-season. There were few cars in the parking lots and even fewer tourists. He drove slowly through the town until he reached a large parking area at the end of the road. Parking the car, he opened the door only to be struck by a brisk northern wind. Randall quickly donned a coat from the backseat and began to casually stroll onto the rocky shoreline, the cold breeze blowing across his face, rustling his hair.

Before him was a rocky plateau at the eastern edge of the entrance into St. Margarets Bay. On the plateau was the Peggys Point Lighthouse. Randall carefully negotiated the fractured stone surface of the natural jetty, the sharp rocky edges dulled and worn by tides and time. After a few minutes, he made it to the lighthouse. It was a simple structure of white-painted concrete formed in an octagonal shape. Randall stood at the base and looked up at the light. The lighthouse was not particularly tall, he estimated, perhaps no more than fifty feet in height. Randall then continued to walk on the granite outcropping until he neared the water's edge. He gazed out onto the cold sparkling blue ocean. Eight miles away, he thought, just eight miles to the final resting place of the *Loch Gillelli*. That was the reason for recording the coordinates on the slip of paper kept in the jeweled *Rubaiyat*. The ship rests here, not in an unknown spot in the North Sea. Someone, a long time ago, knew it and remembered it, he concluded.

Randall began to feel the chill of the early autumn wind and quickly returned to his car. Shivering, he gazed out the windshield at the white-capped waves. He suddenly remembered his first visit to the area of Peggys Cove. Just beyond the horizon, he thought. It was about this time, seventeen years ago. He remembered the frigid water as he dove to the wreckage of the airliner. Shattered airplane. Shattered lives. Randall closed his eyes and tried to suppress the slumbering dragon within him. It was time to leave Peggys Cove.

As he made the return trip to Halifax, Randall dwelled only briefly on the past. It was now the present, and two tasks remained for the day. The first was his visit to CFB Shearwater. The second task was related to the second set of geographic coordinates recorded on the faded slip of paper. He didn't know what those numbers meant. But he would soon find out.

* * *

The time for the return trip to Halifax seemed to pass much more quickly. Ahead of schedule, Randall paused at a restaurant on the edge of town for a leisurely lunch. Then he proceeded to drive through the downtown area. People were out on the sidewalks in droves, scurrying about at the end of the lunch hour. The autumn air was filled with the sounds of traffic, blaring horns and loud shouts. After a few days of passing quiet, pastoral settings, to Randall the change of scenery was welcome.

He drove east on the MacDonald Bridge, crossing over Halifax Harbour and into the other side of the city. Recognizing the landmarks, Randall drove south along the harbor's edge until he came to the main entrance to CFB Shearwater. He turned left past the air museum building and proceeded to the guard gate. He was greeted by a uniformed security guard who checked his identification and instructed him to make an immediate left and drive to the parking lot. First building on the right, the guard concluded with a smile. Randall moved past the gate and turned left, passing buildings on the left and right with empty parking lots. The military airbase seemed to be absent of any activity. He finally reached the parking lot. It, too, was almost empty. Randall parked and exited the vehicle. As he approached the main entrance to the designated headquarters building, the only sound he heard was that of the blowing wind.

Randall passed through two sets of doors and entered an unoccupied foyer and reception area. As he began to scribble his name on the unattended visitor's log, he heard a familiar female voice call out. "I recognize that man," she exclaimed, "right on time, too!"

Randall glanced up and saw Captain Robin Holland approaching him, a radiant smile on her face. "Hi, Rob," the captain greeted him warmly, extending her hand. "How are you?"

"Omigosh! Commander Holland," Randall responded. "Oh, excuse me," he continued as he stared at her rank insignia. "I mean *Captain* Holland."

"Oh, forget that," she laughed. "It's still Bobbie. Remember?"

"Yes, I remember," Randall admitted with a nod. He quickly studied her. She appeared much the same as in years past. Her hair was slightly longer but just as dark. As before, she was far more cute than beautiful, more perky than pretty. But she still had a million dollar smile.

"Well, it looks like the years have been kind to you," she observed. "What's it been? Seventeen, now?"

"Yeah, just about," Randall replied. "It appears the years have been kind to both of us."

Holland laughed. "You know, we better go back to my office before we just keep standing here, each of us telling lies."

Randall followed the Canadian naval captain down the hallway and into a corner office at the end of merging corridors. She gestured for him to sit on a sofa. "I have to tell you," Holland began, "you caught me just in time. Three more months and I'm out of this place. For good."

"I assume you're retiring," Randall guessed.

"Absolutely," she conceded. "Twenty-six years in the Canadian Navy. That's more than enough. I'm ready for a change."

"What are your plans for retirement?" Randall asked.

"Relax," Holland replied. "Lounge around. Six months in Canada. Six months in Florida. For a while, retirement will be an extended R & R." Captain Holland paused briefly. "In your phone call," she continued, "you told me that you have been retired for a few years. How do *you* like it?"

"I like it fine," Randall replied smiling. "I'm restoring an old boat, a cabin cruiser. Believe me, tinkering with a fifty-year-old boat takes up a lot of time – *a lot* of time."

The phone on her desk suddenly rang. "If you don't mind, I need to get this. I'll only be a minute." Holland picked up the receiver and began talking.

Randall glanced about the office as Captain Holland chatted on the phone. The walls were covered by mementos and memories of a Navy career, each carefully framed and prominently placed. Diplomas and certificates, paintings and pictures, awards and honors, she had a full career, indeed. A brief feeling of envy swept over him.

"Sorry about that," Holland apologized as she replaced the receiver. "Never a dull moment."

"You know," Randall responded, "I was going to ask you about that. When I drove in here, well, it seems like this place is a ghost town. What gives?"

"You're right about the ghost town," she replied. "The flight operations here ended a few years ago. The fixed-wing squadrons moved out to other locations. A few helicopters still operate out of Shearwater, but that's about it for flight ops."

"What is here now?" Randall asked.

"The base has been renamed the CFB Shearwater Annex. It's home to the Fleet Diving Unit Atlantic. The annex is also known as the Shearwater Jetty. We work with Her Majesty's Canadian Dockyard-Halifax." Holland's proclamation was one of pride combined with cynicism. "We supply additional secure dock space."

"I think I catch your drift," Randall remarked, smiling. "You folks here at Shearwater take care of the dockyard overflow."

"Yep, you got it," she replied somewhat flippantly. "We accommodate some of the NATO ships and submarines when they're in port."

"So you're in command of the Annex, right?"

"You are correct," confirmed Holland. "My final command."

Randall shrugged his shoulders. "It's not so bad. Land-based command."

"Actually, you're right," she agreed. "It really is not so bad. After you were here in '98, I moved over to the dockyard. I had a number of positions there, you know, moved up through the ranks. I did a lot of work on providing the dock infrastructure for the Maritime Fleet operations."

"In other words, MARLANT war ships," Randall surmised.

"Exactly," Holland answered ruefully. "Next best thing to being at sea."

Randall nodded but remained silent. He imagined Captain Holland on a ship's bridge, in command of a cruiser. She would have done great he concluded.

"Well, enough about me," Holland announced. "You told me you were doing research on a book. How can I help you?"

"You see, I'm writing a book about the Swissair Flight 111 crash," Randall began. "I'm not so much concerned about the actual investigation. I'm concentrating on the underwater work, you know, surveying the wreckage and recovering it. I want to write about the Boeing 747 crash off the shore of Long Island in 1996 and how surveying and recovery techniques were perfected and utilized two years later. I have spoken with a number of folks from the U.S. Navy with regards to their efforts here in Halifax. I was wondering if you knew of Canadian folks who participated in the recovery of the wreckage. I helped train some of them, but that was a long time ago."

Captain Holland sighed. "I'm not sure I can help much on this one. Basically, I was the Canadian Navy coordinator to assist the Coast Guard, the Canadian Navy, and the American Navy efforts during the survey and recovery efforts. I was never really involved in the actual work."

"Do you know who was?" Randall was treading lightly.

"Uh, there's the captain of the *HCMS Compass*," Holland remembered. "He was in charge of the Navy and Coast Guard efforts. His name was Foster. George Foster, I think. I don't have any idea where he is, though. I might be able to find out."

"If you could, I would appreciate it." Randall decided to change the line of questioning. "Did you know any of the Canadian divers who participated in the airliner recovery?"

"No, not really," Holland answered firmly. "I may have talked to one or two of them during the investigation, but I sure don't remember them. I doubt I would recognize any of them if they walked through the door at this moment."

Randall laughed. "Well, you remembered me."

Holland chuckled. "That's because I saw you every day. Besides, I thought you had the hots for me."

"Is that right?" Randall stammered. "I thought it was the other way around."

"Heavens, no," she laughed. "You seemed so preoccupied during that time." Holland grew solemn. "Actually, I had never known anyone as quiet and as serious as you. You were in your own world then."

"I'm sorry," Randall said softly. "Airplane crashes had that effect on me. It's taken a long time to get over it."

Captain Holland immediately recognized she had touched a nerve. Time to change the subject, she thought. "You know there is one person in town you should talk with while you're here in Halifax. His name is Fredrick Molnar. I'll bet you don't remember this, but the Royal Canadian Mounted Police directed the entire recovery and investigation effort for the Swissair crash. Everything. The Navy units, the Coast Guard, the transportation safety boards, all of it was managed by the RCMP. Molnar was an inspector who was selected to be the director for the entire investigation. He ran the show for four years. He knew *everyone*."

"Interesting. Where is he now?" Randall wondered.

"Oh, he's been retired for years," Holland replied. "He must be in his seventies. You can probably find him at his family's jewelry store in the downtown area on the other side of the harbor. He helps out there. The sign says E. J. Molnar & Sons. If Molnar's not there, his son will know his whereabouts."

Randall smiled. "Thanks. I'll do that." He decided to tread a little harder. "Bobbie, I've got another question for you. When the survey work began for the Swissair plane recovery, a sunken ship was discovered near the crash site. Do you remember that?"

Holland, her dark eyebrows furrowed, pursed her lips. "Vaguely. Maybe. I'm not sure. That sounds somewhat familiar." She shook her head. "I just don't remember. But I do know someone who would have information on any and all sunken ships in the area. His name is Dr. Saul Shlumberg. He works at the Oceanographic Institute here in Halifax. I am positive he could help you on that one."

"Okay," Randall said. "Fair enough."

Randall continued his visit for another hour. He asked additional questions on the Swissair recovery work, but it became painfully obvious Captain Robin Holland had little knowledge of the American and Canadian dive efforts. It felt like he had hit a dead end. At least the visit wasn't a total loss, though. Randall had a date with Captain Holland for dinner later in the evening. But first, though, he had one final task for the day.

* * *

Randall returned to downtown Halifax by way of the MacDonald Bridge. As he passed the apex of the bridge, he looked to the north, searching for the tip of Bedford Basin. He then glanced briefly at his GPS. Randall was searching for the location of the second set of geographic coordinates:

44 degrees 39 minutes 39 seconds North
63 degrees 37 minutes 17 seconds West

Once he entered downtown Halifax, Randall turned to the northwest and drove towards the southern tip of the basin. He meandered through a series of older residential areas and commercial zones, all the while observing the progress towards his destination. Finally, he reached the coordinates and turned right into a small office building parking lot. Sliding into the first available space, he parked the car and walked to the edge of the street. Across from him was a line of trees that bordered the road, their leaves becoming a myriad of colors. To the south of the trees were three square structures made of what appeared to be polished marble, each of them a few stories tall. Randall returned to his car and exited the parking lot, briefly continuing north until he made a U-turn. Slowly driving south, he again studied the GPS. He was at the correct geographic coordinates, he concluded. Of that, there was no doubt. He turned right onto the first side street he came to, driving even slower as he looked to his right, searching for some form of landmark. He quickly found one.

Randall passed two additional marble structures. Instantly, he knew what they were. He drove a few more yards and stopped along the edge of the street, staring at an open gate made of grey granite and black iron. Above the gate, etched in stone, was the name of the location called out by the geographic coordinates. It read Fairview Lawn Cemetery. The second set of coordinates was an old Halifax cemetery.

Once inside the cemetery grounds, Randall turned left onto a narrow paved drive. He moved slowly past rows of grave markers with every type of tombstone imaginable. Tall, short, gray, brown, black, statues and obelisks, some new, many old - Randall imagined he was passing through a stadium of silent stone. Suddenly he saw a small blue and white sign ahead, adjacent to an intersection, an arrow pointing to the right. The sign read *Titanic* Grave Site.

He stopped along the drive and parked the car. He left the vehicle and walked towards an area of dark granite markers, most of them of uniform appearance and mounted on three, curving rows of brownstone. He stepped onto the grass at the first row of graves, slowly moving past the markers. Some of the granite headstones posted the names of the deceased. Many were simply etched with the name *Unknown*. All, however, had an individual number cut into the lower portion of the grave marker. Randall quickly realized the meaning of the last three numbers on the faded piece of paper enclosed in *The Great Omar*. He read the number 229 on a headstone. It was the grave of an unknown.

The grave of a single unknown *Titanic* victim at this particular cemetery is important, Randall thought. But why? And who or what lies beneath this plot of grass, this spot called out in a faded handwritten note of decades past? He sat down on the grass, folding his legs against his chest, his arms around his knees. The wind kicked up the cold autumn breeze rustling the limbs of the trees, the leaves protesting their approaching demise. At that moment, Randall felt very alone. And very mortal.

* * *

The last of the dinner dishes had been removed from the table. The evening crowd in the restaurant was beginning to thin out. Randall once again gazed at Bobbie Holland, studying her features, her countenance. Strange, he thought, she seemed more feminine when she was in uniform. It was as if a uniform with rank and ribbons accentuated her femininity. Now the delicate vestige of the woman seemed muted, almost absent.

"So," she continued, "now I know you're an Eisenhower republican slash John F. Kennedy democrat, whatever that means."

Randall smiled. "That means I'm standing in the middle of the road, and I have no desire to cross over to either side."

Holland laughed. "Very well. If you insist. Just be careful – you might get run over."

"I'll take my chances," Randall responded. "In America, most folks are on either side of the road. And a fair number of them are in the gutters, where nothing moves until there's a storm."

Holland shook her head and then paused, staring intently at Randall. "I suppose you're right. It's the same in Canada."

"Maybe it's the same everywhere," Randall said wistfully. "It's tough to see the road, to see where you've been or where you're going, if you're in a ditch. Or a sewer." Both were quiet for a moment.

"You know, speaking of Canada, Rob, just why are you here? You certainly did not need to visit Halifax for your book, not with computers and cell phones. What's the real story?"

Randall paused, carefully choosing his words. "Like I said, I'm doing additional research. In my mind there are some questions that need to be answered."

"About the Swissair crash?"

"Oh, more about the recovery efforts," Randall replied. "The accident has pretty much been explained. The folks here in Canada conducted an outstanding investigation. Best in the business. I simply wish to know more about the folks that did the underwater surveying and recovery work. That's all. Besides, if I hadn't traveled to Nova Scotia, I wouldn't be sitting here in a great seafood restaurant, having a wonderful dinner with an old and dear acquaintance."

Holland laughed. "Well, it still sounds like you're up to something nefarious. I'll have to keep an eye on you."

Randall smiled. "Be my guest. Just remember – a moving target is hard to hit."

The moment the words were out, Randall wondered why he uttered them. He had been uncomfortable the entire evening, at times casually looking over his shoulder, attempting to appear inconspicuous. But he felt like a bug under a microscope, continually being observed, being studied, being examined for dissection. Careful, old man, he mused to himself, you're becoming paranoid. Then Randall remembered the bomb in the car and Paul McDowell enjoying the permafrost in Maine. The uneasiness continued to grow within him, alive and unabated.

When dinner was over, Bobbie Holland asked Randall if he would like to go to her place for a nightcap. Randall begged off, explaining his schedule for the following day. Seeing her subtle disappointment, Randall promised to call for another date. Satisfied, she gave him a peck on the cheek before walking to her car.

Randall watched her for a moment. Then he glanced about the parking lot. I feel like I'm being watched, he thought. I've been watched the entire night.

He was right. He had been watched the entire night.

Chapter 11

The lobby was filled with fish. Big fish. Little fish. A tuna in one corner, a shark in the opposite corner. Fish the colors of a rainbow, others a bland grey or brown. All were swimming in an ocean of air. Randall studied them as he gazed upward, the fish slowly moving in an unseen current, the wires suspending them from the ceiling barely visible.

He sat across from the reception desk in the visitors' waiting area for the Halifax Oceanographic Research Center. The lobby was three stories high with the outer walls made of smoked glass. Appropriately, the two inner walls were painted a deep azure blue. Randall was kept company in the waiting area by very small fish swimming about in a very large aquarium, back-lit with subtle light and accented by rising bubbles. The fish swam among live plants and an ornate sunken shipwreck.

"Mr. Randall?" The receptionist awakened him from his underwater reverie. "Dr. Shlumberg will be with you in just a few minutes."

"Thanks," Randall said, nodding his head. He stared at the aquarium, observing the fish as they wiggled and darted about in their submerged world. He again slipped into his watery daydreams. It seemed like just a brief moment before he was awakened by the sound of a bell and an opening elevator. Out stepped someone who could only be described as a kindly old man.

"Mr. Randall," he said smiling as he offered his hand. "I'm Saul Shlumberg. I'm sorry I kept you waiting."

"Dr. Shlumberg," Randall responded, "I'm the one who should be apologizing, asking you to see me on such short notice. It's very kind of you to visit with me this morning."

"Oh, my," Dr. Shlumberg said with crinkling eyes behind dark, thick horn-rimmed glasses and a wide smile framed by pink cherubic cheeks, "when you told me yesterday you had worked on the aircraft recovering effort off St. Margarets Bay, I just knew I had to see you. Why don't we go up to my office?"

Dr. Shlumberg gestured to the elevators. Randall followed him, noticing the somewhat unkempt white hair surrounding a small crown of baldness. "I hope you didn't have any trouble finding us," Shlumberg said as the elevator doors closed before it began the climb to the third floor.

"No, not at all," Randall responded. "Your instructions were fine." Actually, the GPS guidance was much better, Randall mused gently.

The elevator doors opened to reveal a large room with a central bullpen of cubicles and offices on the periphery. They strolled down a corridor to one of the offices.

"Please," Dr. Shlumberg gestured to a single chair in front of his desk, "have a seat. May I get you anything?"

"No, thank you. I'm fine."

"Very well, "Shlumberg said, maintaining the smile. "Now, Mr. Randall, how may I help you?"

"As I told you over the phone, "Randall began, "I want to find out more about the seafloor where the Swissair plane was discovered. I was told that when it comes to the ocean floor surrounding the coastline of eastern Canada, you are the man with the knowledge."

The perpetual smile broadened even more. "Oh, I don't know if I have all the knowledge, but I think I can be of assistance to you." Shlumberg paused briefly, examining his glasses. "You see," he said as he replaced his glasses on his face, "I am an oceanographer. My specialty is underwater bathymetry. Do you know what that is?"

"Vaguely, at best," Randall replied.

"Hm-m-m. Well, bathymetry is the study of underwater topography, you know, the sea floor terrains of oceans and lakes. Bathymetric work involves measuring ocean depths at numerous locations and, from the depth measurement data, we can develop seafloor maps that show the contours of the underwater terrain. Mountains, hills, valleys, plains, just like the earth's land masses."

Randall nodded in silence as Dr. Shlumberg continued. "Years ago, bathymetry was a very inexact science. In the old days, folks would simply lower graduated ropes or cables over the side of a ship and let their weighted ends sink to the bottom. That technique was not at all accurate, as you can well imagine." Shlumberg's eyes crinkled and twinkled as he told the story. "Today, we have so many tools and resources at our disposal for making really accurate topographic maps of seafloors using very precise instruments. It really is quite amazing."

"How so?" Randall asked in rapt attention. "I mean, how is it done, now?"

Shlumberg laughed. "Well, when I started out, oceanographers utilized sonar technology to map the seafloors. We used echo sounders mounted on boats, pinging the sea bottoms with sound, like trying to find submarines. The seafloor reflected the soundings, and we would have an accurate measurement of depth. Now it is so advanced. We use laser technology called LIDAR combined with global positioning systems to create underwater topographic maps. Oceanographers can develop extremely accurate maps covering wide swaths of the seafloor from boats or from aircraft, even from satellites in orbit high above the earth. All of the data is collected and interpreted by computer to produce the maps. The technology is very advanced."

Randall shook his head. "Sounds like it," he remarked. "It's all beyond me."

"You know," Shlumberg continued, "it used to be that the maps we produced were used primarily in surface and subsurface ship navigation." He sighed. "They still are. But now, oceanographers map underwater volcanoes, earthquakes faults, even locations of sunken ships."

"Actually Dr. Shlumberg," Randall interjected, "that is in part why I am here. As I told you over the phone, my intent is to learn about the seafloor where the airliner crash occurred. But I also want to discuss an additional portion of ocean floor with you. You see, during the survey and recovery work on the aircraft wreckage, the wreck of an old cargo ship also was discovered. I don't know if you were aware of the shipwreck."

Shlumberg smiled. "Oh, my heavens, yes," he said with that twinkle in his eyes. "There was a grand to-do about it, and it was somewhat of an embarrassment to the Oceanographic Center."

"An embarrassment?" Randall interrupted. "Why is that?"

"Well," Shlumberg replied, "we had never identified that particular shipwreck before its discovery."

Randall gave him a quizzical look. "What do you mean?"

"I know I'm not being clear on this," Shlumberg continued. "You see, the shipwreck indeed was annotated on the bathymetry charts that were completed in 1989. We knew the ship was there. But that particular ship had not been specifically identified. You must remember, Mr. Randall, there are more than twenty thousand shipwrecks along the coastline of Nova Scotia and Newfoundland! We assumed, including myself I'm sorry to say, that the wreck already had been identified and named. It was not. Certainly a mistake on our part."

Randall nodded. "So it wasn't until after the Swissair airliner accident that someone really took an interest in the shipwreck."

"That is correct," Shlumberg agreed. "It was as if the wreck had never been discovered."

"Incredible," Randall sighed.

"Yes," Shlumberg nodded, "incredible. The ship was finally identified and formally recorded. Unfortunately, the name of the ship escapes me."

"The ship was christened the *S.S. Loch Gillelli,*" Randall said quietly.

"Yes, yes," Shlumberg remembered. "The *Loch Gillelli.* Charming name, don't you think? A good name for a ship."

"Very much so," Randall responded with a wistful smile.

"Let me show you the most recent topographic map of that area of the ocean floor," suggested Shlumberg. "You will have a better picture of the wreck site. After all, as we say around here, a map is worth a thousand words." He snorted at his own remark. "Please, come with me."

Randall followed Dr. Shlumberg out of his office and down the corridor to a cubicle marked Bathymetry Files. Shlumberg approached a large file cabinet with wide drawers containing sheet files. He glanced at a notebook resting on top of the cabinet. "Let's see," Shlumberg said as he leafed through the binder. "Entrance to St. Margarets Bay." He paused a moment. "Ah! Here it is." He bent down and opened a file drawer labeled D. Shlumberg rummaged through an orderly pile of large thirty-six-inch by forty-eight-inch colorful maps. "Yes, this is the one," he announced. He pulled a map from the drawer and placed it on a flat table illuminated by a fluorescent light fixture in the cubicle. "This is the entrance to St. Margarets Bay," Shlumberg said as he gestured at the map. "You'll notice this area here colored light tan. That is the natural channel into the bay."

"How deep is St. Margarets Bay?" inquired Randall.

"Oh, anywhere from forty to seventy meters," Shlumberg replied.

"About two-hundred-thirty feet," Randall surmised.

"Correct," Shlumberg responded. "Now, you'll notice here to the left of the channel," he pointed," this slightly lighter color here, right on the edge, that is the rise where most of the aircraft wreckage was found. It is slightly shallower. The water depth here varies from one-hundred-twenty to one-hundred-eighty feet."

"And this profile here," Randall pointed to the map, "this small elongated oval object with the line in the middle. Is that the shipwreck?"

"That is correct," confirmed Shlumberg. "That is the hull of the ship."

"Seems rather innocuous," Randall concluded. "It could just as well be an outcropping of rock as the hull of a ship."

"Yes, you're right. It is difficult to discern the two. It does take a seasoned eye." Shlumberg smiled as he touched his glasses with a pointed finger. Randall returned the smile, nodding in agreement. "As you can observe," Shlumberg continued, "we knew an object was there. Probably a ship. We simply didn't know if it *definitely* was a ship, and if it was, which one."

"I understand, Dr. Shlumberg," Randall sighed.

"You know," Shlumberg exclaimed, "if you are interested in the shipwreck, there is someone here at the Center you need to visit. Let's go back to my office. I'll see if I can find him."

Dr. Shlumberg returned the underwater map to its drawer and led Randall out of the cubicle and down the corridor to his office. As Randall again took his seat, Shlumberg lifted the phone receiver.

"Benjamin, my boy," Dr. Shlumberg declared, "can you come to my office? I have a visitor here I want you to meet." He paused as he listened to the response. "Fine. See you in a few." He replaced the receiver on the phone.

"Ben Quigley is a marine archaeologist here at the Oceanographic Center," Shlumberg explained. "If anyone here knows anything about the *Loch Gillelli* it will be he."

Without fanfare, Benjamin Quigley arrived at Shlumberg's office a few minutes later. However, he certainly was no boy. Quigley appeared to be in his mid-forties, tall, and built like an Olympic weightlifter. "Hey, Dr. Saul," his deep voice boomed.

"Ben, I would like for you to meet Mr. Robert Randall. He is visiting us from Washington, D.C."

"Well," Quigley smiled, "you've come from away. Happy to meet you." His handshake was like being grabbed by a pair of vice grips.

"Mr. Randall is a retired investigator with the National Transportation Safety Board. He was here in Halifax in 1998 assisting the Canadian Transportation Safety personnel during the Swissair accident investigation. I am sure you remember it."

"Good Lord, yes," Quigley responded, nodding his head. "Ghastly. It was terrible."

"When Mr. Randall first contacted me," Shlumberg continued, "he talked about his work on the airliner recovery efforts. He helped train both the American and Canadian dive teams. Mr. Randall is hoping to obtain more information on the ocean floor conditions where the airliner wreckage was found. We've reviewed topographical maps of the area. He also wanted to discuss the discovery of a shipwreck which occurred during the initial stages of the airliner recovery."

"Yes," Quigley interjected, "you're speaking of the *Loch Gillelli*?"

"That is correct," Randall nodded.

"Being a marine archaeologist, Benjamin does a great deal of deep sea diving throughout the area." Shlumberg chuckled. "That is why we call him Quigley down under. You know, like the movie." Shlumberg laughed loudly.

Quigley closed his eyes and shook his head. "Lord, give me strength," he pleaded in a whisper.

"Look at it this way," Randall mused. "It's not any worse than Gentle Ben."

"O-h-oh!" Shlumberg bellowed. "Excellent! I never thought of that one!"

"Thanks a lot," Quigley said, continuing to shake his head.

"Sorry about that," Randall apologized.

"You're forgiven," Quigley sighed. "Dr. Saul is like that. He is a regular laugh riot."

"Well, as a diver," Randall changed to a serious tone, "perhaps you have been down to the *Loch Gillelli*?"

Quigley nodded. "Yes, the Center received a report from the Coast Guard that a shipwreck was observed just west of the Swissair crash site. We checked it out and discovered the sunken ship had not been formally recorded or identified. That struck me as odd, very odd, considering the shipwreck's location at the entrance to St. Margarets Bay. After the airliner recovery efforts were completed, I visited the *Loch Gillelli* on two separate occasions, the first in November of '98 and the second in the spring of the following year."

"And what did you discover?" Randall asked.

"Well," Quigley replied, "the wreck appears to be that of an old cargo ship. Not very big – certainly no more than three hundred feet in length. Maybe a beam of forty feet. Gross tonnage – perhaps two thousand tons. Like I said, not very big."

"Coal burner?" Randall wondered.

"Yes, absolutely. Smokestack at the stern. Coal bunker amid- ships. Small bridge amidships. Single screw. Draft – maybe twenty feet."

Randall nodded. "What condition is she in?"

"She's sitting upright on the bottom with a slight list to starboard. The wreck's not in real bad shape – you know, the usual corrosion, silted over, incrustation." Quigley smiled. "It's funny. When I first visited the wreck, almost all of the ship was covered in fishing nets. It appeared that hulk was gobbling up nets as quickly as they were being cast. On both visits, I spent most of the time hacking away at those darn nets."

"What did you find underneath?" Randall pressed him for more details.

"Just a one-hundred-year-old shipwreck. The bridge structure is pretty much gone. The ship's hull is in fair condition. The decks are mostly rotted away, but that's to be expected. The cargo holds were empty when she sank."

"Benjamin," Shlumberg interrupted, "were the ship's anchors in place?"

"Yes, Dr. Saul. The anchors were hoisted and stowed."

"Ben," Randall asked, "you said the hull was intact. No breaches?"

"No," Quigley replied with a smile, "and I know what you're thinking. Why did she sink? Well, I don't know the reason. I found no areas on the hull that were open to the sea."

Randall thought a moment before continuing with the questions. "So you found no evidence of damage from heavy storms or rough seas. And no evidence of collisions or capsizing. Did you notice anything at all unusual?"

Quigley nodded. "Now that you mention it, I did find something unusual. And knowing that the *Loch Gillelli* sank sometime around 1912, it makes it even stranger. I found a deck gun on the ship. The gun is mounted on the fo'c'sle at the bow of the ship. The artillery piece isn't very large. It's not like a big turret. The gun carriage is mounted on a flat, circular platform on the fo'c'sle. It is certainly unusual, considering World War I was three years off in the future. But I do believe the *Loch Gillelli* was prepared to do battle with a U-boat on the high seas."

"Or maybe a surface ship," Randall thought aloud. He quickly changed the line of questioning. "You have not visited the shipwreck since 1999. Is that correct?"

"Yes," Quigley replied.

"Do you believe a lot of divers have visited the wreck site?"

"No," Quigley smiled. "After the Swissair plane wreckage was recovered, the Coast Guard made that area a no-dive zone. And they enforced it, too - for a long time. The souvenir hunters immediately flocked to the crash site searching for bits of wreckage or personal items from the passengers or, God forbid, human remains."

"Human remains were left behind?" Randall interrupted.

"Unfortunately, yes," Quigley replied. "On my first dive, I filled a plastic bag with remains. And on my second dive, I found the upper portion of a spine." He pointed to his neck. "It contained all of the cervical vertebrae and a portion of the skull at the attach point."

"Please, Benjamin, enough," Shlumberg admonished, holding up the palm of his hand. "No more."

"Sorry, Dr. Saul," Quigley remarked somewhat remorsefully.

"What did you do with those remains?" Randall quietly asked.

"I gave them to the police," Quigley quietly replied. He turned to Dr. Shlumberg and mouthed the word, "Sorry."

"How did you identify the wreck as that of the *Loch Gillelli*?" Randall continued with the questions.

"Believe it or not," Quigley replied, "the name of the ship was still visible on the starboard side of the bow."

"What did you do after you identified the ship?"

"I formally notified the Canadian maritime authorities that a cargo ship by that name had been discovered in the Atlantic in front of the entrance to St. Margarets Bay." Quigley shrugged his shoulders. "What happened after that, I have no idea."

Randall furrowed his brow. "You never pursued it on your own?"

Quigley laughed. "No. If the shipwreck had been filled with treasure, I'm sure someone would have been out there searching for it long before me." He shook his head. "No. To me, it was just another sunken hulk."

"I guess you're right," Randall responded, smiling. "Still, I probably would have yanked that deck gun off the wreck, cleaned it up, and set it out in front of the building here. It would have made a great conversation piece."

Both Dr. Shlumberg and Quigley laughed at the suggestion. "You know, Ben, he may have a point. If not here, we could park it next to the Peggys Point Lighthouse. You know, guarding the entrance to the bay."

Quigley continued laughing. "Great idea, Dr. Saul. I'll see what I can do." Then he became serious. "Actually, Mr. Randall, if you're interested in learning more about the *Loch Gillelli* there is *someone* you should visit while you're here in Halifax. Her name is Claire DuBois. I believe she and her husband did some research on the ship. I know they did some diving on the wreck a few years ago just before he passed away. Together, they owned a dive shop south of town. She runs the shop now."

"Where is the shop?" Randall asked, trying to hide his interest.

"It's easy to find," Quigley replied. "Just drive south on the shoreline road that runs along the western edge of Halifax Harbour. You'll pass through Herring Cove and Portuguese Cove. You'll see the dive shop sign just before you enter Ketch Harbour. You can't miss it."

"Thank you, sir," Randall responded. "I'll try to visit her tomorrow."

Randall concluded his meeting at the Oceanographic Center by profusely thanking his hosts and promising to see them again before leaving Halifax. As he walked to his car, he tossed around the information from the morning meeting in his mind. Randall knew just enough to know he still knew very little. But every little bit helps, he concluded.

Randall hoped his next meeting also would be at least somewhat productive. He would be disappointed.

* * *

The parking meters in Halifax were very selective. Beyond any doubt, the devices discriminated against those who attempted to place American coins into them. The small warning imprinted on each machine advised "Canadian Coins Only". Randall rifled through his pockets, collecting the correct coinage to buy at least one hour. He bought forty minutes. Disgruntled, he accepted his parking plight and strolled down the sidewalk towards the intersection.

After a long, relaxing lunch, Randall had traveled through downtown Halifax, searching for a jewelry store on the southern edge of the city's older community. The store was located on the main north-south route into downtown. Although it was an older area of Halifax, the shops were no less than beautiful, the storefronts displaying historic pride and dignity. Randall stopped just before the intersection and glanced up to a sign above the corner shop. It read "E.J. Molnar & Sons Jewelry, est. 1915". He entered the shop.

Randall was greeted by a loud buzzer that sounded until the door was closed. A young man behind the far glass display case looked at him and smiled. "Good afternoon. Welcome to Molnar's. May I help you?"

"Well, I hope so," Randall replied. "I wanted to speak with Mr. Fredrick Molnar. By chance, is he here today?"

The young man continued to smile. "Yes, he is. Let me find him for you." The young man moved around the display case to an open entrance to the rear of the shop. Randall looked about the store as he waited. It was larger than he had anticipated. The walls were lined with glass display cases. In addition, the center of the room contained an island of displays. Walking about, gazing at the jewelry and the watches, Randall immediately recognized the shop as a "top drawer" retailer. Only high quality items with hefty price tags were being offered.

"Sir, I am Fredrick Molnar. May I help you?"

"Yes," Randall turned and replied. "Perhaps you can. My name is Robert Randall." He gazed at the older gentleman as he offered his hand. Fredrick

Molnar looked every bit of his seventy-plus years. Somewhat bent over, he tried to straighten slightly as he shook hands, attempting to swell with dignity. His faded cold blue eyes stared at Randall, a wary expression lost in the wrinkles on his face.

"Mr. Molnar," Randall continued, "we have never been formally introduced, but I saw you many years ago while you were a member of the Royal Canadian Mounted Police. I was here in Halifax during the latter part of 1998. At that time, I was an investigator with the National Transportation Safety Board out of Washington, D.C. I provided assistance to the Canadian team investigating the crash of Swissair Flight 111." Randall smiled, hoping the old man would forgive him for the intrusion. The old man returned the smile.

"Yes," Molnar responded in a grave but soft voice. "I remember American personnel participating in the recovery and investigation efforts. I'm sure your help was very much appreciated."

"Thank you for your kind words," Randall said. "If you have a few minutes, I would like to ask some questions about your work during those recovery efforts."

"Surely," Molnar responded. "If you don't mind, I would like to sit down. My pins aren't as strong as they once were." He moved to a chair in front of one of the glass cases. Randall sat next to him.

"To begin with, I believe you were a superintendent with the RCMP," Randall began. "Is that correct?"

"Actually, I was an inspector here in Halifax," Molnar replied. "I was the commander for the Sheet Harbour Detachment, and later, I commanded the Halifax Stanfield International Airport Detachment. When the Swissair accident occurred, the RCMP was given complete jurisdictional control over the entire rescue and recovery effort. Because of my prior work history and extensive experience with the two detachments, I was promoted to superintendent and selected to command the recovery effort."

"A massive task, to say the least," Randall reflected. "I believe I first saw you at Sheet Harbor when the aircraft wreckage was being recovered."

"Yes," Molnar agreed. "You probably did. I moved around a lot during that time." His smile became more pronounced.

"The aircraft recovery work and the crash investigation have been well documented," Randall continued. "I know of the American Navy diving and salvage efforts. Did you and the RCMP work directly with the Canadian salvage team?"

"No, not really," Molnar said, shaking his head. "The underwater salvage work was controlled by the Coast Guard. The Canadian Navy and the U.S. Navy answered to the Coast Guard. With them, my job was one more of coordination than control."

"Yes," Randall said with a nod. "I thought that's the way it was." Molnar gave a brief shrug of the shoulders. "One other question I wanted to ask you, Mr. Molnar. During the Swissair recovery work, do you remember that a shipwreck was discovered adjacent to the crash site? The shipwreck was later identified as that of the *S.S. Loch Gillelli.*"

It was almost imperceptible, but a subtle change in Molnar instantly happened. He seemed to stiffen, the faint smile fading as if a shadow had fallen upon him. "I really don't remember a shipwreck being discovered. That might have occurred. I just don't remember it. You will have to ask the Navy about it. Sorry."

"That's all right," Randall reassured him. "It was a long time ago. And like you said, you didn't interact with the Navy." He decided to end the questioning on the shipwreck.

"You have a beautiful jewelry store," Randall complimented Molnar. "I noticed on your sign that the business was established in 1915. Is this the original building, or did you have to relocate in 1917?"

"Oh, so you know about the harbor disaster?" Molnar said in surprise.

"Just a little bit," Randall responded. "I learned of the story on my first visit to Halifax in '98. It was my understanding that much of the city at that time was either destroyed or severely damaged."

Molnar nodded. "That is correct. The disaster occurred in early December of 1917, right in the middle of World War I. A French cargo ship carrying munitions and explosives for the war was accidentally struck by a Belgian relief vessel in the Narrows of Halifax Harbour. The munitions ship caught fire and exploded. The blast devastated the Richmond Industrial District of Halifax. Over two thousand people lost their lives and thousands more were injured. Fires everywhere. Hundreds upon hundreds of buildings collapsed. Giant waves swept the harbor shoreline. Northern Halifax was obliterated."

He paused for a moment. "We were fortunate, though. Our shop location here was sufficiently south of the explosion in the harbor so that the building was only damaged slightly. We were indeed very fortunate, unlike so many others."

Randall smiled and nodded. "Well, sir, I have taken up enough of your time. Thank you for taking the time to talk with me. Perhaps I will come by your store again before I leave Halifax."

"Any time, Mr. Randall," Molnar said as the smile returned. "You would be welcomed."

Molnar watched Randall leave the store and disappear past the front window. He then quickly headed into the back room and picked up the phone. It was time to issue a warning. Molnar was confident Randall knew far more than he was letting on, and that conclusion scared him to his core.

Chapter 12

It was another beautiful early autumn morning in Halifax, the third successive day of sunshine and wispy clouds. The waters of Halifax Harbour were smooth with only tiny splashes of water striking the rocky coastline. Even the seagulls seemed serene as they glided on cool, gentle breezes.

According to the GPS, Ketch Harbour was approximately ten miles south of Halifax on Route 349. Rob Randall caught glimpses of the Atlantic Ocean as he passed by Herring and Portuguese Coves before the road turned inland towards Ketch Harbour. He drove slowly, enjoying the short jaunt from Halifax. It ended too quickly as he drove into the outskirts of the fishing village.

Just as he spotted the harbor, Randall came upon the dive shop. It appeared exactly as Ben Quigley had predicted. He turned left onto a gravel drive and parked in front of the building. Randall quickly studied the structure. The shop resembled a weathered, rustic log chalet. A sign on the sloped roof read "DuBois Dive Shop". As he emerged out of his car, Randall noticed the rear of the building faced the northern tip of the cove. The gravel crunched under his shoes as he walked to the main entrance at the end of the building.

As he quietly entered the shop, Randall noticed there was no bell, no buzzer to announce his arrival. The store was deathly quiet. "Hello?" he called out. "Anybody home?"

Suddenly, off to his right halfway back, a head and shoulders popped up from behind a set of shelves. "Good morning! You sort of sneaked in on me!" A woman came from behind the shelves and stood next to them, cleaning her hands on a rag.

"Sorry about that," Randall apologized. "I didn't mean to scare you." He smiled at the woman, attempting to appear benign.

"You're my first customer of the day. Can I help you?" She tucked the rag into the back pocket of her blue jeans.

Randall stared at the woman as he quickly studied her. He estimated she was in her mid-forties. Her face was built around large brown eyes set widely apart with heavy eyelids making her appear somewhat sultry. Her nose was small and thin, and the lips were full and complemented her high cheekbones. Her fair complexion was framed by dark auburn hair pulled back into a ponytail. She wore a red plaid shirt and somewhat tight jeans that accentuated her curves.

"Perhaps. My name is Robert Randall. I was hoping to speak with a Claire DuBois, if she is here."

"Well," she acknowledged, smiling, "I'm not *a* Claire DuBois. I'm *the* Claire DuBois. And, again, how may I help you?"

Randall sighed heavily as he slowly approached her. "I've been here in Halifax for three days meeting with a number of folks about a plane crash that occurred seventeen years ago. But I'm tired of putting on a front. Quite honestly, I want to talk to you about a sunken ship. Her name is the *Loch Gillelli*."

The smile on the face of Claire DuBois instantly evaporated, only to be replaced by lips naturally formed into a perpetual frown. "What do you want to know about the *Loch Gillelli*?"

"Everything you know," Randall replied with a completely serious and sober countenance.

"Why?" she asked, her guard up.

"Why?"

"Yeah, why?" she again asked, acting like a coiled snake ready to strike.

"Because someone tried to kill me over that ship," Randall replied, "and I believe others have died as well."

Claire DuBois stared at Randall. She appeared as if she were trying to decide whether the police should be called. She said nothing.

"There are others that have been threatened as well," Randall continued. "I want to stop it. All of it. Will you help me?"

DuBois continued to stare into Randall's eyes in suspicion and contemplation. Randall noticed her breathing was rapid and shallow as if she was gripped by fear. He gave her a brief, faint smile, wondering if she could be trusted. She continued to gaze at Randall, eyes wide and unblinking, for what seemed like an eternity. Then her gaze shifted slightly, as if she was staring at a different place and in a different time.

"Yes," DuBois answered in resignation as she gestured at Randall to follow her. She walked to behind the counter at the back of the shop. Randall sat on a stool to the side of an old cash register on the counter top. "Where are you from, Mr. Randall?" she asked nonchalantly.

"I'm an American. I live outside of Washington, D.C."

"Do you work in law enforcement?" Dubois was still wary of him.

"No," Randall replied, attempting to appear as relaxed and non-threatening as possible. "Actually, I am retired from the National Transportation Safety Board."

"You are?" DuBois seemed puzzled.

"Yes," Randall replied. "I worked in aircraft accident investigation." DuBois nodded but remained silent. "That's what originally brought me here to Halifax," he continued. "You may remember the crash of a Swissair airliner in 1998. It went down near Peggys Cove at the entrance to St. Margarets Bay."

"I remember it well," she said softly.

"I along with a team of investigators was sent to Halifax to assist the Canadian authorities in the airliner recovery efforts. I helped train the divers from the Canadian and American Navies to conduct the underwater survey and salvage work."

"Then you must have met Jason. Jason DuBois." She suddenly became excited. "He was my husband. Jason was a member of the Canadian dive team that worked at the crash site."

"I probably did," Randall responded smiling. "I provided training to all of the divers. I also helped in the identification of the aircraft wreckage as it arrived on shore. It was a very busy time."

"Yes," she said, finally displaying a smile. "We had only been married a few years." Then the smile faded. "That was a difficult time for Jason. It was very hard, you know, recovering all of the victims. It changed him for a long time." She shook her head.

"I know," Randall agreed. "Believe me, I know exactly what you're saying. Some folks never get over it. It stays with you forever."

DuBois gazed at him. "Voice of experience?"

Randall smiled. "Something like that."

"So you are a diver?" she decided in a more relaxed tone.

Randall again smiled. "I still have my certifications. I participated with both the Canadian and American Naval personnel in some of the dives during the recovery efforts." DuBois nodded but remained silent. "It's my understanding your husband made some dives on the *Loch Gillelli?*" Randall continued.

"Who told you that?" she asked, again becoming tense.

"A fellow from the Halifax Oceanographic Research Center. His name is Ben Quigley. He is a marine archaeologist."

"I know Ben," she responded, the faint smile returning. DuBois paused a moment before continuing. "Jason never made a dive on the shipwreck when it was first discovered. I'm not even sure any Canadian divers did, perhaps with the exception of Ben. My husband didn't visit the wreck site until after he retired from the Navy. Honestly, I'm not sure why he made the first dive on the *Loch Gillelli*. The Coast Guard at that time was enforcing a no-dive zone designation on the wreck site. I know my husband petitioned the RCMP to allow him to dive on the shipwreck."

"Hold it a moment," Randall interrupted. "The *police* issued the no-dive designation, not the Coast Guard?"

"That's correct," DuBois responded. "The Coast Guard simply enforced the directive from the police."

"You wouldn't happen to know who specifically issued the directive, would you?" Randall began fishing.

"Well, yes, I do," she replied. "It was Superintendent Molnar of the Canadian police. I'm sorry. I don't remember his first name."

"It's Fredrick," Randall reminded her.

"Yes, you're right. In fact, it was Superintendent Molnar that helped Jason get permission to dive on the *Loch Gillelli*. The only condition was that whatever he saw or found on the shipwreck was to be reported to Mr. Molnar personally."

"My God," Randall exclaimed. "I visited with Fredrick Molnar yesterday afternoon. To hear him tell it, he's never even *heard* of the *Loch Gillelli*." Randall shook his head in disbelief. "Tell me, Ms. DuBois . . ."

"It's Claire," she interjected.

"Okay, Claire," Randall smiled, "when did you husband begin diving on the shipwreck?"

"Oh, about four years ago, I guess. He read some newspaper article about old shipwrecks in the area and their impact on marine life. The article mentioned the *Loch Gillelli*. He was curious about the wreck, you know, being off-limits to divers. It must have taken Jason six months to obtain permission to go to the wreck site."

"Your husband Jason is passed now?" Randall asked as delicately as possible.

"Yes," Claire responded, looking away from him. "My husband disappeared in July of 2013. His boat was discovered beached just above Northwest Cove at Leeward Point in St. Margarets Bay. He was never found."

"No idea of what happened?" Randall asked.

"No, not really," Claire replied, sighing.

"Did anyone accompany your husband on the diving excursions to the *Loch Gillelli* wreck site?"

"Yes, I did. On a number of his dive trips."

"So you've been to the wreck site and seen the ship?"

"Yes," Claire nodded. "I'm very familiar with the wreck site."

Randall decided to start trolling. "Did you see or find anything unusual on the wreck?"

"Such as?"

"Oh, anything unusual," Randall casually replied.

Claire laughed. "Well, I remember a whole lot of dives where all we did was clear the wreck of a gazillion fishing nets."

Randall joined in the laughter. "Okay. *After* that."

"Well, as you can imagine," Claire responded, "the ship is in poor condition. After all, it has been over a hundred years. The wooden deck structures that still exist are pretty fragile. The hull is hanging in there. I did venture a few times below decks. That scared me half to death. I'll never do that again."

Randall smiled and nodded. "Yeah, I can only imagine. Find anything interesting?"

"No, nothing unusual. Except for a deck gun. Jason was totally intrigued by that deck gun."

"Yes," Randall mused. "I heard about the deck gun from Mr. Quigley. I suggested to him that the gun should be recovered and placed on the lawn in front of the oceanographic building."

Claire laughed as she nodded. "That sounds just like my husband. Jason wanted to haul up that cannon and stick it in front of our store. He said he would clean it up so he could fire off ceremonial tributes. You know – birthdays, anniversaries . . ."

Randall laughed. "Your husband sounds like he's my kind of guy."

"Yeah," she admitted, "he was awfully crazy at times." Claire paused a moment as a memory returned to her. "Actually, we did find something else unusual. Really strange."

"What was it?"

"We found a box, strictly by accident," she said, her face covering a mind struggling to remember. "On one of our dive trips, we anchored the boat about one hundred feet west of the shipwreck. Just by happenstance, the anchor landed next to an old wooden box wrapped in a rusted chain. When we descended the anchor line, Jason and I found the box. Somehow, it came from the *Loch Gillelli*."

Randall displayed an expression of disbelief. "That can't be. A wooden box that old would have rotted away."

"I know," Claire replied. "That is why it was so unusual. Under the rusted chain, the entire box was coated with a thick layer of pitch, you know, tar. Really thick and hard as a rock."

"What was in the box?" Randall asked, finding it difficult to suppress his excitement. "Did you open it?"

"Well, we sort of had to break it open," she grimaced.

"And?"

"Inside the box were the logbooks of the *Loch Gillelli*" she replied softly. "Dry as a bone."

Jackpot, Randall thought. Finally! "Where are they now?" The excitement bubbled to the surface.

"I don't know," Claire answered regretfully.

Bang! No jackpot. The bubble burst. Randall simply closed his eyes and shook his head.

"The logbooks are around here somewhere, though," she continued. "Jason hid them not long before his disappearance. I still search for them. All the time."

"And you have no idea where they are located?" Randall asked, stifling his disappointment.

"My husband said he hid the books in the store – in plain sight," she replied to his dismay, "but he did not tell me where he placed them. Sorry."

"Oh, it's not your fault," he responded, shrugging his shoulders.

"I can show you what's left of the box if that will help."

Randall gave DuBois a faint smile. "Sure. Why not?"

He stood and followed her around the sales counter, through the store office and into a back workshop. Randall noticed a large tool bench, a parts bin against the wall, a lathe, circular saw, and pipe-fitting equipment. He also saw an acetylene tank and oxygen tank attached to the wall by chains, the welding and hose equipment wrapped around the tank fittings.

"My husband did repair work on dive equipment," Claire said as she pointed about the shop, "but since he's been gone, I farm out the repairs to other folks in town." She walked to the far corner of the shop and gestured towards the floor. "There it is."

Randall glanced down at old pieces of wood in a pile, tar covering some of the boards. On top of the pile were wooden splinters. He picked up one of the boards and examined it. "I see what you mean about the pitch coating," he noted. "It really did keep the interior of the box high and dry. Even the ends of the nails are in good condition." He carefully returned the wood to the pile.

Randall followed DuBois back through the store office. He glanced about the small room, a desk and file cabinets on the left. "Hey, wait a second!" Randall suddenly exclaimed. He pointed to a photograph among a group of framed pictures mounted on the wall above the desk. "I've seen that photo before."

Claire turned and peeked around the corner at the pictures. "Which one?"

"This one," he reported, pointing at a picture of a group of men taken on the shore of a bay or lake.

"Yes," she acknowledged, "it's a picture of the Canadian dive team that worked on the airliner salvage. You know, you trained them." Claire reached in front of Randall and pointed to a tall man smiling from the back row in the photograph. "There's my husband." She turned to Randall. "Where did you first see the picture?"

"I saw it just a few days ago. I noticed it hanging on an office wall at the Shearwater Naval Annex. Captain Holland's office. She's in charge of the annex facility."

"Yes," Claire agreed, "that's the home of the Canadian Navy dive unit for the Atlantic."

"Yeah, I know," Randall said quietly. "Strange. She told me she didn't know any of the Canadian salvage divers. According to her, she wouldn't even recognize them. But she has their picture hanging on her office wall." He grimaced. "That doesn't make sense."

"Holland," Clair repeated. "I think I've heard that name before, but I don't remember where or when. Sorry."

Randall sat down on the chair in front of the desk. "Claire, did your husband ever mention a man whose name was Reece?"

"No," she replied with a puzzled expression. "I don't think so."

"His last name might have been Devero. D-E-V-E-R-O." Claire remained silent, appearing confused. "Look," Randall continued, "do you have the names of the men in this picture?"

"Sure," she replied. "The names are on the back of the photograph." Claire reached past Randall and removed the picture from the wall. Turning it over, she carefully slid the cardboard backing from the frame and removed the photo. Then she placed it face-down on the desk top in front of Randall. "See," she pointed, "there's my husband's name. Jason DuBois."

Randall looked at his name and then quickly glanced down the list. He stopped and returned to the top of the list of names, slowly reviewing each one.

"Wait a second!" he suddenly exclaimed. "Wait a second!" He placed his finger down on the photo. "Look at this. The name listed directly above that of your husband. See?" Randall said in excitement as he showed it to Claire. "Maurice Devoreux. *Reece Devero!*"

"Maury?" Claire seemed shocked.

"You know this guy?" Randall asked in disbelief.

"Yeah," she replied loudly, "I know him. His last name is pronounced *De-vor-a*. You know, a French pronunciation. But his name isn't Reece. It's *Maurice*. Everybody calls him Maury."

"Not everybody," Randall cautioned Claire. He turned over the photograph. "Show me who he is in this picture."

Claire pointed to an individual next to her husband. Thin. Blonde hair. Sharp features. Just as Nigel Sheffland had described him. "That's got to be him," Randall proclaimed, nodding his head. "How do you know him? Have you seen him lately?"

"No," Claire replied, shaking her head. "Not since my husband disappeared. I first met him when they were members of the same dive unit. They went diving together. Not all the time. Just once in a while."

"Did he visit the shipwreck with your husband?" She nodded her head but remained silent. Randall closed his eyes. "Does he still live here in the area?"

"I don't know," Claire replied. "Like I said, I haven't seen him in years." She paused for a moment. "Mr. Randall, what's going on?"

He gave the photo to Claire. "I'm not sure." He rubbed his chin. "I wish I knew." He silently watched Claire place the photograph back into the frame and return it to the wall.

"Tell me, have you heard the name Paul McDowell?"

Claire brought her right hand to her mouth. "Yes! He went diving with Jason and Maury a few times."

"On the *Loch Gillelli*?"

Claire nodded her head. Randall sighed. "Paul McDowell was a U.S. Navy diver who was part of the American team providing assistance to the Canadian folks during the airliner recovery efforts in 1998. He was the first to dive on the *Loch Gillelli* shipwreck in October of that year."

"I don't believe Jason knew that," she whispered.

"Claire, Paul McDowell is dead. He was murdered a month ago in Maine. I know his death is tied to the *Loch Gillelli*. It's very possible your husband's disappearance is also connected to the ship."

Claire DuBois now appeared stricken. "Mr. Randall . . ."

"Rob," he interrupted softly. "Call me Rob."

She smiled slightly. "Rob, there are some things I haven't told you about the shipwreck of the *Loch Gillelli*. To begin with, the ship didn't sink due to some accident. She was scuttled. The seacocks were open. The ship was opened to the sea. She was sunk on purpose."

Randall shook his head in disbelief.

"And there's something else," Claire continued. "During one of his dives, Jason found eight pairs of boots and shoes on the floor of the forward cargo hold. They weren't placed neatly together. Each pair of boots looked as if the man wearing them was lying flat on his back. No bones, no clothes, just remnants of shoe leather."

Randall nodded in understanding. No bones. No clothes. Just shoes. The only thing remaining of a man in a watery grave after one hundred years.

"My husband found some personal items in the silt. Belt buckles, buttons, a few pocket watches, stuff like that. And one additional thing." Claire reached in front of Randall and opened a desk drawer. She pulled out an envelope and gave it to Randall. He opened the flap and looked inside before pouring its contents into his hand. He stared down at what appeared to be two old lead bullets, each one corroded and deformed. "There's a slip of paper in the envelope, too. My husband had one of his dive buddies from the police department analyze the slugs. He wrote down what they were."

Randall extracted a folded sheet of paper from the envelope. He carefully opened it. It simply read Webley 455.

"Do you know what that means?" Claire asked.

"Yes," Randall replied. "The bullets were most likely fired from a Webley revolver, an old British handgun. The number 455 refers to the caliber of the bullet. An old .455 caliber Webley revolver." He sighed. "Makes sense. One hundred-year-old murders committed with a one hundred-year-old firearm." He returned the folded slip of paper and the slugs to the envelope and placed it back into the desk drawer. Claire reached down and closed it.

"That ship holds secrets," Claire said with a strange expression on her face, a combination of fear and loathing. "Terrible secrets. From the moment I first laid eyes on it, I knew."

"I'm afraid you may be right," Randall agreed. "Terrible secrets. Dreadful stories."

"Rob, do you want to visit the shipwreck? Would you like to see the *Loch Gillelli*?" Randall furrowed his brow, appearing confused. "Look, you told me you're a diver. I'll take you to the shipwreck. It's not far from here. We can do it tomorrow. The good weather is supposed to hold for another day. I have all the dive equipment we need for the two of us. I want to return to the ship. I want you to see the *Loch Gillelli* too."

Randall hesitated for a moment and then spoke. "Well, okay," he replied, "but what about your shop? Your business here?"

"Oh, it's the slow time of the year," Claire replied. "Winter's coming on. The water's getting colder. Heck, you're my only customer so far today. Closing the store tomorrow won't be a big deal. How about it?"

"All right," Randall agreed. "We'll do it. Tomorrow."

If Randall had known another terrible secret of the shipwreck would be revealed to him and Claire DuBois the following day, he never would have ventured to the ocean grave of the *Loch Gillelli*.

Chapter 13

The wave from a passing fishing skiff slapped against the hull of the dive boat, causing a slight rolling motion. Rob Randall watched Claire Du-Bois maintain her balance as she topped off the boat's eighty-gallon fuel tank. "There we go," she announced. "Now we have enough gas to go all the way to Newfoundland."

"I don't believe we need to go that far today," Randall responded. "St. Margarets Bay will do fine."

Randall gazed at Claire as she finished fueling the boat. She wore a yellow windbreaker over a one-piece bathing suit that left little to the imagination. She definitely was easy on the eyes. Ah, to be young again, he thought. At least a little younger, anyway.

She moved past the pilot's seat to the bench at the front of the boat and sat next to Randall. "Here's your receipt," she said, handing the paper to Randall. "Thanks for buying the gas."

"My pleasure," he said smiling. "It's the least I could do."

"At one time we had a couple of dive boats," Claire reminisced fondly. "Our big dive boat was a forty-two-footer. We used it for our classroom dive training. When we filled that boat with gas, it cost us an arm and a leg. This boat is only a twenty-six-footer. It's not nearly as bad, believe me."

Randall smiled as Claire stood and moved back to the pilot's bench.

"You can cast off the bowline," she instructed him. When he returned to the bench, Claire started the engine.

"What kind of motor do you have in this boat?" Randall asked as it rumbled to life.

"It's a Cummins QSB. Three hundred-fifty-five horses. Plenty big enough for around here."

"I wish I had a couple of them in my old cabin cruiser," Randall said as the dive boat slowly began to pull away from the fueling dock. He stood and moved next to Claire as she negotiated a smattering of boats anchored nearby.

"This morning you told me about getting your open water dive certification while you were at Annapolis," Claire reminded Randall. "Did you get your advanced dive certification there, too?"

"No," he replied. "Actually, I received that certification while I was on active duty in the Navy. A friend of mine in our squadron talked me into it. He persuaded me with thoughts of hunting for sunken treasure."

"Who was your friend?" she asked.

Randall smiled. "A fellow by the name of Kilby. John Kilby. But we call him Jack."

"You still know him?"

"Oh, yeah," Randall replied. "He's my best friend. We were classmates at the Naval Academy. I've known him over forty years."

"You're very fortunate," Claire said with a tinge of regret. "Are you married?"

"No," Randall responded, also with a tinge of regret. "I guess you could say I'm a widower. I lost my wife Laurel many years ago."

Claire advanced the throttle lever. The bow of the boat lifted slightly as the roar of the motor became more pronounced. "Well, I guess you could say we both have something in common," she casually remarked. "You lost your wife. I lost my husband."

Randall gazed at the shoreline of Ketch Harbour. He turned to Claire. "Yesterday, you told me your husband disappeared a few years ago. What were the circumstances surrounding his disappearance?"

"That's the problem," she replied. "Nobody really knows. When it happened, I was visiting my mother in Montreal. I didn't know of his disappearance until after his boat was found in St. Margarets Bay. It was *this* boat. The

Coast Guard has no idea what happened. No idea, whatsoever."

Randall nodded and returned his gaze to the shoreline. Claire navigated the boat through Ketch Harbour to the open sea beyond. As they passed the harbor entrance, she turned the boat to the west. Randall returned to the bench to sit down as the ocean swells increased.

The dive boat rode the waves well. The autumn wind across the water was cool. Randall zipped his jacket over a swimsuit purchased the previous day. He stretched out on the bench, the hull of the boat cutting the blowing wind. The bright morning sun slowly warmed him to the point he became sleepy, the rhythmic rocking of the boat adding to his reverie. Randall drifted off, losing track of time, slumbering to the sounds of the sea.

He was suddenly awakened when Claire cut the throttle to the dive boat's engine. The bow dropped down as the boat came to a stop. "Hey, Rob," Claire called out, "we're here. Go ahead and tie us off with the anchor." Randall checked the rope on the cleat and tossed the anchor over the bow. He then walked back to Claire still sitting on the pilot bench.

"According to the GPS, we should be directly over the *Loch Gillelli*." Claire pointed to the northern horizon. "See. We're just about equidistant between Peggy's Cove Lighthouse on the right and the point of Aspostagan Peninsula on the left."

"Yes," Randall nodded, "I remember the position of the airliner wreckage. It should be just a few hundred yards east of us."

Claire went to the bow of the boat. Randall followed her and together they sat on the bench. "Did you have a good nap?" she chuckled.

"Oh, yeah," Randall replied. "I could sleep in the middle of a battlefield without much trouble."

"So I noticed," Claire responded, shaking her head. "So, now that you're fully rested, we can talk about the dive plan. Okay?"

"Sounds good," Randall smiled. "Plan the dive. Dive the plan."

"Yes," she agreed, "and my dive plans are very conservative. I always try to eliminate any risks, or at least minimize them. Since you're certified for it and you've used it many times in the past, we'll be diving on Nitrox today. But we'll be setting our dive computers for regular air. We will dive to the wreck and stop there for twenty to thirty minutes. Thirty minutes – *tops*," she emphasized. "We will then ascend to a safety stop depth of fifteen to twenty feet for four minutes before we surface. The dive tables say we should have no problems for an eighty to one hundred foot depth during the dive. Okay?"

"I got it," Randall responded.

"Good. Now, you know the emergency routines. We'll be diving together the entire time. No separation. I lead. You follow." Randall nodded but said nothing. "Back at the shop, we checked our air tanks," she continued. "Each has a pressure above three thousand psi, and the oxygen content exceeds thirty-one percent. We're good to go. So let's suit up."

Both Randall and DuBois donned dry diving suits. He noticed the suit was slightly snug as he zipped it up. I guess I better lose some weight, he thought. They sat on the bench and pulled their dive equipment from underneath it.

"I've programmed our dive on the computers," Claire said as she gave one to Randall. "We'll have continuous monitoring of our depth and time down at those depths. Again, one hundred feet – twenty to thirty minutes. Max."

"Got it," Randall said as he put on his gloves. "No sweat."

Both stood and moved to the air tank rack on the opposite side of the box. Each inspected their air tank before slipping into their rigs and adjusting their weight belts. "I gave you the ankle weights," Claire said as she inspected Randall's tank regulators. "A lot of divers don't really like them, but to me, they make diving in a dry suit a lot easier."

"Yeah," Randall agreed smiling. "Who wants to float around – upside down?"

After Randall and DuBois checked the others' dive rig, they maneuvered to the platform at the stern of the boat. DuBois lowered the hinged ladder into the water as Randall rinsed his mask with spittle. He then checked both mouthpieces and placed the lanyard of his dive light on his wrist.

"Are you ready?" Claire called out. Randall nodded. "Good. We'll descend on the anchor line. Follow me." DuBois lowered her mask into position and carefully entered the water. Randall followed.

For Randall, the entrance into the ocean world never changed. He always felt a wonderful transformation of existence into a new and vast universe. It was almost like flying, but instead of sailing through a sky made of air, he was sailing through a marvelous realm of water. He immediately purged the second stage regulator and checked the other mouthpiece. He also checked the inflator valve on his suit and the pressure relief valve on his wrist.

Randall and DuBois glanced at each other and gave the "Okay" signal. They slowly moved to the anchor line, Randall glancing up at the hull of the dive boat. At the anchor line, they again gave each other the "Okay" signal. Then, DuBois gave Randall a hand gesture with a thumb pointing down. The two began their descent, each watching the other.

Intermittently, Randall gazed down past his fins to a watery world slowly changing. The world gradually darkened, bright colors becoming shades of grey. He listened to his own breathing, the sound almost seeming mechanical and labored. Once he looked upward, but the boat's hull already had disappeared. But mostly, he observed DuBois staring at him, the wide eyes unblinking behind the mask.

Slowly, a form took shape below them. Off to their right, the shipwreck of the *Loch Gillelli* became visible. It appeared the dive boat anchor had landed amidships next to the portside of the hull. Randall and DuBois stopped their descent at deck level and together began to swim to the ship's bow.

The shipwreck was covered in silt. Lots of it. Various thicknesses of brown silt covered a wooden deck all but rotted away. Masses of greyish-green barnacles protruded from the silt, their irregular globs of growth masking the definition of the ship's features, hiding its edges and curves. Any metal to be seen was covered in tubercles of rust, the face of the ship seemingly scarred by leprosy. Randall was struck by the notion. The ship, once beautiful, was no more than a leper in death, a rotting corpse already forgotten.

DuBois swam to the corroded form of the deck gun. Had it not been so closely attached to the edges of the bow, it too would have fallen into the ship. As it was, the gun mount had partially broken away, the barrel of the artillery piece skewed upward. Randall studied the deck gun as he approached it. The question in his mind was not that of the gun itself, but why was there an old artillery piece mounted on the forecastle deck to begin with? Why a deck gun on the *Loch Gillelli*?

DuBois motioned to Randall to follow her along the ship's deck to the stern of the craft. They swam slowly, their halogen dive lights dimly illuminating the wreck. They stopped briefly at midpoint of the ship. Randall glanced over the side and studied the rusting hull. The metal plates, once straight, appeared to have gradually bowed and warped over the years, the undulations of the riveted plates now matching the irregular surface of the seafloor beneath them. They continued down the length of the ship to the stern. Once there, Randall noticed the wooden structures on the deck were gone. He turned and looked towards the ship's bow. No bridge. No wheelhouse. No Captain's quarters. All had either rotted away or fallen into the hull. Now it was no more than a jumbled mass of silt-laden debris.

Randall swam past the edge of the stern and glanced downward. He directed his dive light below the stern. In the shadowy gloom, he saw the ship's rudder and the top of the single propeller, both half buried by silt. Laying on the seafloor surrounding the stern, Randall noticed piles of fishing nets, their lines extending away from the ship wreck and disappearing in the darkness.

Suddenly, Randall noticed the current had become much stronger. It seemed to carry DuBois and him back across the stern of the ship. He looked down at a few sea fans anchored to the thick silt deposits covering what remained of the deck planks. The sea fans began to sway slowly to and fro like fallen leaves and grass in a gentle breeze.

Randall and DuBois approached the fallen smokestack once mounted on the stern. It had collapsed onto the starboard side of the wreck. The stack had broken where it struck the edge of the ship's hull. Now the outer portion of the stack was leaning downward to the seafloor while the upper portion rested on the hull. The corroded support cables once bracing the stack were draped across the stern. Randall swam closer to the fallen stack. He shone his dive light into the end of the stack leaning against the wreck, being careful not to become entwined in the web of the cables. He noted the upper portion of the stack was almost crushed. Randall turned and pointed the light into the end of the lower portion of the stack lying on the stern.

For a moment, he saw only darkness. Then the light illuminated a polished metal surface. He moved closer to the broken edge of the stack, gazing at the bright reflection. The object appeared to be ten or twelve feet into the dark tunnel. At first Randall couldn't discern the shiny reflection. He entered the end of the broken stack, being careful to avoid its jagged edge. Suddenly, he recognized the object. It was an aluminum SCUBA diver's tank.

Randall recoiled in horror. The tank was attached to a body in a black dive suit! He could see the arms, the legs, and the head and torso of a person wearing a full dive rig. As he backed away in a flurry of bubbles, it appeared the diver was not wearing a mask. Just as he was exiting the stack, Randall felt a firm handgrip on his leg, pulling him out and away from the broken stack. He turned and observed Claire DuBois wagging a gloved finger at him as if scolding an errant school child.

Randall shook his head and gave her a thumbs-up gesture to ascend to the surface. She looked past him to the stack opening. He moved in front of her, shook his head, and again gestured her to ascend. Together they returned to the dive boat's anchor line and slowly began their ascent. It was when the shipwreck slowly disappeared from view that Randall heard it.

At first the sound was like a high-pitched voice singing a melodious rapture. Then the sound seemed to be transformed into the stroking of a lyre, the music a cry from a soul. Randall heard the sound for only a moment, the song both wonderful and awful. In an instant, it was gone.

The two divers stopped their ascent at twenty feet and waited for the prearranged four minutes before surfacing. They swam to the back of the dive boat and boosted themselves onto the stern platform. DuBois removed her mask and mouthpiece and glared at Randall. "Just what the hell were you doing down there?" she exclaimed. "Going into that stack. You knew better than to do that!"

"I'll tell you about it in a second," he sputtered. "Just let me get this rig off."

Randall and DuBois climbed from the dive platform and onto the boat deck. They immediately moved to the bench at the bow, each fighting to keep their balance as the boat rocked in the ocean's swell. Randall sat down, alternately coughing and pinching his nose.

"Are you all right?" Claire asked, showing concern.

"Yes," Randall replied, "I'm okay." He smiled at her. "Just not quite as young as I once was." He removed the SCUBA tank and placed it in the tank rack, securing it in place with a bungee cord. He then returned his equipment to a bin under the bench. Seemingly exhausted, he simply sat there in his dry suit.

Claire sat next to him. "Are you sure you're okay?"

"Yeah, yeah," he replied. "I'm fine." Randall paused a moment. "Claire, do you have some type of ship-to-shore radio rig on this boat?"

"Sure," she responded. "Why?"

"You asked me about looking in the smokestack."

"Yeah," Claire said, vigorously nodding. "What was that all about?"

Randall sighed and gazed at a beautiful, innocent face with wide-open eyes and down-turned lips. "Claire, there is a person's body in the stack. It's a diver. He or she is wearing a full rig. Tank, dive suit, fins, weight belt, the whole smash. I think the person's been in there a while."

Claire raised her head and covered her mouth. "Could you tell if . . ." she asked, eyes pleading for an answer.

"No, no," Randall replied, returning his gaze downward at the deck. "You better contact the Coast Guard. Tell them what we've found. I'm sure they will contact the appropriate law enforcement authorities." Claire didn't move. Randall again gazed at her, the perpetual frown more pronounced. "Go ahead," he reassured her in a soft voice. "It will be all right. We'll stay here until they arrive."

Claire DuBois nodded and quickly returned to the boat's pilot bench. Staring at the deck, Randall slowly unzipped his dry suit. He had no further desire to dive on the *Loch Gillelli*. Not ever again.

* * *

The late afternoon autumn sun was failing to warm the now cold northern ocean breeze. The sea swells were growing in size, vigorously rocking the dive boat to the point the wave tops were at times splashing over the edge of the stern. Randall reclined on the bow of the dive boat, resting against the railing. He watched the Coast Guard activities occurring no more than a few hundred feet from the moored dive boat.

A Canadian Coast Guard helicopter was the first to arrive on scene less than a half-hour after the initial radio call was made. The helicopter hovered above them until a Coast Guard cutter appeared an hour later and anchored next to the dive boat. The cutter was not particularly large, perhaps no more than fifty feet in length. The cutter's red hull contained a large, gleaming-white enclosed bridge and wheelhouse structure with Rescue/Sauvetage painted on the sides. C.C.G.C. personnel were congregated on the ship's stern, monitoring two divers in the water.

Claire sat on the dive bench in front of Randall. Both remained silent after the Coast Guard divers had entered the water. The two divers had been submerged for more than thirty minutes. Randall stared at the profile of Claire DuBois. What was she thinking, he wondered. It probably was the same thing as what he was thinking, what he already had concluded. Randall had little doubt that the body he discovered on the shipwreck was that of Claire's missing husband, Jason DuBois. What was she feeling, he wondered. Fear? Anger? Relief? Sadness? Probably all of the above. He closed his eyes and shook his head. I hate this, he thought.

Randall turned his attention back to the cutter when he heard loud voices. The three Coast Guardsmen at the stern were gesturing as a diver popped to the surface behind the ship. Soon, the second diver appeared. Between them was a wire-frame litter containing a large, black bag. A line from a stern winch was dropped to one of the divers. Moments later, the litter was hoisted from the surface and lowered onto the stern deck. The two divers then emerged from the water and briefly rested on the dive platform, conversing with the Guard personnel on the deck.

He glanced at Claire. She stared downward. Randall closed his eyes and waited. He felt the ocean wind chilling him to the bone. The autumn sun was low on the horizon when he heard the Coast Guard cutter's engines cough to life. He watched as the cutter slowly turned and maneuvered alongside the dive boat. One of the C.C.G.C. personnel, apparently an officer, moved to the ship's railing across from the dive boat.

"If you don't have any objections," he shouted, "I would like to request one of you come on board and return with us to Halifax. I'm sure you understand."

DuBois turned and looked at Randall sitting on the bow. He gave her a brief, understanding smile and nodded. "If you want, Claire, go ahead. I can take the dive boat back to Ketch Harbour. It's a lot smaller than my old cabin cruiser. I won't have any problems."

Claire gazed at him with a grateful smile and mouthed the words, "Thank you." Then she turned and stepped over the dive boat railing and onto the cutter, the Coast Guard officer carefully assisting her. Randall watched the cutter slowly pulling away from the dive boat to begin its return voyage to Halifax Harbour. After a few minutes, he retrieved the anchor and he climbed from the bow to the pilot bench. Starting the boat's engine and engaging the prop, Randall steered the craft to the east, following the cutter as it gradually disappeared into the distance.

Randall entered Ketch Harbour as the sun was lost to the western horizon. When he tied the boat to the dock, a sea fog was beginning to darken the night. He transferred the dive equipment to the dive shop's rear entrance and closed up the store. As he got in his car, Randall felt exhaustion overwhelm him. All he wanted now was to warm himself with a hot shower and sleep. And forget.

For Randall, the sleep would not come easily.

∗ ∗ ∗

The lights across Halifax began to dim and flicker in the thickening fog, the harbor's edge obscured by the mist. Randall stared through the hotel window as he sat at a small table, waiting for his laptop to power up. He had already taken a lengthy shower, allowing the chill to be swept away by the cascading hot water. The chill was gone, but the cold he felt inside remained. He turned his attention away from the view of downtown Halifax and focused it on the computer screen. Immediately, he noticed an e-mail sent by Alex Sheffland. Randall opened it and read the contents.

> "Hello, Rob. I hope this note finds you well and in good spirits. I am truly sorry it has taken so long to respond to your request of me during the visit to Portsmouth, but I returned to London only yesterday. Please forgive me for my tardiness. However, I was able to determine if brother Nigel had any visitors at the prison in the days following your meeting at Wandsworth."

Randall paused and rubbed his eyes, dried and irritated by the salt water and the sea winds. He continued reading."

> Your unspoken intuition was correct. Nigel had a visitor after your visit to the prison."

Randall blinked, trying to refocus his vision. "Mother of God," he whispered as he read the name of the prison visitor. "Lord Almighty. Now I know the name of Huey the Duck. Baby Huey." *The puzzle is beginning to come together,* he thought. *Of that, there is no doubt.*

Randall immediately forwarded the e-mail message to Jack Kilby. He provided further instructions.

> "Jack - Please follow up on this guy. I'm sure he's the ringleader of this entire extortion plot. Also, check out a Maurice Devoreux. He was a Canadian diver back in 1998. He's absolutely in on the plot. And while you're at it, please check on Fredrick Molnar. He is a retired superintendent with the RCMP here in Halifax. Make sure you investigate his family history. I'm positive he's in on it, too. I'm not sure how, but he is."

Randall paused, then ended the message.

> "I found another murder victim today. I believe he is Jason Du-Bois. He disappeared two years ago. Pretty sure there's a connection. More to follow.
>
> Rob"

He sent the e-mail message and powered down the laptop.

Randall returned his gaze to the lights of downtown Halifax. He thought about Claire. *Where is she at this moment,* he wondered. *Was the body that of her dead husband?* Laurel briefly flashed into his mind, the feeling of loss after more than twenty-five years ever present.

And then his thoughts shifted to the shipwreck. Randall remembered the sights and sounds of the Swissair airliner recovery. The wreckage of a sleek, beautiful airplane. The pieces. The victims. It was as if he once again had returned to those moments of long ago. So now, more wreckage. More victims. More death. The feeling of dread arose within him. Randall closed his eyes and breathed deeply, trying to suppress the dragons. But now they were sirens of the sea, guarding the grave of the *Loch Gillelli* caressing him with their songs.

Randall opened his eyes. His gaze wandered to a Bible lying next to his computer. Obviously, a member of the housekeeping staff preferred the book to be kept *on* the table, not hidden in a drawer. He slid the Bible over and looked at it. The Old Testament was open to the Book of Psalms. He glanced down the pages until he recognized a verse in *Psalm 42*.

> *"Deep calleth unto deep at the noise of the waters;*
> *all thy waves and thy billows are gone over me."*

Randall closed the Bible. It was now the moment to rest.

Chapter 14

The fog had lifted over Ketch Harbour only to be replaced with low clouds and intermittent drizzle. The shoreline, bathed in sunlight the previous four days, was now awash in dreary and dismal shadows, the water cold and forbidding. It was an inevitable reminder that the onslaught of winter was fast approaching.

To Randall, the visage of the harbor accentuated his mood. Even though he had slept well, the rest did little to placate the sadness and the emptiness. He had debated whether to visit Claire DuBois. After a small breakfast and a few moments of internal deliberation, he decided on making the short drive to Ketch Harbour. As he parked his car in front of the dive shop, Randall glanced at his watch. It was almost eleven o'clock. He exited his car, looking about the area. The store appeared empty. He walked to the entrance. A closed sign was posted behind the window on the door. He reached down and turned the brass doorknob. The door opened.

"Claire?" Randall called out. His greeting was met with silence. "Claire, are you here?" More silence. He took a few steps into the store. "Hey, Claire?"

"Quit your shouting," came a voice from behind him. "I'm right here."

Startled, Randall whirled about. Claire DuBois stood at the doorway, staring at him, holding a cardboard box in her arms. "I just went across the street to the house. I had this box of computer printer paper in the trunk of my car."

"Here," Randall said, "let me get that for you."

"I got it," Claire exclaimed. "Just close the door after me." She walked past Randall to the office entrance behind the store counter. Closing the door, Randall sighed and followed her into the office. "I was wondering if you were going to show up today," Claire grunted as she placed the heavy box on the floor next to the printer stand.

"I didn't know if you would be in the shop," Randall responded. "I decided to come out and check on the dive boat. You know, make sure it was okay."

"The boat's fine," Claire said smiling. "Thank you for taking good care of her. And thanks for bringing the dive equipment inside the shop."

"Any time," Randall nodded. He gazed at her. She appeared tired but determined. "What happened last night?"

"Honestly, not much," she replied. "The Coast Guard folks and the police asked me some questions. Why were we diving on the wreck? How we found the body - that sort of thing." Randall nodded as she continued. "Don't worry," Claire said as if reading Randall's mind. "I didn't tell them much about you. You were just a visitor to Halifax doing research on the 1998 plane crash. That's all."

"Thanks," he said gratefully. "I appreciate that."

"Yeah," Claire responded as if she had second thoughts.

Randall watched as she turned and opened the box and retrieved a ream of paper. She began tearing off the wrapper and then stopped, silently looking down at the printer.

"Are you okay?" Randall asked softly. She nodded her head briefly. "I'm sorry I dragged you into this," he continued. "If I had known . . ." his voice trailed off.

"It's all right," Claire responded, her voice cracking. "I'm not angry at you." She turned and faced Randall, her eyes shining with tears. "Quite the contrary. Had it not been for you . . ." she again turned away from Randall. "I know we found Jason. I know it. Now I can bring him home." Randall remained silent as Claire loaded paper into the computer printer. When she was finished, Claire glanced at him. The tears were gone.

"I have to leave in a few minutes and drive into Halifax," she said in a steady, emotionless voice. "The police want me to track down my husband's

dental records. They told me that an autopsy on the body we found will probably be completed tomorrow. I should be back to the shop by the end of the
afternoon."

"If you don't mind," Randall requested, "I'd like to stay here at the shop
for a while. Maybe look around for those hidden logbooks. Okay?"

"Sure," she nodded. "Just lock up the shop when you leave." Claire
quickly brushed past him into the store. Randall heard the door at the main
entrance open and close. The shop fell silent. Randall sighed. "Well, that
didn't go so well," he said aloud to himself as he walked out of the office
and into the store.

The drizzle outside had turned to a hard rain, the sound on the roof accentuating the feeling of emptiness. Randall slowly strolled throughout the
dive shop, browsing the aisles and scrutinizing the merchandise. Everything
a diver could want or use, he thought.

He walked to the front of the store and turned around, gazing at the merchandise racks and shelves. The logbooks of the *Loch Gillelli* were hidden
in plain sight, Jason DuBois had told his wife. The books certainly were not
hidden *within* the walls for the walls were the wooden timbers that formed
the structure of the rustic log chalet. Randall glanced at the flooring. It, too,
consisted of wood in the form of long, narrow planks. The floor, covered
with layers of old varnish, was otherwise unblemished. He looked up to the
ceiling. Suspended high above from thin wires mounted in the center of the
A-frame ceiling was a mannequin wearing a dive mask and snorkel, wet suit,
and swim fins. Randall studied the diver swimming through the air. No, not
there, he concluded.

Randall once again slowly migrated through the length of the shop, eval-
uating the store shelves and racks for possible hiding places. He found no
spots that could be used for purposes of concealment. As he approached the
rear of the store, he glanced at dive decorations mounted on the back wall.
In the center, hanging above the entrance to the office, was an antique canvas
and leather diving suit, complete with a copper helmet, its windows protect-
ed by brass wires. The helmet appeared empty. Next to the suit on either side
were items such as old dive fins and masks, a Navy surplus set of aluminum
SCUBA tanks, and items like antique diving knives and a spear gun. The
display items on the wall were framed by a pair of antique harpoons. Randall
drifted to the old SCUBA tanks. The two tanks were vintage U.S. Divers

Twin Navy MKII tanks connected together by two steel-banded frames. The two tank outlets fed a single large circular regulator. The two regulator outlets were connected to the opposite end of a large, flexible, ridged hose with the mouthpiece located in its center.

Randall smiled as he gazed at the SCUBA tanks. It was the exact same type of dive rig he trained on during his tenure at Annapolis. He placed the side of his head against the wall, studying the rear portion of the aluminum cylinders. Immediately, Randall saw it. There was some form of metal patch covering a portion of the backside of the left tank. Beyond his reach, he searched for a step stool or ladder. After finding a stool in the corner of the workshop, he carried it into the store and placed it beneath the tank rig.

Carefully, Randall removed the rig and set it on the floor. He studied the two tanks. There indeed was a metal patch tack-welded over an opening on the back of the tank. The four small welds were at the corners of the rectangular patch. He picked up the tanks and carried them through the office and into the workshop.

Setting down the tank rig on a large bench, Randall looked about for the appropriate tools to remove the metal patch. After selecting a large hammer and chisel, he attempted to fracture the four small welds. The clangs of the hammer blows echoed throughout the store. Within a few minutes, the welds were broken. Randall removed the patch and peered inside the tank. He stared at two, leather-bound books. Carefully, he lifted them from inside the tank and carried the two books into the office. Setting them on the desk, he retrieved his reading glasses from his coat pocket and opened the first book.

"Log of the *S.S. Loch Gillelli*
Artemus Pritchard, Captain"

There was no doubt. The books were the logs of the Sheffland's ship. Randall slowly began to page through the first log. Randomly, he read various entries to the log, attempting to establish a pattern of how the records were written and maintained. The entries appeared to be orderly and recorded by ship's watch. Their contents were typical of civilian cargo vessels. The perfunctory recordings of ship's locations, movements, weather reports, signals and orders were noted. Also included in some of the entries were descriptions of ship stores and cargo and tasks performed by the ship's company.

> "Position 46 degrees 14' N 18 degrees 8'W
> Wind nor'-nor'-west to sou'east
> Breeze–steady, light
> Course laid east by north & northeast
> Est. arrival Southampton within 24 hours"

On this particular voyage of the *Loch Gillelli* according to the log entries Randal was reading, the tramp steamer had departed Boston and was bound for Southampton, England, with a cargo of bales of cloth.

Carefully, Randall continued to examine the logs. The Shefflands had been truthful. The voyages of their ship, although few in number, had transported rather innocuous cargos of textiles and lumber. As he reviewed the entries, Randall concluded that there was nothing unusual in the ship's operations through its final voyage of the year in November of 1911. There appeared to be few discipline problems with the ship's company and no remarkable incidents during its voyages.

Randall paused and rose from the office chair, stretching and massaging his lower back. He was already well into the second logbook. Nothing of interest, so far, he concluded, just one of thousands of cargo ships plying their Atlantic trades back in the early 1900s. He sat again, rubbing his eyes, strained from scanning the faded inked lines. He turned the page, noting the ship remained in Halifax during the winter of 1911 through 1912.

Randall stopped and gazed out the office window facing the harbor. The rain had increased to a steady downpour, the drops hammering the glass. The wind had picked up, the tree limbs swaying, the leaves cascading. He returned his attention to the second logbook. The first entry of the year 1912 was made on the 12th of April.

> "Departed from Halifax
> Course laid east by southeast
> Winds west-nor'west to east
> Breeze steady
>
> Crew duties increased due to reduced numbers. Preparations completed for 14th."

Randall stared at the entry. The *Loch Gillelli* departed Halifax on April 12, 1912, and sailed on an east-southeasterly course. To where, he wondered. Why the reduced number in the ship's company? And what preparations? He continued reading the log. The next few entries documented their voyage to the 14th of April.

"Arrived position 41 degrees 52' N 50 degrees 16' W Orders to maintain position –
increased drift due to empty holds
Crew standing by"

To Randall, this was the confirmation. The *Loch Gillelli* was prepared to intercept R.M.S. *Titanic* on the 14th of April.

"Maintaining position 41 degrees 52'N 50 degrees 16'W Difficulties with forward mount corrected.
Ship and crew prepared for action.
Winds calm slight swell"

During the late afternoon, the ship was in position and ready to seize *Titanic*.

"Position 41 degrees 51'N 50 degrees 16'W
Wind calm smooth sea
Course– stationary
Ship spotted to southeast

Distress call– wireless message received
from R.M.S. *Titanic*. (CQD MGY). Struck
a berg. Down by bow.
Distress rockets sighted.

Orders to stand by"

Randall imagined the scene aboard the *Loch Gillelli*. A dark, cold moonless night, the ocean's surface as smooth as a glass mirror reflecting a billion stars. The captain is standing on the bridge. On the invisible horizon are the lights of the *Titanic*. Rockets from the huge liner in distress are observed.

"Position 41 degrees 51'N 50 degrees 16'W
Wind calm sea slight swell
Orders – ship to come about –
set course for return to Halifax.

Ship's crew ordered to stand down and
resume normal duties. Some unrest."

The seizure of R.M.S. *Titanic* never occurred. The *Loch Gillelli* simply returned to Halifax. Randall read the final entry in the log of the *Loch Gillelli*.

"Position 43 degrees 10'N 54 degrees 22'W
Wind west-nor'west to east
Breeze steady, light
Course laid nor'west by north

Crew unrest increasing due to presumed
loss of remaining ship's company on *Titanic*.
Also loss of Robinson, Mayhew, and Porter.
Seaman Griggs accused of mutinous remarks and con-
fined below decks. Crew refuses to surrender weapons.
God help *Elgie*."

Randall reread the final log entry. Apparently, a portion of the ship's company was already aboard the *Titanic*, along with three additional individuals. Who were Robinson, Mayhew, and Porter, and just how did they fit into the scheme of things?

Randall leaned back in the chair and looked out the office window. The heavy rain had subsided slightly. It is all true, Randall concluded. The *Loch Gillelli* was a pirate ship, and Cyril Sheffland, Sir Geoffrey's grandfather, was set to seize R.M.S. *Titanic* and rob the ocean liner of its fabulous riches. Incredible, unbelievable – but true.

* * *

The tale of the *S.S. Loch Gillelli* read and pondered for a second time, remained as it was. It was a story of grand piracy on the high seas that never occurred. And it ended in the dark whiteness of floating ice on a frigid Sunday night in April of 1912. Randall closed the second logbook. So many answers but still so many questions. His thoughts were interrupted by an opening door to the dive shop.

"Rob," Claire called out, "are you still around?"

"I'm back here in the office," Randall responded.

"I was surprised your car was still parked in front," she remarked as she entered the room. "I thought you'd be gone . . ." her voice trailed off as she looked at Randall and then at the desktop. "You found them," she uttered in a near whisper.

Randall nodded. "Yes. I found them. The logbooks were hidden in one of the SCUBA tanks hanging on the store wall. Your husband was right. The logs were hidden in plain sight."

"Have you read them?"

"Yes. Twice."

"Well, what did they say?" Claire asked, both impatient and perplexed.

"The logbooks *are* from the *Loch Gillelli*. Their contents did confirm the stories of the ship that were told to me." Randall smiled. "I also learned some things that were not told to me."

"Such as . . ." Claire persisted.

"I learned about the final voyage of the *Loch Gillelli*," Randall responded. "And I believe I now know how the ship came to end up in its final resting place."

Abruptly, Randall changed the conversation. "Tell me," he continued, "I believe you said your husband didn't share any of the logs' contents with you. Correct?"

"Yes," she confirmed. "Nothing."

"Do you think he told Devoreux about the logbooks?"

"Probably," Claire replied. "I wouldn't be surprised if he told Maury about them."

Randall nodded. "I suppose you're right," he agreed, puffing out his lips in frustration. "By the way, were you able to find your husband's dental records?"

"Yes," Claire quietly answered. "I gave them to the medical examiner."

"Is the autopsy still on for tomorrow?"

"Yes. It's scheduled for early afternoon."

"Where will the autopsy on the body be performed?" Randall asked, displaying more than a passing interest.

"At the medical examiner's office in Dartmouth, on the other side of Halifax Harbour. Why are you asking?"

Randall feigned a faint smile. "Because I imagine you will want to be there."

Claire sighed. "You're right. I do want to be there." Randall nodded but said nothing.

"Rob," she asked nonchalantly, "have you eaten yet? I bought some groceries while I was in Halifax. Can I fix you an early"No, that's all right," he replied. "You don't need to go to all that trouble."

"It's no trouble," Claire said. "Besides, I could use the company."

Randall gazed at Claire DuBois. She showed a countenance of both determination and vulnerability. She seemed at once tough as nails and soft as flower petals. "Okay," Randall relented, "but nothing fancy."

She smiled and nodded as he gave the two logbooks to her. "Here. These are yours. They belong to you. You might want to stash them away somewhere like maybe in a bank deposit box for safe keeping."

Randall and DuBois left the dive store and walked across the road to her house. The pouring rain was gone but a light drizzle remained.

* * *

The rack of dishes clattered as Claire shoved it into the dishwater and closed the door. "Claire, really, that was a great meal," Randall remarked as he sat at the kitchen table. "Who would have ever thought of adding potato chips to a tuna casserole?"

Claire laughed. "Hey, I said I'd fix you dinner. I didn't say it was going to be a gourmet dinner."

Randall joined in the laughter. The kitchen was just like the rest of Claire's home. Immaculate. It was an older house, a white clapboard structure with black shutters and surrounded by pine trees. The house seemed to suit her. He did notice one thing during the tour of her home. There were no pictures of her husband on display.

"So, once again, let me get this straight," Claire said somewhat in disbelief as she returned to the table. "The *Loch Gillelli* was to intercept the *Titanic* on that Sunday night, the day before her arrival in New York, and stop the ship. The plans were to board the *Titanic* and rob the passengers of their valuables and then sail off into the sunset."

"Probably more like sunrise," Randall nodded, "but you've got the picture."

"But it never happened."

"It never happened," Randall agreed. "The *Titanic* struck the iceberg before the intercept occurred. It appears the captain of the *Loch Gillelli* gave the order to do an about-face and return to Halifax even before the *Titanic* sank."

"And part of the ship's crew was already on the *Titanic*, correct?"

"Yep," Randall replied. "Part of the *Loch Gillelli*'s crew was on the *Titanic* from the get-go. And, I imagine, all of them were lost at sea during the sinking."

"Then, there never was a treasure of the *Titanic*?" Claire surmised.

"That, I'm not sure of," Randall responded. "Some of the valuables on board *Titanic* did make it off the ship. And there were three men mentioned in the ship's logs that apparently also sailed on *Titanic*. Their last names were Robinson, Mayhew, and Porter. On how they fit in the puzzle, I have no clue."

"Maybe they were lost, too," Claire suggested.

"Maybe," Randall said, shrugging his shoulders. "Then again, maybe not."

"What now?" Claire quietly asked. "Hunt for the treasure?"

Randall gazed at her. Before dinner, Claire had changed from the usual plaid shirt and blue jean combination and into a black sweater and white skirt. Her hair was no longer bound in a ponytail but was now loose and falling at her shoulders. She appeared much more feminine, and even more fragile.

Randall sighed. "At this moment, I'm not sure. One person, perhaps two, has died because of some perceived treasure from the *Titanic*. I was almost the third, I'm sorry to say." He shook his head. "No. I'm not concerned about treasure, about what happened over a hundred years ago. My attention is to the here and now. All of this goes well beyond old shipwrecks and treasure chests. It involves present day murders and extortion plots and may even extend to threats on commercial airline travel. In reality, you and I are nothing more than bit players in this mystery."

Claire looked down and then stood and walked to the kitchen sink, an expression of sadness on her face. She seemed to brace herself upright with outstretched hands gripping the counter. Randall watched her take several deep breaths as she stared out the kitchen window.

"I'm sorry, Claire," Randall said, stumbling over his words. "I didn't mean to imply your husband's disappearance was just a, well, a minor detail in this whole story. It's just . . . well . . ."

"I know you didn't," Claire said softly. "Funny. He's been gone over two years. It's terrible not knowing, wondering all the time as to where he is. And when he's found – if he is found – it will begin all over again, as if he had left only yesterday . . ." Her voice trailed off.

Randall closed his eyes for a moment. I hope Sir Geoffrey Sheffland and his two sons appreciate all of this misery and heartache, he thought. If they don't now, they certainly will – damn them.

"Well, it's getting late," he mumbled. "I know you'll want to be at the medical examiner's office tomorrow. Thanks again for dinner. I haven't had a home-cooked meal in quite a while. It was . . ."

"Don't go," Claire interrupted in a forceful voice. She turned and faced Randall. "I want you to stay with me tonight."

Randall stared at her. She was sincere if not deadly serious. He smiled faintly. "Claire, I'm not much for crashing on living room couches anymore. I sort of gave that up after I left the Navy. Besides, I mu . . ."

"I don't want you on my living room couch," she replied even more forcefully. She looked at him with unblinking eyes as if she was displaying a proverbial thousand-yard stare.

Randall was immediately cognizant as to the meaning of her words. "I – I'm not sure . . ." he stammered, searching for the proper response.

"I want you with me tonight," she continued. "I don't want to be alone." She moved closer to him. "I don't want you on my couch. I don't want you in my guest bedroom. I just want you . . ."

Randall gazed at Claire. So beautiful – so open. So terribly sad. He stood and faced her. "All right," he answered her, "but on one condition. Not here. I want you to go with me back to my hotel room. I thought about this earlier today, but I was hesitant to say anything. I'm not sure if it's safe for you to stay here alone – not in light of what has occurred over the past few days. I don't know if you are in any immediate danger, but I believe there is a distinct possibility of it. Okay?"

Claire smiled and nodded. "I'll go pack on overnight bag." She leaned forward and kissed him. "Thanks."

Randall again sat at the kitchen table and waited for Claire. I sure hope I'm doing the right thing, he thought. I'm certainly a far cry from being a knight in shining armor.

"Okay, I'm ready," she declared as she entered the kitchen just a few minutes later. "I'm taking the logbooks with me. Let's go."

Randall and DuBois left the house and scurried through the drizzle to his car still parked at the dive shop. "Great flying weather," Randall observed as he drove out of the parking lot and onto the narrow rain-slick road. "Is this the first day of the typical Nova Scotia winter?"

"No, not really," Claire replied. "If it were, you would be driving through snow right now. We will still have some nice days during October."

"Yeah, I guess you're right. It wasn't bad back in '98." Randall paused. "Have you ever thought of leaving Halifax?" he asked. "I mean, you know, selling the dive shop and moving to a different part of Canada?"

"No," she responded quietly as she stared out the windshield, oblivious to the movement of the wiper blades sweeping the surface of the glass. "I thought that I should be here when my husband returned."

Randall decided to end the conversation. They remained silent as he drove along the west side of Halifax Harbour and into downtown Halifax. Curious, Randall thought as he kept glancing into the rearview mirror. The same car has been following us since we left the dive shop. Randall dismissed the thought as he drove into the hotel parking lot.

He stopped under the alcove in front of the hotel entrance and allowed Claire to exit the car before he searched for a parking spot. As he drove around the lot, Randall observed a car stop along the street in front of the hotel. It was the same vehicle that had followed them from Ketch Harbour. He parked the car and waited a moment before going into the hotel. The automobile on the street didn't move.

Randall quickly trotted across the parking lot and into the hotel lobby. Claire was standing near a group of plush sofas and chairs across from the check-in counter. As he approached her, a voice called out from behind the reservations desk. "Mr. Randall?" He turned and saw a young woman behind the counter gesturing to him. He glanced at Claire and then walked to the desk. "I'm sorry, Mr. Randall," the young clerk said rather breathlessly. "Two gentlemen arrived here about a half hour ago. They were looking for you. I called up to your room, but there was no answer. I told them you were not here at the moment."

"Do you know where they are now?" Randall asked warily.

"Yes, sir," the clerk replied. "They went into the lounge behind you. They seemed like it was urgent that they find you immediately." The young girl smiled. "I told the two gentlemen that that I'd keep a look-out for you."

"Thanks," Randall responded. He turned and casually strolled over to Clair. "Something's come up. I'll be just a few minutes." He reached into his coat pocket. "Here," he said as he gave her his key card. "You go up to the room and get comfortable. I'll be along shortly. The elevators are to the right just beyond the lobby. See you in a few." He tried not to show any apprehension.

Randall watched as Claire walked through the lobby. Then he turned and approached the entrance to the hotel lounge. He slowly entered and looked about, allowing his eyes to become accustomed to the dimly-lit bar. He noticed two men sitting at a table. Randall recognized one of them. The other was unknown to him.

Randall suddenly realized he had been holding his breath. He drew it in even more and closed his eyes. I really must be in trouble now, he concluded.

Chapter 15

Claire DuBois appeared rested and refreshed but not relaxed as she sat down opposite Randall at a table in the hotel coffee shop. She was back to blue jeans and a sweater but no ponytail. "Thank you for allowing me to sleep in this morning," she said in greeting Randall. "I was dead to the world. I don't even remember you leaving the room."

Randall glanced at his watch. It was almost ten o'clock. "I tried to be quiet. I came down here a few hours ago."

"What have you been doing?" Claire asked as she scanned the breakfast menu.

"Homework," Randall replied. "I've been doing some homework. And planning."

Claire stared at him over the top of the menu. "Planning for what?"

"Planning out what to do next?"

Claire lowered the menu. "So what are your plans?"

"I'm not sure," Randall replied with a faint smile. "I'm still in the planning stages."

It was immediately obvious Claire DuBois was buying none of it. "Who were the gentlemen in the lounge last night?"

"Just two men who told me the dangers of sticking my nose in where it doesn't belong and to mind my own business." Randall hesitated a moment.

"Look, Claire, last night at the house, I told you there was a lot more to the story than sunken ships and treasure chests. You must trust me on this. For the moment, the less you know, the better. As God as my witness, I'll explain all of it to you when my work is completed. I promise. My solemn oath."

Claire sighed. "All right – for now. I'll quit asking questions. For now." She raised the menu. "Have you eaten breakfast yet?"

"There you go again," Randall responded laughing, "asking me more questions."

Claire joined in the laughter. "Sorry about that. A wife nagging."

The two were interrupted by the coffee shop waitress. Claire gave the waitress her order and returned her attention to Randall. She became serious. "Rob, thank you for last night. You were very kind, very gentle and very understanding." Claire smiled. "And you're a great cuddler."

"That's what Maggie thinks," Randall interjected.

Claire's smile instantly evaporated. "Who is Maggie?"

"There you go again with them questions!" Randall retorted. "Nag, nag, nag!"

Claire closed her eyes and shook her head. "Fine. But *who's* Maggie?"

"Maggie just happens to be my cat. A stray, no less. And she's also the first mate on my boat. Maggie manages my crew, which happens to be a portion of the local rat population."

Claire scrunched her eyes closed and grimaced. "Ask a stupid question . . ."

"That's not so stupid," Randall responded with a slight smirk. "Maggie's more than a cat." The smirk faded. "In many ways she saved my life," he sighed. "She's a good companion on lonely nights. And there's plenty of them, I might add. People who lose spouses – they're experts on lonely nights." Randall paused. "But I don't have to tell you that. You already know. Maybe it's time for a Maggie in your life, too."

Claire smiled wistfully. "Maybe you're right." She paused in reflection. "But, you know, I think I'd rather have an old, mangy tomcat. The kind that sits on a fence and wails and brings in gifts of dead snakes and offerings of captured mice. That would suit me fine."

"I see," Randall said somewhat dismissively, "you like the masculine but messy type."

"Uh-huh," Claire said as she sipped her coffee.

"Okay, fair enough," Randall relented.

Setting the coffee cup on the table, Claire once again became serious. "What are your plans for today?"

"Well, when we return to my room, I want to send an e-mail to an old and dear friend of mine by the name of Hugh Pierce. He was my boss at the National Transportation Safety Board in Washington. I would like for him to at least try to obtain information on the start-up, the very beginning, of a British commercial air cargo passenger carrier company. The name of the company is British Sovereign Airlines."

"Do they have something to do with the shipwreck?" Claire suddenly seemed anxious.

"In an indirect way, yes." Randall replied. "Very much so." He paused for a moment. "After that I'll take you across the harbor to the medical examiner's office in Dartmouth. I know you want to be there while they're conducting the autopsy on the body we found. I'm going to drop you off, but I'll join you later in the afternoon. I have an errand to run."

"What's that?" Claire asked, somewhat dismayed.

"I want to drive down to your dive shop and return the ship's logs to their hiding place in the SCUBA tank."

"Why do you want to do that?" Now she was confused. "Yesterday you told me we should stash them away safely where they can't be stolen."

"I know," Randall agreed, "but now I'm planning to use the two log-books as bait. Please trust me. I am absolutely sure they will not be taken. The logs will be safe."

Claire's breakfast order was delivered to the table. The meal was con-sumed mostly in silence. When she was finished, Randall and Claire re-turned to the hotel room. As the elevator doors closed on the lobby, Claire made one final remark about the previous evening.

"You know, Rob, when we finished the dive on the *Loch Gillelli* and were back on the boat, you said you weren't as young as you once were. Well, last night, you sure could have fooled me . . ."

With that, Randall's spirits, like the elevator, went soaring toward the sky.

* * *

The lobby, the reception area, the hallways all seemed as sterile and clinical as a hospital. But the building was not a place of life and healing. It was a crypt of death and decay, albeit temporary. Randall walked down a corridor to the medical examiner's office counsel's room, the sound of his footfalls echoing from the empty walls and polished floor.

Randall had brought Claire DuBois to the medical examiner's office and then headed for the dive shop at Ketch Harbour. He placed the two logbooks into the SCUBA tank and then returned the rig to its mount on the wall, the tank opening hidden from view against it. When he was finished, he walked across the street to check on Claire's house. He found it undisturbed. From there he returned to Halifax and his hotel room. After a half hour on the phone with Hugh Pierce in Washington, he drove back across the harbor bridge to Dartmouth.

Randall glanced at his watch as he approached the waiting area. It was half past four o'clock. He immediately saw Claire sitting in the corner paging through a health magazine. Great reading material for a morgue, he thought.

"Sorry I'm a little late," was the apology as he sat next to her. "I've been communicating with Hugh. Any news?"

"No, not yet," Claire replied. "Just waiting." She reached over and took his hand.

Randall looked across the room to two men sitting in the opposite corner. Both stared at Claire and him, their faces cold and void of expression. "Those two gents over there," Randall quietly asked, not taking his eyes off of them, "how long have they been here?"

"They were already here when I arrived," Claire replied. Randall nodded slightly but said nothing.

"Do you know them?" Claire pressed him. Randall nodded. "Who are they?"

Randall turned to Claire. "Those are the two guys that were waiting for me in the lounge last night," he replied in almost a whisper. Randall smiled. "Don't worry, Claire. I'm sure they like you. They just don't like me." At that moment a man in a business suit entered the waiting area and approached Claire.

"Mrs. DuBois, I'm Dr. Nellis with the medical examiner's office. The front desk informed me of your visit." He glanced at Randall briefly and continued. "The autopsy on the body of the diver recovered from St. Margarets Bay has been completed. The identification of the man and cause of death won't be officially posted for a few weeks pending results of tissue and toxicology tests." The doctor sighed heavily and continued. "What I can tell you is the autopsy dental examination was able to match the dental pattern of the victim with the dental records of Mr. DuBois which were provided to our office. In addition, a set of Canadian Naval identification tags on a small chain were found around the neck of the victim after the body was recovered. The tags belonged to Mr. DuBois."

Claire nodded but said nothing, remaining stoic and steady.

"Dr. Nellis," Randall interjected, "was the autopsy work able to identify the cause of death?"

Dr. Nellis momentarily hesitated, glancing at Claire before replying. "We cannot be sure as to the exact cause of death at this time, but I can tell you that entry marks caused by a sharp instrument were found on the victim's dive suit. Also, the air hoses on the diver's tank had been severed." The doctor looked at Randall. "I'm sorry. That's all I can tell you at this time." He turned back to Claire. "Mrs. DuBois, you will be notified when the body has been released to the family for final arrangements. I believe that will occur within the next one to two weeks. I'm sure you understand."

Dr. Nellis nodded and left the room. Randall and Claire DuBois followed. The two men sitting in the corner remained.

"Claire," Randall remarked as they exited the building, "we'll stop at the hotel and you can get your things. Then I'll take you home."

Claire stopped and gazed at Randall. "Will you stay with me tonight?" she asked as a plea. "Please."

"Sure," Randall replied. "I'll stay with you. But the couch better be comfortable." She gave Randall a faint smile as they continued to the car.

∗ ∗ ∗

Randall said little during dinner as he allowed Claire to reminisce about her life with Jason. Even though he had disappeared more than two years ago, she was now entering a delayed part of the grieving process. To Randall it seemed to be a joining of anger and sadness. He gazed at her as the waiter removed the dinner dishes. He remembered his own grieving process over Laurel so many years in the past.

"Thank you for listening," she said softly. "You're a good listener. You don't tell me what to think or do - or especially feel."

"I'm a better listener than talker," Randall confessed. "It's taken a long time for me to recognize when I should just keep my mouth closed and my brain engaged."

"Well," Claire responded, "you do so admirably."

Randall glanced at his watch. "It's almost eight-thirty," observed Randall. "Right on schedule. Time to get you home."

"Right on schedule?" Claire asked, puzzled at the remark.

"Oh, nothing," Randall replied, mentally kicking himself for stupidity. "Just thinking about when I first started dating at the ripe young age of sixteen. Curfews, you know."

"I'm not under a *curfew*," she said, emphasizing the word curfew.

"Yeah, I know," Randall responded. "You're not sixteen. And my acne cleared up long ago."

After paying the tab, Randall and Claire left the restaurant and traveled south out of downtown Halifax and toward Ketch Harbour. The narrow two-lane road seemed especially dark as they turned inland from the western shore of Halifax Harbour. As he continued down the darkened road, Randall came to the realization that they once again were being followed. He remained silent, not wishing to alarm his passenger.

"Claire, I want to check the dive shop before we go up to the house," Randall said as they approached the outskirts of Ketch Harbour.

"That's okay," she responded. "I can go to the house while you visit the shop. Maybe you can . . ."

"No," he interrupted. "I want you with me." He glanced in the rearview mirror just before turning left into the store parking lot. Randall had the car door open as he slid to a halt.

"C'mon, hurry!" he exclaimed. "Let's get in the shop."

They ran to the store entrance. Randall quickly opened the door and they hurried towards the lone lamp illuminating the counter. Randall heard the scrunching of gravel as the car following them came to a halt in the parking lot, the headlights flashing through the shop window and onto the wall.

"Claire, go into the workshop area and hide," Randall instructed her as he heard car doors being slammed. "Don't come out unless I ask you to." Showing fear in her eyes, she hesitated. "Go! *Now!*"

Claire scurried around the counter and disappeared into the darkened office. Randall heard a brief gasp from her as the front door opened and two men entered the shop. It appeared one of the men was holding a gun.

"Please, Mr. Randall, don't move." The two men slowly approached him, the lamp gradually illuminating their faces. He recognized one of them. "As you can see, we are very serious."

"Yes," Randall responded, staring at the handgun. "That's rather apparent."

"Where is Claire?" the man holding the gun inquired.

"She went up to the house," Randall replied.

"We'll see about that," the other man said. He continued. "I'm sorry. We haven't been formally introduced. Allow me to . . ."

"I know who you guys are," Randall interrupted. He turned to the man holding the gun. "I recognize you. Mr. Devoreux. Correct?" The man nodded. "Notice I used the correct French pronunciation." It was immediately apparent Maury Devoreux did not appreciate the gesture. Randall turned to the other man. "And you must be Huey the Duck or Baby Huey or whatever your nickname is. Commander Martin Hewes, U.S. Navy, retired. I've heard a lot about you. Do you prefer Martin or Commander or just plain Huey?"

Hewes stared at Randall, a look of contempt covering his face. "Commander will do," was the cold reply.

"Where is the third member of the group?" Randall continued, gazing past the two men to the shop entrance. "You know, your lovely cohort in crime, your better half?"

Just then the door to the store opened. "There she is," Randall proclaimed, "none other than Captain Robin Holland, currently of the Canadian Navy. And the wife of Commander Martin Hewes, U.S. Navy, retired. She ranks you, Commander. How has that been working out?"

"Shut up, Randall!" the Commander snapped. He turned to his wife.

"She's not in the house," Holland told her husband.

"Okay, Randall. Where is Claire?"

"She's back at the hotel," Randall lied.

"Like hell she is," Hewes cursed. "Where is she?"

"Claire," Randall called to her. "Come on out."

After a few seconds, Claire DuBois slowly emerged from the darkened office and walked around the counter to where Randall was standing.

"Claire, let me introduce these folks to you. The one holding the gun, there, you already know him. None other than Maurice Devoreux, your husband's friend." Randall gestured to the other two. "And this is Commander Martin Hewes, formerly of the United States Navy, along with his wife, Captain Robin Holland."

"You seem to know a lot about us," Hewes observed.

"I've been doing my homework," Randall retorted, "and I believe I have pretty well figured this whole thing out." Randall turned to Devoreux. "To begin with, I believe all of this started with you, Maury. You helped find the shipwreck of the *Loch Gillelli* in 1998. I'm not sure if it was a big deal to you back then, but somehow, the *Loch Gillelli* was linked to its owner, Dr. Cyril Sheffland. Certainly when Claire's husband discovered the ship's logbooks and shared their contents with you, the puzzle began to come together - which leads to Commander Hewes and his wife."

Randall turned and faced them. "There had to be a link between Maury and you two folks. The link was you, Bobbie. Devoreux is your first cousin. He came and lived with your family when he was only twelve. It was either that or Maury living permanently in juvenile incarceration. You're the one that got him into the Canadian Navy when he had just turned eighteen. You even got Maury into the dive unit stationed here at Shearwater. That was good. You could keep an eye on him."

Randall paused and sighed before continuing. "Bobbie, imagine my surprise when I discovered that you have been married to Commander Hewes here for sixteen years. I had no idea. I guess the two of you met back in 1998 when both of you were working on the recovery efforts for the Swissair crash. And to think, Bobbie, I really believed you liked me."

"Not particularly," Holland sniped.

"Yeah, I know," Randall continued, "but it sure was convenient. All of you knew from the very beginning that I would show up here in Halifax - especially after your bomb failed to detonate. Together, you were able to track my every move. Thanks to Bobbie, you even knew what I was thinking."

"It's funny how that worked out," Hewes said smiling, "much to our benefit."

"Except for one tiny mistake," Randall responded. "You screwed up,

Bobbie. When I was visiting your office at Shearwater a few days ago, you told me you wouldn't know any of the Navy divers if they walked through the door. But you had a picture of them on your wall. The Canadian Navy dive unit that worked the Swissair airliner crash. The picture with your cousin in it. The same photograph that is hanging on the opposite side of the wall behind me." He gestured to the darkened office with his thumb. "That got me to thinking . . . so I began doing homework." Randall paused for a moment. "How am I doing so far?"

"You're very perceptive, Mr. Randall," Hewes replied. "Unfortunately . . ."

"Yes," Randall agreed, "unfortunately. Finding the logbooks of the *Loch Gillelli* sure helped, though. I can see how the final entries in the logs allowed you to figure out what happened to the ship and to the *Titanic*."

"True," Hewes said smiling. "By the way, where were they hidden?"

"Just as Jason DuBois said. The logs were hidden in plain sight."

"Please tell us, Mr. Randall," Hewes said with a frown. "I would hate to see Claire experience any discomfort."

"They are hidden in the SCUBA tanks hanging on the wall behind me," Randall acquiesced.

Hewes gestured to Devoreux. "Get them."

Giving his gun to Hewes, Devoreux walked, with a slight limp, to the wall. He grabbed the step stool and lifted the tanks from their mount. He laid them on the floor and removed the two logbooks from their place of hiding. Devoreux said nothing as he returned to Holland and gave her the books.

"You know, I almost forgot," Randall remarked in reflection. "There was a fourth participant in your little cabal of crime - Paul McDowell, or more accurately, the *late* Paul McDowell. Just how did he get started in your extortion plot?"

"Simple," Hewes replied, "he worked for me. Pauly was one of the original U.S. Navy divers that first explored the shipwreck. After he left the Navy, he moved to Maine. We kept in touch. In fact, Pauly worked for me on a few of my salvage operations. You could say he was one of my personal representatives in our efforts here in Halifax."

"Until he became a burden," Randall mused. "I am assuming, Maury, you're the one who left McDowell in a back alley of Calais. But why did you murder him?"

"Because he lacked patience," Hewes answered on behalf of Devoreux. "Pauly didn't want to wait on receiving his compensation and bonus for services rendered. The promise of future riches did not satisfy him. He began making threats. Pauly provided an interesting extortion sub-plot to an extortion plot. Unfortunately for him, we lost patience."

"Is that why you also murdered Jason DuBois?" Randall asked as he glanced at Claire. She stood motionless, again displaying the thousand-yard stare.

"We didn't murder DuBois," Devoreux declared. "McDowell did it. He thought DuBois was going to spill the beans to the police. When Jason finally figured out what was happening, he made it clear he wanted no part of it and threatened to report us to law enforcement. We had to do something."

"So McDowell stabbed DuBois and cut his air hose," Randall retorted, "but you were there, too, weren't you, Maury? You watched your friend die and then you probably helped place his body in the smokestack of the *Loch Gillelli*. For you, it was out of sight, out of mind." Randall paused and smiled. "I'll bet you never thought someone would find Jason - at least not for years and years. But it didn't work out that way. He was found and now *all* of you are facing at least a couple of murder raps."

"Not really," Hewes contended. "Your evidence is all conjecture, all hearsay. And it all rests with you and Claire, here. The police have nothing. They will never have anything. That is because the two of you will disappear, and this time, we will ensure that no one will ever find you."

Randall stared at Hewes and Devoreux and then at Holland. All three appeared cold and expressionless. He glanced at the gun in Hewes' hand, thinking of the holstered revolver tucked in his waist band. No sense in doing anything stupid, he thought, weighing his options. At least, not at *this* moment – at least not until the cavalry shows up.

"Maury," Hewes ordered, "take the concrete blocks and the chains from the trunk of the car and carry them down to the boat." Hewes smiled broadly. "Our friends here are going out on an evening excursion along the coast."

"That won't be necessary," came a loud voice from behind Randall. Two men emerged from the darkened store office. Both were pointing semi-automatic handguns at Hewes. "Please place your gun on the floor, Mr. Hewes, and step away from it. *Now*!"

Stunned, Hewes slowly bent down and carefully laid the firearm on the floor.

"I am Inspector Peter Markay with the Royal Canadian Mounted Police," the man announced. "To my right is Inspector John Kilby of the American Federal Bureau of Investigation." The two men walked around the store counter and moved in front of Randall and Claire DuBois, still pointing their guns at Hewes and Devoreux. "All of you are under arrest for conspiracy to commit murder." Markay paused. "Inspector Kilby, would you please tell the men outside to come into the building?"

Kilby nodded and holstered his firearm before walking to the front entrance of the dive shop and calling out through the open door. Slowly, men dressed in black clothing began streaming into the store, each carrying a military-style tactical assault rifle. They surrounded Hewes, his wife and Devoreux and began restraining them.

Claire turned to Randall. "Those are the two men we saw at the medical examiner's office," she whispered while pointing at Inspectors Maury and Kilby. "Do you know them?"

"I know Jack Kilby," Randall replied. "I've known him for over forty years. I just met Inspector Markay last night in the lounge at the hotel."

"Did you know they were going to be here in the shop tonight?" Claire appeared both scared and angry.

Randall smiled. "Well, I had high hopes." He paused and took Claire by the shoulders. "Look, we had all of this planned out. You and I have never been in any danger. The police knew that we were being followed since last night. We've never been out of their sight."

At that moment Jack Kilby approached them. "Are you guys okay?" Before they could answer, Kilby offered his hand to Claire. "Hi, Claire. I'm Jack Kilby, one of Rob's friends. Pleased to finally meet you. I've heard a lot about you already." He turned to Randall. "Well, that turned out better than expected," Kilby sighed. "We heard every word they said – all of it admissible in court."

"Well, at least it didn't turn out to be like the gunfight at O.K. Corral," Randall remarked, tongue in cheek.

"Yeah, but I knew you had your trusty hawg-leg at your side," Kilby laughed. "I wasn't worried."

"Yeah, right," Randall responded. "In a way, though, it concluded much too early. I still had a thousand questions to ask."

"Such as . . ." Kilby asked.

"Oh, such as what Hewes was really after," Randall replied. "He knew any valuables from the *Titanic* were gone long ago. And I wanted to know how a former superintendent of the Royal Canadian Mounted Police fit into this scheme."

"You mean Molnar?" perceived Kilby.

"Exactly," Randall nodded. "And before I leave Halifax, I'll get the answer to that one."

"Well, don't worry," Kilby reassured Randall. "We'll be asking a lot of questions in the days to come. I'll make sure your questions are answered." With that, Kilby strolled over to Inspector Markay and the two began talking.

Randall turned and gazed at Claire. "It looks like these police folks will be here for a while. I'll take you up to the house, okay?"

Claire nodded and, together, they walked out of the dive shop and to her home. No sooner were they in the house when Claire all but collapsed into Randall's arms and began sobbing. The tears continued for much of the night.

Chapter 16

A Canadian Navy frigate sailed slowly through Halifax Harbour on its way out to sea. Colorful flags and pennants attached to the ship's lines flapped furiously in the strong ocean breeze. Gazing out the hotel window, Rob Randall remembered his summer tours on board U.S. Navy vessels during his days at Annapolis. Wonderful memories, he thought. That is, after he finally found his sea legs.

Randall had returned to Halifax the following morning. He made breakfast for Claire prior to his departure from Ketch Harbour to his hotel. After a shower and a change of clothes he sat down and responded to a lengthy e-mail message from Hugh Pierce at the NTSB. Now he knew the entire history of British Sovereign Airlines. Secrets unearthed and more to come. "It continues," he sighed aloud.

Randall's next task was a return trip to a jewelry store. Leaving the hotel, he retraced his drive through downtown to the south side of Halifax. On this visit, however, he parked directly in front of the store. Randall exited his car, glancing about with the expectation of being followed. He saw nothing suspicious as he entered the jewelry shop.

"Good morning, sir," the same young man as before greeting him. "May I help you?"

"Yes," Randall replied. "Is Fredrick Molnar here today?"

"No, sir," the young man responded politely, "but I expect him at any moment." He gestured to a chair in front of one of the display cases. "If you wish, you can wait for him. I am sure he will be here momentarily."

"Thank you," Randall smiled and nodded.

He did not have to wait long. Fredrick Molnar entered the store just a few minutes later. Wearing a hat and gloves and heavy coat, Molnar seemed even older than only a few days before, his stooped shoulders emphasizing his advanced age. He immediately noticed Randall. "Ah, Mr. Randall," Molnar quietly proclaimed as he shuffled to the store counter. "I knew you would be visiting me again sooner or later."

"You were correct," Randall responded.

"I saw the article in the newspaper and also on television about the discovery of a body on board the shipwreck of the *Loch Gillelli,*" Molnar said as he removed his coat and gloves. "I suppose you're here to ask me about the story."

"Actually, more than that, Mr. Molnar. I know, at least in part, your family's connection to the *Loch Gillelli* and, to a lesser degree, your connection to R.M.S. *Titanic*. The logbooks of the *Loch Gillelli* tell a great deal of the story. I believe you know the rest of it."

Molnar's face became ashen, as if a century-old shadow fell across it. He stared at Randall and sighed heavily as he sat next to him. "I knew it would all come out sooner or later." Molnar sighed again as if he were catching his breath. "My great-grandfather was Edward Molnar. He was born and raised in Halifax. He was a silversmith and metalsmith by trade as was his father. It was through his work that he met and befriended a British doctor also living here in Halifax. The doctor's name was Cyril Sheffland. My great-grandfather made surgical instruments for Dr. Sheffland."

Molnar paused a moment in recollection before continuing. "It was Sheffland's idea to commit the act of piracy against the *Titanic*. Why he wanted to do this, I don't know. But I was told that it appeared to be an act of revenge. Sheffland left England and came to Nova Scotia. I believe that was part of his plan. He established his medical practice here, and at the same time, he started to work in the shipping trade. Dr. Sheffland purchased a tramp steamer, the *Loch Gillelli*. In reality, the *Loch Gillelli* was his pirate ship. The cargo business was just a front. It all was part of the plan."

Molnar paused as he retrieved wire-rimmed spectacles from his pocket and placed them on his face. "It was all thought out very carefully. The ship's crew was trained. The heist was planned. Dr. Sheffland and my great-grand-father along with half of the ship's company would actually be on board the *Titanic* when she sailed on her maiden voyage. They smuggled weapons on board to facilitate the ship's capture. At the designated time on Sunday night, the group would attempt to stop the *Titanic*. At the same moment, the *Loch Gillelli* would intercept *Titanic* and force her to stop."

"The deck gun," interrupted Randall, "that's why they had the deck gun mounted on *Gillelli's* bow."

Molnar nodded. "Members of the ship's company on board *Loch Gillelli* were to storm *Titanic* and help in her seizure. After their work was complete, and the *Titanic* had been disabled, the pirates were to return to the *Loch Gillelli* and sail off into the night."

"But it didn't happen that way," Randall said, mesmerized by Molnar's story.

"No, it didn't," Molnar agreed. "Dr. Sheffland, my great-grandfather, and a second Brit - a fellow named Porter – along with a portion of *Loch Gillelli's* company *did* sail on the R.M.S. *Titanic*. And the *Loch Gillelli* did leave Halifax and sail into position to intercept the passenger ship. But before the piracy plan could be enacted, *Titanic* struck the berg."

"What happened after that?" Randall asked.

Molnar shrugged his shoulders. "Sheffland, Porter, and my great-grand-father stole the contents from the first-class purser's safe. They filled their pockets and suitcases with the safe's contents and went to the lifeboat deck." Molnar paused. "Imagine having all the riches in the world and the mighty *Titanic* sinks to the ocean depths from beneath you."

"But they made it off the *Titanic*, didn't they?" Randall interjected.

"Yes," Molnar responded. "Sheffland, Porter and my great-grandfather made it into the last collapsible lifeboat. Dr. Sheffland and Great-grandfather lived, but Porter died from exposure before they were rescued. The ship's company from *Loch Gillelli* that was on board *Titanic*, they all were lost that night."

"And there was no record of them because everyone used assumed names," Randall concluded.

"That's correct," Molnar agreed. "My great-grandfather assumed the name Mayhew. That was his mother's maiden name. Sheffland assumed the name of Robinson. I don't know Porter's real name. Only the name Porter is on the *Titanic*'s passenger list."

Randall pondered the story. "After that night, Dr. Sheffland and your great-grandfather were taken by the *Carpathia* to New York, and from there, they returned to Nova Scotia. Correct?"

"Yes," Molnar replied. "They returned to Halifax with the valuables they stole from the *Titanic*. No one was the wiser. My great-grandfather eventually used his ill-gotten worth to begin the jewelry and precious metals business. Our family has owned this store from that time until now." Molnar paused, raising his eyebrows. "Unfortunately, my great-grandfather paid for his sins."

"How so?" Randall asked.

"In the great Halifax disaster of 1917, the ship explosion in the harbor, my great-grandfather was severely injured. He lost the use of his legs. He was partially paralyzed for the remainder of his life."

Randall sighed and shook his head. "So the Molnar family has hidden the secret of the *Titanic* for over a hundred years."

Molnar nodded in agreement. "My brother continued the jewelry business. I joined the RCMP and became a policeman."

"And as a member of law enforcement," Randall said, "you were able to help keep the family secret a secret, especially when the wreck of the *Loch Gillelli* was discovered, right?"

"That is correct. I was as surprised as anyone when the shipwreck was found. Our family never really knew the fate of the *Loch Gillelli*. When it was discovered, I was in a position to make sure nobody investigated the wreck. The airliner crash provided the perfect excuse to prohibit diving on the area of the crash site."

Randall smiled and nodded. "Absolutely perfect," he agreed. "And by the time Jason DuBois decided to dive on the *Loch Gillelli* a few years ago, you were already retired from the Canadian police force. You probably thought no one would ever uncover your family secret."

"That's right," Molnar said in resignation. "I never imagined the *Loch Gillelli* would relinquish her secret and thus the secret of my family."

"Or that of Dr. Cyril Sheffland," Randall added. "What happened to him?"

"I don't know what he did with his share of the stolen valuables from

Titanic. I suppose he gave them to his family in England. I do know he remained in Halifax. From what I've been told, he lived a very modest existence. But he also became a leader of the medical service organization to care for the indigent. He provided for the poor and downtrodden. In fact, he became famous here in Halifax after the 1917 disaster. He led the medical team that attended to the victims of the explosion. They numbered over two thousand. He became known as the *Canadian Saviour of Christmas 1917*." Molnar paused a moment. "If you wish to see him, Mr. Randall, there is a statue of Dr. Sheffland adjacent to the main entrance of Halifax Regional Hospital. He founded the medical center in the 1920s."

The store was silent. The young man behind the store counter was enthralled by the story, his eyes wide in amazement.

"Mr. Molnar," Randall finally asked, breaking the silence, "do you know what happened to the *Loch Gillelli*?"

"Only what I was told as a very young boy by Grandfather," he replied, "but I have never forgotten the story of the *Loch Gillelli*. The ship was a small cargo freighter. Her captain's name was Pritchard. Artemus Pritchard. I was told Captain Pritchard was more than a taskmaster. He was a cruel man, even sadistic. He drove his ship. He drove his crews. He was the captain of the *Loch Gillelli* on the night *Titanic* sank." Molnar paused, his expression becoming one of rage. "Captain Pritchard, from the wireless messages he received from *Titanic*, knew the great liner had struck an iceberg and was sinking. The *Loch Gillelli* was less than ten miles away from *Titanic*. There was more than enough time to go to the aid of that huge stricken vessel and save the crew and passengers. But Pritchard did nothing. He let those people perish. He did nothing. Fifteen hundred people dead – and the bastard did nothing."

Randall drew back, recoiling in horror. Molnar continued. "I'm not sure what happened to the *Loch Gillelli* after that night. I don't believe anyone really does know. I was told the ship returned to Halifax, but there is no record of it. My grandfather told me – or at least he believed this – that the crew on board the *Loch Gillelli* attempted a mutiny because Pritchard didn't try to help their fellow crewmembers who were on *Titanic*. I suppose it's possible a mutiny occurred."

"I believe it is more than possible," Randall concluded. "Does anyone know what happened to Pritchard?"

Molnar shook his head. "No. To my knowledge, no one ever knew the fate of Captain Pritchard." Molnar stopped and stared into space. "No," he whispered, "I don't think anyone will ever know."

Randall gazed at the visage of Fredrick Molnar, his back and shoulders stooped, his countenance one of sadness. He was going to ask Molnar about the grave of the unknown *Titanic* victim in the cemetery at Halifax, but he decided against it. Enough was enough.

At that moment, Randall came to the realization that the most burdensome possession a man can keep in life is a secret too terrible to contemplate.

Chapter 17

The overcast skies of the early afternoon matched the hue of the granite tombstones. A small group of people stood in front of one of the markers, their voices hushed as if trying not to disturb the dead resting in their graves. Rob Randall and Claire DuBois remained well away from the cadre of law enforcement officials and cemetery staff, choosing to stand under an oak tree near the edge of the drive. They observed a white panel truck pass by them and stop on the asphalt, the driver being careful not to encroach on the thick carpet of grass. Two men in dark blue jumpsuits exited the vehicle and walked past them to the knot of people, the voices suddenly becoming more prominent. After a few minutes of discussion, the two men returned to the back of the truck and began to off-load equipment. Another man left the group at the graveside and approached Randall and DuBois.

"I guess the show is about to begin," Jack Kilby announced dryly. "The cemetery folks have been laying down the ground rules to Inspector Markay."

"And they are . . ." Randall said somewhat impatiently.

"Basically, we take a look-see with the GPR," Kilby responded. "After that, we'll decide what to do next. But under no circumstances can we open the grave and exhume the body. That is, unless we have a court order."

"Good luck on that," Randall remarked. "We would have to find some-

thing extraordinarily compelling in order to get a court order for exhuma-
tion."

"That's for sure," Kilby agreed. "I'm surprised that Markay approved
even this test." He chuckled. "But, Rob, you did provide a pretty convincing
case to examine this particular grave of a *Titanic* victim – especially with the
victim being unknown."

"Actually, I believe that helped," retorted Randall. "No family to worry
about."

"Yeah, you're probably right," Kilby concurred. "By the way, how did
the morning's research go?"

Randall sighed. "Claire and I visited the local historical society and the
maritime museum. We found a lot of information on the *Titanic* victims that
were recovered and brought here to Halifax. The records included old pho-
tographs of funeral hearses lined up at the docks, waiting to transport the
victims to funeral homes or cemeteries. The hearses were ornate carriages
made of wood and glass and drawn by horses. There were well over three
hundred victims recovered in the weeks following *Titanic*'s sinking. Over
one hundred are buried in this cemetery alone."

Kilby nodded. "Did you find anything on the disappearance of the *Loch
Gillelli*?"

"No, not really," Randall replied. "I believe a lot of the maritime records
were destroyed in the 1917 explosion and fire."

"And nothing on Captain Pritchard?"

"No," Randall responded. "Nothing. Like he never existed." Randall
shook his head.

Kilby remained silent as they watched the two men standing at the rear
of the panel truck carefully assemble what appeared to be a large electric
push mower. The men attached a handle to the unit and connected cannon
plug wiring before pushing the gadget across the drive and towards the group
of men standing at the grave.

"Is that the GPR test equipment?" Claire asked.

"Yep. That's it," Randall replied.

"Funny," Claire observed, "I thought there would be more to it than that.
It looks like a lawn mower."

"C'mon," Kilby said. "Let's see why somebody thought this old grave was important enough to make sure it was remembered for more than a century. Shall we . . ."

Randall, Kilby and DuBois quietly walked to the grave site, being careful not to interrupt the two men introducing themselves to the group. "I'm Ken Asper and my assistant here is Blake Asper and, yes, we're brothers," he said smiling as he introduced himself. "We're from Geotechnical Investigations here in Halifax. This is a mobile ground penetrating radar system. For those who don't know how this works, let me explain its function to you." Asper moved to the side of the unit.

"A GPR system uses radar pulses to create images of what is below the surface of the ground. It sends radio signals down into the earth and it detects the reflected signals from subsurface structures, such as tree roots, rocks, buried objects, and the like. GPR can be applied to subsurface media such as rocks, soil, ice and water. Depending upon soil conditions, GPR can detect voids and cracks in the soil in areas where soils have been disturbed, even in excavations done hundreds of years ago."

"Will GPR disturb the subsurface conditions?" Inspector Markay asked.

"No," Asper responded, "not in the least. The system is totally non-destructive in nature. This investigation method is classified as NDI - non-destructive inspection. This test method utilizes electrical energy rather than acoustic energy. It detects changes in subsurface electrical properties rather than mechanical properties - you know, seismic properties."

"I'll take your word for it," one of the group chimed in. Everyone laughed.

"The use of GPR has numerous applications. It's used to locate buried structures, underground utility lines, changes in soil conditions. The technology is used by geologists, archaeologists, even the military."

"How far down can that system see?" Kilby asked, pointing at the unit.

"Depending on the soil conditions, this unit can provide images down to thirty feet." Asper glanced about, awaiting more questions before continuing. "This device will provide a profile of the subsurface. The profile will be displayed on this small screen on the handle. To the untrained eye, it will appear to be just a bunch of dark squiggly lines. For Blake and me, however, we will be able to interpret the meaning of those lines."

Asper moved to the rear of the unit. "We will profile the graves on each side of the target area for comparison. Then we'll profile the middle grave and we'll see what we get."

The group quietly agreed and retreated from the grave site to the drive. The Asper brothers began their silent scan, slowly moving the wheeled device over the two peripheral graves. When they were finished, they called Markay and Kilby over to the units to review the results. Randall tagged along behind them.

"Gentlemen," Asper began, "you'll notice the lines on each of the two scans are fairly similar. They show the profiles of the graves. You'll notice, for each grave, the lines here at approximately the two-meter level . . . see, right here . . . curve upward in the form of an inverted U. This indicates a material change in subsurface conditions at the depth of approximately six feet. These are typical profiles of graves."

Randall and the two others stared at the black squiggly lines painted on the GPR unit screen. If you say so, Randall thought.

"Now we'll scan the grave in the middle," Asper continued, "the one you're interested in."

Randall, Kilby and Markay moved back as Ken Asper and his brother slowly moved the unit back and forth across the grave. When they had completed the GPR scan, they motioned the group to return to the grave site.

"Okay," Asper began, "we finished the inspection. On the screen you can see what appears to be a change in subsurface conditions at the two-meter level beneath the surface. That is the same as the graves to either side. However, there is an anomaly at about the one-meter level. From these inverted U-shape lines on the profile, it appears there are two distinct changes in subsurface conditions roughly three feet down."

"Another coffin?" Markay asked in disbelief.

"No, I doubt it," Asper replied. "The profile is not indicative of two coffins in one grave. The objects at the one-meter level are rather small although one is definitely larger than the other. But I assure you, there definitely is something down there in addition to a body in a casket."

Inspector Markay remained silent as he looked about the group as if attempting to guess their thoughts. Finally Kilby broke the silence. "There may be something down there that could add to active murder investigations."

Markay stared at Kilby for a moment. Then he sighed heavily. "Well, we're not going to exhume a body from its grave. But I don't see a problem with digging down a few feet and determining if something has been placed in a grave after the fact." He glanced about, waiting for objections. When no rebuttals from the group were forthcoming, Markay nodded his head. "Very well. Let's proceed with carefully digging down a few feet into the soil and see what we find."

An elderly gentleman from the cemetery staff left the group and walked to a pick-up truck parked on the drive. He then returned with two men carrying shovels and a large drop cloth. As the group moved away from the grave, the two men from Geotechnical Investigations returned to their truck, pushing the GPR device. It really did resemble a lawn mower, Randall thought as he, Kilby and DuBois moved to the backside of grave marker 229. It was from there that they observed the two cemetery workers begin to dig carefully into the earth and place the dirt on the drop cloth.

"I wonder what they'll find down there," Claire said in almost a whisper.

"We'll know soon enough," Randall responded.

"I just hope it isn't Jimmy Hoffa," quipped Kilby. "We'd have a whole new set of problems on our hands."

The hole in the earth gradually deepened. The small group of people surrounding the excavation remained quiet. Suddenly, the deathly silence was broken by one of the men digging into the grave. "I've got something here," he exclaimed as he placed the shovel on the drop cloth and bent down, brushing away dirt with his hand. "It looks like a bone."

Markay leaned forward and looked into the hole as the worker brushed away more dirt. "Another bone," the worker exclaimed.

"Those appear to be ribs," Markay quietly observed as the second man in the hole began to brush away the dirt at his feet.

"It looks like a skull here," the first gravedigger announced.

"Yes, that appears to be the crown of a skull," Markay agreed.

"I've got something," the second digger said. "It looks like a button of some sort." He reached up and gave it to Markay.

Inspector Markay examined the object. "It's too large – too thick – to be a coin. I believe he's right. It may be a button."

"May I see it?" Randall requested. Markay reached across the grave marker and handed it to Randall. He looked at it. "Anybody have a bottle of water?" A water bottle instantly appeared from the group and was passed to

Randall. He poured the water over the button and proceeded to clean away the moistened dirt with his thumb. After an additional wash, he studied the object.

"I've got another button here," came the announcement from the excavation. Markay took the round bit of brass.

Randall could see that the object indeed was a brass button. On it was what appeared to be a ship's anchor encircled by stars.

"Ladies and gentlemen," Randall said in a loud voice as he stared into the freshly-dug earth. "Let me introduce to you Captain Artemus Pritchard, late of the S.S. *Loch Gillelli*." He glanced at Markay and then at Kilby. "I'll explain it when we're done here." Randall then looked at the two men standing in the hole. "You'll probably also find at least one slug from an old Webley revolver down there." He glanced at Markay. "That seemed to be the weapon of choice back then."

The group continued to watch the two men sweep away the dirt from the bottom of the hole. "Hey, we've got something else here" one of the diggers exclaimed. "It looks like a box." Soon the man lifted the small rectangular object from the hole and gave it to Inspector Markay.

"It's a metal box all right," Markay said as he examined the dirt-encrusted object. "This looks like an old lead-lined tin box that was used years ago for storage of valuable papers." Markay set the box down on the ground and attempted to pry open the lid. Portions of the corroded outer tin casing broke apart as he finally removed the lid. Inside was a stack of documents. Markay removed the contents from the box and paged through them.

"Is that money?" someone in the group asked.

"No," Markay replied. "They appear to be old bonds and stock certificates." He paused as he studied them. "Yes, old bonds and certificates of stock," Markay reiterated. "Very old, indeed."

Randall glanced at Kilby. He said just one word. "*Titanic*." He then noticed that Claire DuBois had returned to beneath the tree at the edge of the drive. "Here," Randall said as he gave the button to Kilby. "Evidence. I guess this place is now officially a crime scene." With that he left a somewhat bewildered Kilby and walked to where Claire was standing.

"Are you all right?" Randall casually asked, trying not to show concern or worry.

"I'm fine," she replied unconvincingly. "I just didn't want to be around another dead body."

Randall smiled faintly. "I know what you mean," he said as he placed his arm around her shoulder. Together they watched as the group of people at the graveside slowly began to disperse. "Well, now it's time for the police to take over," he remarked quietly as if in resignation. "We're finished here."

Claire turned and faced Randall. "So, what's next for you?" she asked, her face one of sadness.

Randall shrugged his shoulders and sighed. "My work here in Halifax is pretty much done. I have one task remaining. I need to go to England for a day or two to complete the job. Just a day or two."

"Will you come back to Halifax?"

Randall smiled. "Absolutely. After all, I need to help you clean up the dive shop. I left a mess on the work bench. And I'm sure there will be more loose ends to tie up."

His smile faded as he turned and observed Inspectors Markay and Kilby standing at the side of the open grave, discussing their future work. One task remaining, Randall pondered, one last thing that must be done before all of the graves are filled in and forgotten. One final act.

Chapter 18

Rob Randall stared out the window of his railroad coach, observing the countryside of rural England. Autumn was now in full bloom, the colorful leaves a visual symphony of changing seasons. The rhythmic clacking of wheels on rails lulled him into a sense of serenity. After the six-hour flight from Halifax to London, a journey on rails into central England seemed a welcome relief.

Randall had one final task to complete before meeting with the Sheffland family at Banhaven, their country estate. He was traveling by train to the village of Kempston where he was to visit with Mrs. Edna Colquist. He had lingering doubts about his trip to Kempston – whether the visit to Mrs. Colquist would yield any benefits in his work. Nothing ventured, nothing gained, he concluded. Maybe there was something further to be learned.

Randall's relaxing reverie came to an end as the train approached Kempston, the melodious sounds of the coach wheels becoming slower and slower until finally ceasing. He stood and stretched before grabbing his overnight bag and stepping off the train. The station at Kempston, except for the wooden platform, appeared completely restored. Randall passed through the station interior and secured the services of a taxi at the train station entrance. After no more than a ten minute cab ride, he arrived at the home of Edna Colquist. Randall paid the taxi driver and asked him to drop off his bag at the hotel where he would be staying for the night.

The house was a modest abode at the edge of Kempston. It stood close to the narrow road passing by the premise, separated only by a thin wall of hedges. Randall approached the door and pulled the string attached to a small brass bell. After a brief moment, the door was opened by a quintessential little old lady.

"Hello, Mrs. Colquist?" Randall asked in a somewhat shy manner. "I am Robert Randall. I talked to you by phone about possibly visiting here today." He prayed she would remember.

"Yes," Mr. Randall," she replied in a high, breathless chirpy voice. "I have been expecting you. Please come in."

Randall entered an old English homestead that had been impeccably and lovingly cared for. It was light and warm and cheery, furnished with a collection of antique furniture pieces and keepsakes gathered over a lifetime. Mrs. Colquist gestured to her right. "Let us go into the parlor." She then briefly giggled. "Actually, I don't really have a parlor, but it sounds good."

Randall laughed. "Parlor, living room, den – whatever it is, it's fine."

"May I serve you some tea?" she offered in her squeaky resonance.

"No, thank you. Perhaps later." Randall sat on one of two straight-back chairs.

Mrs. Colquist took the other chair and began the conversation. "Mr. Randall, when you called, you told me of your visit to London with regards to your work at British Sovereign Airlines. Am I correct?"

"Yes, that is correct," he replied. "And thank you for seeing me. I very much appreciate it."

"It's my pleasure," Mrs. Colquist said smiling, "but I don't believe I can be of much help to you. I know only of the beginning of the company when I was very young. Now, all I know of it is what I read in the newspaper. And unfortunately, British Sovereign has been in the news quite a bit of late."

"Yes," Randall agreed, "very unfortunate for all." He immediately decided to change the direction of the conversation. "Actually, the beginning of British Sovereign Air Cargo Service in 1947 is what I'm interested in. That's the reason for my visit."

"Well, I can tell you what I remember of it," she said smiling.

"I know your father was instrumental in the start-up of the cargo carrier business," prodded Randall.

"Yes, that is true," she nodded. "My father was Horace Weller. He was born into a family comprised of generations of tool makers. My grandfather Weller, though, went to work for the British government during the First World War. He participated in the procurement of war materials for the British Army and Royal Navy. My father continued his father's work in that endeavor. Prior to America's entry into World War II, he helped procure everything from destroyers for the Royal Navy under lend-lease to textiles and coal. When America came on board in the war, the procurement efforts greatly expanded to include airplanes and tanks and bombs and bullets – just about everything." Mrs. Colquist shook her head. "I was almost nine-years-old when World War II began. Those days were terrible." She closed her eyes as if trying not to see the past.

"And after the end of the war?" Randall asked.

Mrs. Colquist opened her eyes and smiled. "After the war," she continued, "my father was in charge of the disposal of surplus war material in the possession of the Royal Air Force. Everything from aircraft to ammunition - as he used to say."

"Many of the airplanes, at least, the larger air transport planes, were sold at that time," Randall reminded her.

"Yes, that's true," she concurred. "The airplanes and all of the spare engines and tires and I guess all of the spare parts."

Randall nodded in agreement. "The RAF had a large number of American C-47 aircraft in their inventory at the end of the war. The Brits called them Dakotas. They were sold off at bargain-basement prices. One of the buyers was a man named Howard Sheffland. He was a former RAF bomber pilot who decided to start his own airline company on the wings of those surplus Dakotas."

Mrs. Colquist nodded. "You are correct. I remember it. That was about a year after the war ended. I believe I was fifteen at the time. Mr. Sheffland purchased a large number of the aircraft along with truckloads of spare parts. He began his company operations at one of the military airfields closed at the end of hostilities. There were a lot of them, you know."

"Yes," Randall agreed. "Actually, it was an airfield north of London. I passed the area on my trip here to Kempston." He paused briefly before continuing. "I'm curious. Why do you remember Howard Sheffland and the purchase of the aircraft for his new cargo company?"

Mrs. Colquist smiled. "I met Mr. Sheffland. He came to our house once. I remember him to begin with because he was very handsome, very dashing." She giggled like a young school girl. "I instantly fell for him like an old iron anvil." Randall laughed as she continued. "I remember him for other reasons," she said as she grew serious. "His cargo company became famous in 1948 during the Berlin Airlift. Mr. Sheffland dedicated every one of his cargo planes to the airlift effort. His planes flew day and night hauling cargo into Berlin. They said he sacrificed an incredible amount of time and money in the effort to feed the starving people of Berlin. Imagine - it was just a few years after he was at war with Germany, dropping bombs on the people of Berlin. I believe his work during the airlift was the most eloquent expression of humanity – as if he was trying to compensate for the sins of that conflict."

"Yes," Randall murmured in a whisper. "His sins, and the sins of the father too . . ."

"What was that?" Mrs. Colquist asked, leaning towards Randall, cupping her ear.

"Oh," he replied, "I said sins of the father. You know, that old expression." He changed the conversation. "Mrs. Colquist, you said you remembered Howard Sheffland for a number of reasons. In addition to being drop-dead handsome and his efforts during the Berlin Airlift, why else do you remember him?"

Mrs. Colquist displayed a faint, distant smile. She hesitated a moment before speaking. "I have something to show you." With that, she rose and left the room. Randall heard her footfalls on the staircase to the second floor of the house. She returned a few minutes later, clutching a small, red box in her hands.

"After the war was over and the surplus equipment was for sale, the British government accepted only cash for the purchases of surplus items. That was true for everything, even old ships like the British Corvette sub-chasers. The airplanes, with all of their ancillary maintenance equipment and spare parts, could only be obtained by paying cash. That is how Mr. Sheffland bought the planes. He paid cash."

She paused for a moment. "Would you like some tea now?" she again asked.

"No," Randall smiled, "thank you. I'm fine."

"Very well," she responded. "Now, where was I? Oh, yes, buying the airplanes."

Randall nodded as she continued. "As I said, Mr. Sheffland purchased the planes with cash. In a way, that was unusual for those times. He definitely was not a war profiteer. They're the ones who had all the money. Those planes cost hundreds of thousands of pounds, but he was able to find the cash to pay for them."

Mrs. Colquist glanced down at the box in her hand. "I don't think I would have ever remembered Mr. Sheffland except for what happened after the transaction." She sighed. "A number of spare aircraft engines were found after the sale was complete, and Mr. Sheffland wanted them. He had some remaining money in reserve, but he was short a few hundred pounds. Since Mr. Sheffland needed those airplanes motors, and they would be available only for a brief time, he made up the shortfall with this." She gave the box to Randall. He opened it.

"Lord, Almighty . . ." he exclaimed in a whisper. Inside the box was a dazzling jeweled ring. The centerpiece of the setting was a massive marquise-cut diamond surrounded by sparking blue sapphires. The gems were mounted on a large white gold band.

"Yes, Mr. Randall," she laughed, "before you ask the question, I will answer it. The gems are real."

"This is perhaps the most spectacular piece of jewelry I've ever seen," he uttered in a low voice as he carefully removed the ring from the box. "It defies description. Unbelievable!"

"That is what my father thought," Mrs. Colquist mused. "The value of that ring certainly covered any cash shortfall."

Randall examined the ring closely. "Mrs. Colquist, you should never show this ring to anyone," he warned her. "This jewelry belongs in the Bank of England!"

She laughed. "I keep it in a safe upstairs. And I'm not worried. You appear to have a trustworthy face."

"Well, thank you for that," Randall responded, joining in the laughter. He suddenly grew serious as he examined the ring. "Were you aware that there is an inscription on the inside of the band?"

"Yes," she replied. "I believe it's some initials."

"You're right," Randall said as he strained to discern the letters. "It reads

To MTA from *JJA.*" He paused for a moment, contemplating the inscription. Suddenly he knew its meaning.

"God," he sighed as he closed his eyes. "God in heaven."

"What's wrong, Mr. Randall?" she asked.

"Madeleine," he replied quietly. "I believe her name was Madeleine."

"Who?" Mrs. Colquist persisted. "Madeleine who?"

"Madeleine Astor," he answered softly. "*To Madeleine Astor from her husband, John Jacob Astor. J-J-A.*"

"Astor?" Mrs. Colquist pondered, "John Jacob Astor? I have heard that name before – somewhere."

"Yes," Randall agreed, "John Jacob Astor. He was an American businessman, an industrialist, at the turn of the last century. He was very prominent, very wealthy, one of the richest men in the world. His wife's name was Madeleine. Very young. Very beautiful. This ring must have been a gift to her from her husband."

"What happened to them?" she wondered.

"John Jacob Astor and his wife sailed on the maiden voyage of the R.M.S. *Titanic* in April of 1912. He was lost at sea when *Titanic* floundered after striking an iceberg. Madeleine Astor was rescued, but she died at a relatively young age, probably in part from, as they say, a broken heart."

Randall placed the ring in the box and returned it to Mrs. Colquist. "Strange," she said, "to think that my father ended up with this ring. I wonder how Mr. Sheffland came to be in possession of it."

"I don't know," Randall lied. "Perhaps it was passed down through the generations. Perhaps it's just a story from a past era." He smiled. "I do know that I would cherish that ring forever. It speaks of another time."

Randall spent the remainder of the afternoon with Edna Colquist. They talked about their lives, about England, about America, and about the *Titanic*. And Randall would finally have that cup of tea.

Chapter 19

Evening rush hour in London seemed to be the same as rush hours in every large American metropolitan area. The journey from downtown London to the Sheffland's estate at Banhaven seemed especially long and arduous after an early morning train ride from Kempston. What made it even more difficult was negotiating the traffic in southwest London all the while remembering that Brits drive on the left side of the road. No limousine for Rob Randall on this trip. He was on his own this time around.

Randall had contacted Alex Sheffland after his arrival in London the previous morning, informing Sheffland that the work in America and Canada was completed. He gave Sheffland scant details on the results of his investigation, simply assuring the Sheffland family that they would be thoroughly briefed on his efforts.

As Randall drove into the English countryside, the traffic congestion lessened until, finally, he seemed alone on the two-lane road to Banhaven. It was dark when he reached the entrance to the Sheffland estate. Passing through the open gate, he observed deer darting along the winding drive as he approached the manor house. Randall parked his rental car in front of the main entrance. As he exited the vehicle, he felt the autumn chill. No doubt about it, Randall thought. Early winter has arrived at Banhaven.

"Good evening, Mr. Randall," Simon's salutation was accompanied by a broad smile. "It's so nice to see you again."

"Good seeing you, Simon," Randall returned the greeting as he entered the foyer to the manor. "It's getting really cold outside. I hope the guest bedroom fireplace is lit."

"Yes, sir," Simon nodded. "We have a number of fireplaces going. These large stone houses always seem to have a chill in them. It is especially bad as autumn passes."

Simon paused for a moment, gesturing towards the hallway. "May I take your coat, Mr. Randall? Young Mr. Sheffland awaits you in the study."

"Thank you, Simon," Randall responded. He walked to the doors of the study. Knocking twice, he slid one of the doors open and entered the room. Randall was immediately greeted by a crackling fireplace and a warm handshake from Alex Sheffland.

"Hello, Rob, welcome again to Banhaven. It's wonderful to have you once more visit us."

"Alex," Randall responded. "Thank you for having me."

Sheffland gestured to the chair near the fireplace. "Please, have a seat. My father knows of your arrival. He will join us in a few minutes. May I get you anything?"

"No, I'm fine," Randall replied. "Fed and watered earlier today."

Alex Sheffland sat down on the couch facing Randall. "Well, from what little I've heard, it appears you've been having quite a go of it."

At that moment the study doors opened and Sir Geoffrey Sheffland entered the room. "Hello, Rob," Sir Geoffrey warmly greeted Randall, grasping his hand firmly. "Thank you so very much for returning to Banhaven."

"My pleasure, Sir Geoffrey," Randall said smiling. "And thank you for having a fire in the fireplace. I may actually begin to warm up."

Sir Geoffrey laughed. "It's the least we could do considering our recently dreadful weather." He sat down on the couch next to his son. "I hope you had a good flight to London."

"It was okay. Of course, not nearly as good as a flight on British Sovereign Airlines."

"Well," Sir Geoffrey said somewhat dismissively, "with Halifax, beggars can't necessarily be choosers." He paused. "Not that you're a beggar," he added.

"I know what you mean, Sir Geoffrey," Randall assured him. "No offense taken." All three men laughed briefly and then became serious.

"Rob, my son has told me you have made some progress over the matter at hand," Sir Geoffrey said hopefully.

"Yes, Sir Geoffrey," Randall responded. "As of a few days ago, the attempt of extortion against your family and the threat to your airline is no more."

Sir Geoffrey closed his eyes and bowed his head. "Thank God" he uttered in almost a whisper.

"What happened?" Alex quietly asked.

"A few nights ago," Randall began, "three individuals involved in the extortion plot were taken into custody in Halifax, Nova Scotia. Martin Hewes, a retired U.S. naval officer, was the ringleader of the plot. Hewes was the commander of the Navy dive unit that first explored the wreck of your ship, the *Loch Gillelli* during the Swissair airliner recovery efforts in 1998. Commander Robin Holland of the Canadian Navy, also Hewes' wife, was one of his accomplices. She, too, worked on the Swissair airliner recovery. There was a third man, the one you knew as Devero. His name is Maurice Devoreux. He was one of the principal Canadian divers who visited the *Loch Gillelli* shipwreck when it was first discovered. He is a cousin of Commander Holland. It was through Devoreux's efforts that the extortion plot blossomed."

"You said they were taken into custody . . ." questioned Alex.

"Yes," Randall responded. "I believe they will be charged with two counts of first degree murder and one count of attempted murder."

"Who did they murder?" Sir Geoffrey wondered.

"Well, to begin with, it appears the group murdered one of their own," answered Randall. "There was an American Navy diver. His name was Paul McDowell. He was the 'Pauly' you made reference to during our initial discussions. McDowell worked for Hewes and Devoreux. He, too, was one of the divers who first explored the *Loch Gillelli* shipwreck in '98."

"Who was the second person to be murdered?" Alex asked in bewilderment.

"The man's name is Jason DuBois. He was a Canadian Navy diver at one time. DuBois was not part of the extortion plot." Randall paused for a moment. "DuBois visited the shipwreck a number of times. His big mistake was discovering the actual logbooks of the S.S. *Loch Gillelli* and sharing their

THE SIREN OF THE LOCH GILLELLI

contents with Devoreux. That is what really started the extortion plot against you. That and finding the wreck of the *Loch Gillelli* in the first place."

Sir Geoffrey shook his head in disbelief. "And they tried to kill you, too."

"Yes," Randall agreed. "Which leads me to the next revelation, a truly nasty one. There was another participant in the extortion plot, the one whose complicity contributed to this whole sordid affair."

"Nigel," Sir Geoffrey blurted out, interrupting Randall.

"Correct. Nigel," Randall nodded. "Son and brother." He paused momentarily, collecting his thoughts. "You know, four months ago, after the DyNational counterfeit parts fiasco, I wondered why Nigel would take such incredible risks with his family and with the company. He entered into the counterfeit aircraft parts scheme and, ultimately, attempted to kill his own father and brother. I was told it was all because of a gambling problem." Randall shook his head. "But I didn't believe that for a second. It just didn't make any sense. And I was right. In reality, Nigel actually wanted to either sell the airline outright or at least take it public in an IPO. Either way, he would make a fortune. The deal with DyNational was to make the airline vastly more profitable, thus making the company much more attractive for purchase and, at the same time, jacking up the purchase price. But then, not only did I enter the picture in May to mess up the parts scheme, but along comes Martin Hewes and company to demand a piece of the action. Hewes knew there really wasn't a *Titanic* treasure for the taking. But he did figure out that the hands of the Sheffland family were collectively covered in the blood of those that died on board both the *Titanic* and the *Loch Gillelli*. The Sheffland family watched as fifteen hundred people, many of them fellow countrymen, died a terrible death while the family stole their worldly possessions." Randall shook his head. "Wow, what would have happened to the value of British Sovereign Airlines had that little gem been made public?"

Randall stopped and stared at Sir Geoffrey and then at Alex Sheffland. "But I believe both of you knew this long before my first visit to London a few weeks ago. You may not have known about Hewes until after his meetings with Nigel at Wandsworth Prison. But by then, you were able to figure out that Maury Devoreux wasn't the head guy in this extortion scheme, or blackmail scheme, or whatever it was. The Shefflands wanted me to, as American sports fans would say, run interference for you. I was to try to figure all of this out while the family's name was kept away from the action. Nigel attempted to kill the two of you because you never would have considered selling the airline to the highest bidder or the wealthiest investors. After all, it's a family business. Your family's business. Your treasure from the *Titanic*."

Sir Geoffrey and Alex Sheffland sat in stunned and embarrassed silence as Randall continued. "Which brings me to the final subject, the so-called treasure of the *Titanic*. The treasure of the *Titanic* was gone long ago. It exists no more with perhaps the exception of *The Rubaiyat*. And I believe you knew that, Sir Geoffrey. You knew what happened to the treasure – probably when you were still a very young man. Am I correct?"

"Yes," Sir Geoffrey answered in a quiet yet anguished voice. "Many years ago."

Randall nodded. "While I was in Nova Scotia, I contacted Hugh Pierce. By the way, he wanted me to say hello to you. I asked him to find out the early history of British Sovereign Airlines. He obtained the information – in great detail – and sent it to me. The company, the airline, the treasure of the *Titanic*. Your grandfather, Dr. Cyril Sheffland, stole the valuables from the wealthy passengers because he believed that the family had been slighted in some manner by the British aristocracy."

"It was not, as you phrased it, some slight by the British aristocracy," Sir Geoffrey angrily retorted. "It was more than that. Much more than that."

Sir Geoffrey paused, shaking his head, his countenance caught up in a sigh as he collected his thoughts and his anger. "In 1899, Great Britain entered the Second Boer War in South Africa. My grandfather was just twenty-three at the time. Grandfather Cyril had a brother nine years his senior. His name was Chadwick Sheffland. Cyril idolized his older brother, and Chad was Cyril's confidant, his guide, and his guard. Chad kept Cyril out of trouble during those years of childhood, and from what I was told, Cyril was a rather rambunctious and unruly child."

His voice now subdued, Sir Geoffrey smiled at his revelation as he continued. "Chadwick Sheffland became a doctor, and because of his medical training, he was conscripted into the British army at the beginning of the Second Boer War. That was in 1899. As with all of the army, he was not prepared for his duties when he was sent to Africa. He was a doctor assigned to attend to refugee camps. The camps were filled with civilians suspected of colluding with guerrilla forces. In reality, those refugee centers were nothing more than concentration camps. Unfortunately, most of those refugees, as they were called, were women and children."

Sir Geoffrey paused for a long moment, closing his eyes as if he did not want to see the vision in his mind. Then, he continued. "The camps were poorly administered. The spread of disease among the refugees was rampant due to poor food and terrible hygiene and sanitary practices. Tens of thousands of men, women and children died in those refugee camps, mostly from typhoid and cholera and dysentery. What made the situation worse was that disease spread to the British troops. Far more soldiers succumbed to disease during the war than those thousands lost in battle."

Sir Geoffrey visibly stiffened. "The army's hospitals were under-staffed and overwhelmed." His voice was now loud and firm. "After the war, a liberal, so-called, Facilities Commission investigating the military and civilian deaths placed the blame, in part, on Dr. Chadwick Sheffland for dereliction of duties in not preventing the terrible loss of life. As you Americans are want to say, blame indeed does roll downhill. His medical career, his reputation, and ultimately his life were destroyed by the upper crust of British civilization. In 1904, Chadwick Sheffland took his own life. My Grandfather Cyril was enraged and embittered over his brother's demise. He could never move past the loss."

"All right," Randall responded, "so be it. He wanted revenge. But on the night of April 14, 1912, he and his compatriots watched as fifteen hundred people perished in the frigid Atlantic. After that, your grandfather wanted nothing to do with his portion of the ill-gotten gains. He sent it to the family members here in London, and he remained in Nova Scotia – a guilt-ridden shell of his former self. Cyril Sheffland spent the remainder of his life trying to forgive himself for his terrible transgressions. Your family knew that."

Sir Geoffrey nodded but said nothing – simply staring at the fireplace.

"The family also knew thirty-five years later, the treasure of the *Titanic* was used in part to start British Sovereign Air Cargo Company. Your father, Howard, purchased a number of surplus U.S. Army Air Force C-47 aircraft from the British government after the end of World War II. I believe you British called the C-47, our old DC-3, the Dakota. Sir Geoffrey, how many aircraft did your father purchase?"

"Eleven," Alex interjected. "The company was started with eleven Dakotas."

"And from those eleven aircraft, the Sheffland family built an international airline." Randall shook his head. "You know, it's funny. In the information Hugh sent to me, he included a picture of one of those original C-47s marked in the BSA livery. On the tail of the plane was painted a single large, gold coin. A British sovereign. Just exactly like the British gold sovereign you keep in your safe. The one you showed to me. The single gold sovereign from the *Titanic*. How appropriate. How utterly appropriate."

Randall glanced at Alex and then at Sir Geoffrey. Alex appeared downtrodden. Sir Geoffrey was on the verge of tears.

"Well, that's about it," Randall concluded. "Thus endeth the story. Nigel's in prison, quite honestly, where he belongs. The Canadian extortion conspirators will soon be in prison, quite honestly, where they belong. And, finally, the Sheffland family secret will continue, for the most part, to be a secret. The shipwreck of the *Loch Gillelli* will remain undisturbed and forgotten in its watery grave. All that is left to you are a very fancy book, a shiny gold coin, and your own individual thoughts."

Randall stared at the two silent Sheffland men, their faces illuminated in the flickering firelight. Strangely, they seemed at once broken in family spirit but not in family resolve. Sir Geoffrey stood and walked to behind the desk. He swung away the painting on the wall and opened the safe. Retrieving the British gold sovereign coin, he returned to the couch and gave it to Randall.

"Here," he said, his voice almost choking. "I believe this belongs to you now, the last bit of our treasure from the *Titanic*. You have earned it, Rob."

Randall took the coin and studied it, the brilliant patina shining in the blaze. If it could speak, Randall wondered, what story would it tell? The *R.M.S. Titanic* once again was sailing the ocean, and it was a Sunday night in April of 1912. The strains of ragtime music drifted across the water, only to be replaced by the sobbing of a mournful Episcopal hymn. And Randall thought of the *S.S. Loch Gillelli*, its fate forever shared with that of *Titanic*.

The sounds of the sirens were no more. The final song of the *Loch Gillelli* was *Autumn*.

Epilogue

Jack Kilby was about to step onto the stern deck of the cabin cruiser when he noticed Rob Randall was sitting on the end of the wooden dock, his back resting against one of the support posts. Kilby quietly approached him. Randall's eyes were closed.

"I'm not disturbing you, am I?" came Kilby's announcement of arrival.

One eye cracked open. "Just when I got rid of all the squawking seagulls, another one shows up." He briefly stared at Kilby with the single disparaging eye before again closing it.

"What are you doing down here at the end of the dock?" Kilby asked nonchalantly.

Randall's eyelids remained closed. "Oh, I had an auto detailer working on the stern of the boat. I was being overcome by paint fumes, so I came here to get some fresh air."

"An auto detailer?" repeated Kilby. "What? Are you customizing the cabin cruiser? Next, you'll tell me you're tricking out the engines and turning it into a drag boat."

"That's not a bad idea," Randall mumbled. "At least I'll be able to get to the good fishing spots a lot quicker." Randall opened his eyes and squinted at Kilby. "What brings you down here? Shouldn't you be off chasing bank robbers or catching international terrorists?" He then closed his eyes. Again.

"Hey – wake up," Kilby said as he gently kicked Randall's foot. "I'm here on official Bureau business."

Randall opened his eyes. "Like hell you are. You just wanted to get out of that bureaucratic puzzle palace for a few hours."

"Well, actually, I haven't been in the office for a couple of days. I just returned from another visit to Nova Scotia."

"Okay," Randall responded. "So, what's happening in Halifax?"

Kilby leaned against the post opposite Randall. "Just finishing up our portion of the investigation. It looks like we'll be able to pin the murder rap on Devoreux for the death of Paul McDowell without much trouble. By the way, Bobber Cork says hey."

Randall smiled. "That's the name for a professional fisherman, not a police chief."

"Yeah," Kilby agreed. "You would think. Anyway, we've got all three for the murder of Jason DuBois. It's an open-and-shut case for Devoreux, Hewes and his wife. And, by the way, Captain Holland *really* doesn't like you."

"Wow, imagine that!" Randall said in feint pain. "Another stab to the heart."

"You know," Kilby continued, "I think retired Superintendent Molnar had an idea of what was going on all those years, but he kept quiet about it."

"Sure," Randall said, "he wanted to keep *his* family secret hidden – at least until he was no longer around." He paused a moment. "What about the bomb in my car? Any progress on that?"

"Yeah. Hewes planted the device himself. You'll never believe this. While you were at the airport waiting for *your* flight to Boston, Hewes was there waiting to return to Halifax."

Kilby paused and began to laugh. "One thing is for sure. You've got Inspector Markay all bent out of shape. At the cemetery grave site, you told Markay that at least one slug from an old British Webley revolver would be found with the body. Well, you were right. They found not one but two bullets – each a .455 caliber from a Webley. Markay believes either you're a psychic or you murdered that guy yourself even though he was dead and buried over a hundred years ago."

Randall joined in the laughter. "Tell Markay I'm older than I look. Tell him I did it because of a deep-seated grudge." As the laughter died away,

Randall became serious. "I wonder if the authorities will ever be able to identify the bones in the grave as those of Captain Artemus Pritchard?"

"I don't know," Kilby replied. "They certainly will try. As to whether or not they'll be successful is anyone's guess." Kilby paused a moment. "Rob, who do you think murdered Captain Pritchard?"

Randall sighed as he gazed out over the water. "I believe Dr. Sheffland did it. I think Pritchard was single-handedly responsible for the sinking of the *Loch Gillelli* and the death of the ship's crew. And in a way, Pritchard was responsible for the deaths of the *Titanic*'s passengers and the ship's company. All those crew members, all those passengers." He returned his gaze to Kilby. "I know Cyril Sheffland believed it. And he killed Pritchard for it."

"You remember the box found with the body at the grave site?" Kilby quietly reminded Randall. "Well, the folks in Halifax were able to identify the contents of the box and its owner. The box contained bonds and stock certificates. There were two hundred thousand dollars in bonds and one hundred thousand dollars in preferred stocks. That was their value in 1912. The stocks and bonds belonged to a Major Arthur Peuchen. He was a first-class passenger on board the *Titanic*. After the liner struck the iceberg, Peuchen left his cabin, C-104, and went to the lifeboats. He did not take the box with him. It remained on the table in his room. Peuchen lived to tell the story. And the box . . ."

"And the box was pilfered from the cabin," interrupted Randall. "Either Sheffland, or Molnar, or Porter stole items from first-class cabins in addition to the contents of the purser's safe while the passengers on *Titanic* were gathering around the lifeboats. What a bunch of great guys!"

Randall shook his head before continuing. "Dr. Sheffland may have believed Captain Pritchard killed all of those people, but deep down inside him, Sheffland knew in his heart he was responsible for their deaths. The *Titanic*. The *Loch Gillelli*. All those people. It gnawed on that heart for the remainder of his life."

"And the Sheffland family now," Kilby reminded Randall.

"Yes, they've lived with it. All these years." Randall smiled. "The sins of the father. Families, those wealthy and famous and those impoverished and unknown, all suffer to some degree the sins of the fathers." He paused for a moment. "Funny. Sir Geoffrey gave to me the single British gold sovereign remaining from the treasure of the *Titanic*. It was as if he were paying a tribute for the tax on his soul, on the souls of his family."

"He paid the tax," Kilby said softly. "His son Nigel, his daughter Lydia. He already paid for the sins of the fathers. The gold sovereign? It's just a piece of metal that belongs in the ocean deep, where it will never again be seen, where it never again will be touched. It will only be remembered."

"Perhaps you're right, Jack. Perhaps you're right." Randall laid his head back against the post and closed his eyes. "Speaking of the ocean deep, I can't help but keep dwelling on something that occurred during my trip to Halifax. Deep down, it's bothered the heck out of me."

"What's that?" Kilby asked.

Randall opened his eyes and gazed at his friend. "Claire and I were diving on the shipwreck of the *Loch Gillelli*. We had just discovered the body of her husband. As we were swimming over the deck of the ship to begin our ascent to the surface, I heard the damndest sound. I can't even begin to describe it. It was as if someone combined the thrumming of a harp and the singing of an aria. I have never heard anything like it. The sound was beautiful and melodic. Irresistible. Haunting. Almost frightening."

"How long did it last?" Kilby asked.

"Only for a handful of seconds," Randall replied.

"Did Claire hear it?"

"I'm not sure. She never really said, and I didn't ask," Randall paused. "You know, I remember one of our instructors at Annapolis. He was an English literature teacher. You remember Sam?"

"Yeah," Kilby responded with a smile. "I remember him."

Randall laughed. "Just like all of our other instructors, anything taught to us had to be related to nautical subjects. *Moby Dick, Captains Courageous, The Cruel Sea* . . . wonderful if not waterlogged." Kilby joined in the laughter as he nodded his head. But then Randall became serious. "I remember Sam taught us Fagles' translation of Homer's *Odyssey*. I was always fond of that story – even when I was a kid. Sam talked about the irresistible sound of the Sirens, the song capturing the souls of unsuspecting sailors, the melody drawing them into the sea."

Randall stared at Kilby. "I've convinced myself that the sound I heard was caused by the changing ocean currents sweeping through the shipwreck." He paused for a moment. "But I swear to God, Jack, if I didn't know any better, I would believe I heard the Sirens inhabiting the wreck of the *Loch Gillelli*."

Kilby looked at Randall with a jaundiced eye. "Rob, you're not having a relapse, are you?"

"No," Randall adamantly answered. "I don't need a return to the rubber room." He rose from the deck, brushing himself off. "But that moment on the wreck did inspire me."

"Oh, I almost forgot to tell you," Kilby said in passing as they strolled towards Randall's boat. "I had dinner with Claire while I was in Halifax. She informed me of her pending visit with you in a few weeks. I think Claire said she wanted to spend a month or so down here. You know, see the boat, meet Maggie, have a few laughs."

"Whatever you're thinking," Randall interrupted, "you're wrong."

"Sure, Rob, sure." Kilby suddenly stopped, staring at the stern of Randall's boat. "Good grief!" he exclaimed. "You named your boat! You finally named her!"

"I told you I was inspired," Randall responded.

Kilby looked at the sweeping gold and black cursive letters adorning the boat's stern. "You named her *Laurel's Song*. Yeah. *Laurel's Song*. I like that."

Randall and Kilby stepped onto the stern deck of the cabin cruiser. "Let me grab Maggie and we can get out of here," Randall said. "I'm through for the day."

After buttoning up the canvas cover over the rear deck, the two sauntered to their cars, Maggie the cat in Randall's arms.

"You know, Rob, during Claire's visit, you need to bring her over to our house for Sunday dinner. Helen can meet her. They can talk about *you* while we watch football."

"Is Helen going to grace us with another superb meal of chicken chop suey?"

"It was chow mein." Kilby reminded Randall. "It was chicken chow mein. Not chop suey."

"Right, right," Randall agreed. "It was chow mein. I get chop suey and chow mein mixed up."

"How can you do that?" Kilby scolded Randall. "They're completely different."

Randall sighed. "Look, let's just have pot roast, okay?"

The two friends disappeared into the fading light of another October afternoon. A small boat passed by the dock, the ripples of water from its wake gently rocking *Laurel's Song*, the rolling motion like that of a cradle. Randall's sanctuary from storm-swept seas was now in a safe harbor.

Charles Knotts was born and raised in Ohio and did his undergraduate and graduate work in engineering at Purdue University. He is a veteran of the United States Air Force and a retired design engineer. He and his wife Jewell, and their two orphaned cats make their home in Florida. This is his third novel in the Rob Randall aviation mystery series.

Made in the USA
Las Vegas, NV
08 July 2021

26129442R00134